LIFE'S A WITCH
A WICKED WITCHES OF THE MIDWEST MYSTERY BOOK SEVEN

AMANDA M. LEE

WINCHESTERSHAW PUBLICATIONS

Copyright © 2015 by Amanda Lee

All rights reserved.

No part of this book may be reproduced in any form or by any electronic or mechanical means, including information storage and retrieval systems, without written permission from the author, except for the use of brief quotations in a book review.

❀ Created with Vellum

PROLOGUE

"That's not going to happen."

Tillie Winchester placed her hands on her hips and glared at Willa, all pretense of coming to an amiable compromise flying right out the window in the face of her sister's defiant attitude. She didn't like Willa. She was pretty sure she never liked her. Even as children they fought ferociously. This dispute wasn't going to be on the level of and cats and dogs, but if Tillie had nuclear weapons at her disposal she knew right where she would drop them today.

"I don't care what you think is going to happen, Willa," Tillie said, anger coursing through her. "You're not taking those girls. They're staying with me."

"They're not staying with you," Willa scoffed, matching Tillie's stance and staring her down. She was a bully, but Tillie was a bigger bully. Both women knew this wouldn't end well. "You don't have children. I do. I can take those girls and raise them right."

"Are you suggesting I can't raise them right?"

"I'm suggesting you don't know the first thing about taking care of teenage girls," Willa shot back. "Let's face it, Tillie, you've been nothing more than the fun aunt who gives them whatever they want, whenever they want it up until this point. With Ginger gone ...."

Tillie narrowed her eyes to dangerous slits. Ever since her sister Ginger's death two days earlier she'd been locked in battle with Willa over the fate of her nieces Winnie, Marnie and Twila. There was no way she would relinquish the girls to a dismal life with Willa.

"Don't talk about Ginger like you knew her," Tillie spat. "You don't even live in Walkerville anymore. You haven't lived here in decades. You barely know those girls. You don't have any claim to them."

"Ginger was still my sister," Willa sniffed. "I think she'd want to know that her daughters were being raised in a safe environment."

Tillie rolled her eyes. "What? Do you think I'm going to teach them how to juggle with knives? They're long past the running-with-scissors lecture. Winnie is an adult. She doesn't have to go anywhere. Marnie will be a legal adult in a month."

"Well, then I'll take Twila," Willa said. "I'll give Marnie and Winnie the option of going with me. If they prefer to stay with you and your … lax attitude … I guess that's on them. Twila still needs guidance, though."

"Twila is staying with me," Tillie argued. "She just lost her mother. She doesn't want to leave her home. We're all staying together."

"I'll take you to court if I have to." Willa knew the girls would never agree to go with her, and she played the one trump card she thought she had.

"You're not going to want to do that, Willa," Tillie said. "If you take me to court, I'll go. I'll tell the court every little thing you've worked so hard to hide since you moved away from here. I'll put it out there for public consumption. I know how worried you are about people thinking ill of you."

"Oh, really? What can you possibly tell the courts about me?" Willa scoffed. "I'll tell the judge that you dance naked under the full moon, let underage girls help you make wine, and teach them about … dark arts."

Tillie snorted. "Dark arts?"

"Everyone knows you're a witch, Tillie," Willa countered. "I'll make sure no court deems you fit to keep Twila."

"If you even try taking that girl I'll … ."

"What's going on?" Calvin Hoffman poked his head into the room, his gaze nervously bouncing between the two women. "The girls are right outside. They don't need to hear this."

Tillie studied her husband for a moment, conflicted. Ginger's death was a surprise. She'd felt poorly for months, but was bouncing back when the unthinkable happened and a massive coronary stole her in sleep. Winnie found her and was having trouble dealing with it. Still, Tillie wasn't one to hide things from her nieces – and she wasn't about to start now.

"Willa is insistent on taking Twila," Tillie informed Calvin. "She's going to let Winnie and Marnie decide, which is pretty funny since they're both adults."

"I could take Marnie for a month, too, if you really want to be obnoxious about it," Willa hissed. "I think you're worried that if I take her she'll never return. You've got them under your thumb here. Freedom might change their outlooks."

"Don't be stupid," Calvin chided, his everlasting patience wearing thin. "Those girls barely know you, Willa."

"And whose fault is that?"

"It's your fault," Calvin charged, not missing a beat. "You chose to leave Walkerville. You haven't talked to Tillie in close to ten years and you only talked to Ginger once in a blue moon. Those girls don't know you and they certainly don't love you. They don't want to leave their home."

"I don't understand how you think you're even a part of this, Calvin," Willa snapped. "Just because you married my sister doesn't mean you get to make family decisions."

Calvin was taken aback. "Really? Who took care of Marnie when she had strep throat last year and was down for ten days? Who helped Twila build set designs for her school play? Who helped Winnie build a doghouse when she was ten? I don't remember you being there for any of those things."

"I'm still a more suitable caregiver than Tillie," Willie said. "I won't let those girls run wild through the fields. I'll turn them into proper ladies."

"They don't want to be proper ladies," Tillie countered. "Why can't they just be who they want to be?"

"With you as a role model that's a terrifying thought," Willa countered. "I'm not giving in on this. I'll take you to court if I have to."

"Well, you'll have to," Tillie said. "I promise you won't like the outcome. We won't see a courtroom until well after Marnie is legal. That means the judge will basically ask Twila who she wants to live with. Do you think that's going to be you?"

"I think that Twila will be happy to get out of here if given the option."

"That's not true!"

Tillie's eyes snapped to the door where Twila, Marnie and Winnie gaped in abject horror.

"I don't want to leave," Twila said, hurrying into the room. "Please tell me I don't have to go with her."

"You don't have to go anywhere," Calvin said, soothing Twila as she cried.

Winnie and Marnie were more defiant than their younger sister.

"You can't take her from us," Winnie warned, her blond hair flying as she bobbed her head. "She's our sister. She wants to stay here."

"And we want to stay with Aunt Tillie," Marnie added. "If you try to take her ... ."

"You'll what?" Willa challenged. "Are you going to cast a spell on me like your precious Aunt Tillie?"

"No," Marnie replied, shaking her dark head. "We'll go the old-fashioned route. We'll burn your house down."

Tillie pursed her lips to keep from laughing. She loved a good threat.

"And that's exactly why the judge will give Twila to me," Willa said, rolling her eyes. "Thanks for giving me all the ammunition I need in court, girls."

Tillie took a step forward, her gaze menacing. "We all know why you really want Twila," she said. "It's not out of love or familial obligation. You think you'll have access to some of Ginger's estate if you take her. There's one little problem with that scenario."

Willa's shoulders straightened. "If you honestly think this is about money ... ."

Tillie cut her off. "When Ginger first got sick, we went to an attorney to set up trusts for the girls," she said. "All of that money is tied up in a way that you can never touch it. All three girls got equal stakes in the inheritance, and they can't touch that money until they're twenty-five. Ginger didn't want them blowing it when they were too young to realize what they were doing."

"But ... ." Willa's face shifted. "How did Ginger expect anyone to take these girls on if there's no money to raise them?"

"We also talked about that," Tillie replied, nonplussed. "The house and property reverts to me upon Ginger's death. I'm the sole owner of the land now. I'm taking care of the girls with my money. I don't need Ginger's money to keep them. I'm keeping them because ... ."

"You love us," Twila supplied.

Tillie cocked her head to the side, considering. "Most of the time," she finally conceded. She turned back to Willa. "I know what you're really doing here and there's no way I'm handing over any of these girls. If you want to take this to court, then we'll take it to court. You won't like what I have to say when we get there, though."

"Tillie is right," Calvin said, trying to calm the women. "Twila will choose to stay with Tillie and me. A judge isn't going to hand her over to you when she doesn't want to go."

"And I'm going to guess that without any money in the mix, you'll lose interest in Twila pretty darned quickly," Tillie added.

Willa's face contorted. "I ... well, I guess you've got it all figured out, haven't you?"

"I have," Tillie replied smoothly. "Now get out of my house."

"I grew up in this house," Willa argued. "It's still my house."

"Not according to the land deeds and law," Tillie said. She leaned in closer so only Willa could hear. "Don't you ever come back here, Willa. We might've grown up together, but we're not family. Those girls are my family, and there's nothing you can ever do to take them away from me."

Willa pulled back, tugging on her suit coat as she squared her shoulders. "Girls, if you ever want a proper role model, you know where to find me."

"I'm guessing it's someplace where people don't notice that big stick hanging out of your behind," Marnie offered, causing Willa to scowl.

"Don't think this is over, Tillie," Willa said. "You'll regret this one day."

Tillie made a face that would've been comical under different conditions. "Don't let the door hit you in the ass on your way out, Willa," she said. "Have a nice life ... and remember what I said. Don't ever come back here again. If you do, I'll be dancing on your grave. I might even do it naked."

ONE

"I don't think this is legal."

"It's legal," Aunt Tillie replied, nonplussed. "Now put your back into it. You'll never get that box into my truck if you don't exert some effort. You need bigger muscles or something. You're a weakling."

I brushed my blond hair from my forehead and looked up at my great-aunt wearily. She was in a mood today. That wasn't saying much, because I can't remember her not being in a mood. This one was entirely annoying, though.

"I could leave this box here and let you figure out how to get it into your truck on your own," I threatened.

Aunt Tillie rolled her eyes. "We both know that's not going to happen," she said, not worried in the least I would abandon her to her own dirty work. "If you leave this box in the middle of the floor your mother or one of your aunts will trip over it. They're at the age where a hip injury could lay them up for weeks, and that means you would have to take care of them instead of fawning all over your boyfriend. Do you really want to serve your mother breakfast in bed instead of cuddling up to your long-haired love muffin?"

I scowled, frustrated. She had a point. I didn't want to encourage her, though. "Is there a reason you couldn't have packed this wine in three separate boxes? I would rather make three trips with lighter loads than one trip with a box that makes me think my back is about to go out."

Aunt Tillie shot me one of her patented "I'm going to curse you if you don't shut up" looks. "Why are you still talking?"

"I honestly have no idea," I muttered, groaning as I strained to lift the box again. It was too heavy. There was no getting around it. I wasn't strong enough to move the box from the foyer of The Overlook, the inn my mothers and aunts run, to Aunt Tillie's truck in the driveway. I'm aware of my limitations and I'm not afraid to admit them. "We need help to do this," I said finally, straightening so I could brush the sweat from my forehead.

Summers in Michigan vacillate wildly. One day can be seventy degrees and beautiful. The next can be ninety and so humid you feel as if you're roasting in an oven. Today was an example of the latter.

My name is Bay Winchester and I'm a witch. No, you read that right. I can talk with ghosts and cast spells. The only things I can't do are control my great-aunt and the weather. She can control the weather. I'm not powerful enough. I would take control over one of those things in a heartbeat right now. I'll let you guess which one.

"You're starting to tick me off," Aunt Tillie said, wagging a finger in my face. "You're young. You should be strong. Now … suck it up and lift with your legs. You're really starting to bug me."

"Aunt Tillie, it's too heavy," I whined. "I physically cannot do what you're asking me to do. I'm sorry."

"Fine," Aunt Tillie sputtered. "Where are your cousins?"

That was a good question. It was Thursday night and Thistle and Clove were supposed to be here an hour ago. Unlike me, they must have realized Aunt Tillie had chores in store for everyone. I either missed that realization – or they purposely didn't tell me what they suspected because they wanted me to do all of the heavy lifting. I leaned toward the latter.

"I don't know where they're at," I replied. "We have a big group of tourists in town for the summer festival. Maybe they got a last-minute rush at the store."

As co-owners of Hypnotic, Hemlock Cove's magic store, my cousins often managed to use their business as an excuse to dodge Aunt Tillie duty. Because I'm the editor of the town's weekly newspaper, I don't have that crutch to lean on. Everyone knows my schedule. It's a real drag sometimes.

"They're hiding," Aunt Tillie muttered. "I told them I needed their help and they're hiding. I'll curse their bottoms blue."

I pursed my lips to keep from laughing. I had no idea whether that was possible – although she'd managed to pull off some truly inventive curses in her time. I was just glad I was putting out observable effort so I would hopefully be free from this week's curse. "Can't you curse them to make them appear and help? We need to get this box in your truck before Landon gets here. If he sees what we're doing … ."

"If who sees what you're doing?"

I froze when I heard the new voice, swiveling quickly to find my boyfriend, Landon Michaels, surveying us from across the room. He had a cookie in his hand, which meant he'd entered the inn through the back door and ran into my mother and aunts in the kitchen.

"Hi," I said, pasting a bright smile on my face. "You're early."

"Uh-huh." Landon's gaze bounced between Aunt Tillie and me. As an FBI agent, he is trained to know when people are lying. I'm a horrible liar anyway. If I were ever held and interrogated I would give up everything and everyone in the first hour. What? I'm not good under pressure.

"I think he came early because he missed you," Aunt Tillie said, opting to take over the conversation in her own way. "He gets little hearts in his eyes when he looks at you."

"I did miss her," Landon agreed.

His office was in Traverse City, so he spent at least three nights a week away from me. It's frustrating, but we're dealing with it. Any case that takes him close to Hemlock Cove – which is more than an hour from Traverse City in northern Lower Michigan – he gladly takes so he can spend the night with me at the guesthouse Clove, Thistle and I share. It's on our family's property but still far enough away to offer privacy. Okay, sometimes we have privacy. More often than not the older women in our family simply barge in whenever they see fit.

"I told you," Aunt Tillie said. "Your love muffin can't stand to be away from you."

"I don't think he likes it when you call him that," I suggested.

Aunt Tillie shrugged, beyond caring. "He'll get over it. Now ... come on. Move that box out to my truck."

I glanced at the box again, frustrated. I bent over to pick it up but Landon nudged me away with his knee.

"What's in the box?" Landon asked.

"It's private," Aunt Tillie replied, narrowing her eyes as he moved closer to it. "You stay out of there, Fed. You need a search warrant to go through my private things, and even then I'll curse you with ants in your pants if you try to touch my stuff."

"Ants in my pants?"

"That's what I said," Aunt Tillie sniffed. "I'll make them those red ones that sting. I don't think you want stinging insects around your manhood."

Landon snorted. I can never tell how he'll react to Aunt Tillie and her threats. Sometimes he finds her funny. Other times he wants to throttle her. His face was unreadable now.

"Tell me what's in the box and maybe I'll lift it for you," Landon suggested.

"It's private," Aunt Tillie shot back. She knew darned well Landon wouldn't agree to help if he knew the contents. "It's woman stuff."

"Woman stuff?"

"You know ... tampons and pads and stuff," Aunt Tillie said, warming to her lie. "I need an industrial supply because I have estrogen issues."

As far as lies go, it wasn't Aunt Tillie's finest effort. She labored under the delusion that all men feared a woman's monthly cycle and you could terrify them with discussions about periods and cramps. Of course, with Aunt Tillie in her eighties the threat didn't hold a lot of weight in this particular scenario.

Landon wasn't about to be dissuaded by a bad lie. "Are you seriously trying to tell me that this box is full of tampons and that's why Bay can't lift it?"

"She's a weakling. What can I say?"

Landon scowled and turned to me. "Do you want to tell me anything?"

He knew I was in a bad spot. I had promised to tell him the truth ... even when it hurt. He was aware of our witchy ways and accepted them. He was aware of Aunt Tillie's penchant for breaking the law and, well, "accepted them" isn't the correct way to put it. Still, he takes her antics in stride most of the time. The problem was that Aunt Tillie was downright nasty and vindictive when put on the hot seat.

"You're very handsome and I love you," I offered, hoping my smile would be enough to distract him.

"You're cute," Landon said. "I love you, too. I still want to know what's in this box."

Crap! "It's ... ."

"I already told you it's tampons," Aunt Tillie said, cutting me off. "Why do you always have to stick your nose in stuff that's none of your concern?"

"Because you keep doing illegal things," Landon shot back, nonplussed. "I know there aren't tampons in there. I also know you only said that because you think I'm afraid of tampons. Here's a tip: Only boys under the age of twenty are afraid of tampons."

Aunt Tillie wrinkled her nose, her hands on her hips as she stared him down. "Do you want me to show you the tampons?"

Landon swallowed hard. He was pretty sure the box was tampon free, yet he was equally sure Aunt Tillie could conjure a bevy of female hygiene products if she felt like it. Aunt Tillie can make almost anyone back down. Landon is one of the few exceptions. "Show me."

Aunt Tillie sighed. "You asked for it."

"Wait!"

Landon glanced at me, feigning patience. "Yes, Bay."

"She's got wine in the box and she's trying to get me to load it into her truck so she can sell it at the festival this weekend," I blurted out. "She doesn't want you to know because you'll try to confiscate it. I really hope you don't do that, though, because I can't spend another weekend trapped in a book."

Landon nodded. "I had a feeling that's what was in the box." I watched him as he considered how to proceed. The last time he tried to stop Aunt Tillie from hawking her homemade wine she cursed us into a book of fairy tales. No one wanted to go through that ordeal again.

"That's my wine," Aunt Tillie said. "I can sell it if I want to."

"Fine," Landon said, giving in as he bent over and hoisted the box off the ground. He moved toward the front door and I hurried around him to push it open.

Aunt Tillie and I followed him down the driveway, watching as he pushed the box into the bed of Aunt Tillie's pickup truck and latched the tailgate in place. When he turned, he seemed surprised to find us right behind him.

"That's it?" Aunt Tillie cocked an eyebrow. "You're not going to fight me on this?"

"I'm not going to fight you on it," Landon conceded, pulling me in for a hug. "I did miss you this week, Bay." He gave me a quick kiss and then moved back toward the inn.

Aunt Tillie scampered after him. "I'm going to sell it."

"I don't care." Landon linked his fingers with mine. "What's for dinner tonight? I'm starving."

"They're making kebabs, rice, hummus and some other stuff," I answered, waiting for him to blow. He was too calm. He was never this calm.

"That sounds good."

"I'm going to sell it and make a lot of money," Aunt Tillie called to his back. "Then I'm going to roll around in it naked."

Landon sighed. "I don't care what you do with the money," he said. "If you're going to roll around naked in it, though, make sure you give us notice. I don't want to see that. I'll have nightmares."

LIFE'S A WITCH

"Why aren't you fighting her on this?" I asked, genuinely curious.

"I don't want to get trapped in a book, and I figure if she's selling alcohol at the town festival that doesn't fall under the purview of the FBI," Landon replied. "That's Chief Terry's problem. I have a three-day weekend ahead of me and I'm not getting involved in any of this crap. I want to relax, eat and spend time with you. That's all I want to do."

Landon is handsome in everyday circumstances, but when he's romantic and sweet he doubles his appeal. "That's sounds nice," I said.

"Nothing is going to ruin this weekend," Landon said, leading me up the steps and pulling up short when my mother appeared in the doorway. Her face was white and she clutched her hands together. "Yeah, I think I just jinxed us."

I had a feeling he was right. "What's wrong? Aunt Tillie has been with me. She couldn't possibly have done something terrible." I shot Aunt Tillie a worried look. "You haven't, right?"

Aunt Tillie scowled. "When are you going to learn that I can do anything I set my mind to, including being in two places at once? That being said, I haven't done anything bad in weeks."

Landon arched a challenging eyebrow.

"Fine! I haven't done anything bad today," Aunt Tillie conceded. "What's wrong, Winnie?"

Mom is generally good under pressure. She takes on all of life's little oddities – and Aunt Tillie's big transgressions – with an air of confidence and calm I often admire. She looked positively apoplectic, though.

"We got a call a little bit ago," Mom said, hopping from one foot to the other. "I ... well ... we have two guests who will be arriving for ten whole days starting tomorrow."

"The way you're acting you'd think it was one of those oasis buggers over in the Middle East," Aunt Tillie replied, already bored with the conversation. "If that's the case, don't worry. I'm sure I can handle them."

"ISIS, not oasis," I corrected.

"It's worse than that," Mom said.

What's worse than that? "Mom, you're starting to worry me," I said. "What's wrong? Who's coming?"

"Aunt Tillie, you're really not going to like this," Mom said.

"Then you should've told them they can't come," Aunt Tillie replied. She wasn't showing signs of being particularly bothered by Mom's worrywart nature. "Stop being dramatic. Who is it?"

"Aunt Willa and Rosemary are coming to town for the festival, and they're staying here," Mom said. "I felt caught and I told them it was fine. I'm sorry. I ... ."

For a moment, it was as if all of the oxygen had been sucked from the Earth's atmosphere and we were about to implode. Then Aunt Tillie broke the spell and erupted.

"Over my dead body!"

TWO

"Aunt Tillie, you need to calm down." Mom was atwitter with nervous energy. "Pitching a fit won't help matters."

"Says you." Aunt Tillie stalked toward Mom, but Landon snagged the back of her shirt and hauled her back before she could get close enough to slip her hands around Mom's neck and start squeezing.

"Tell me why this is such a big deal," Landon instructed, refusing to release Aunt Tillie's shirt even as she bucked and yanked against his efforts.

"Let me go!"

Landon ignored her. "Is this the same cousin and aunt we met in the horrible fairy tale world?"

I nodded. "Aunt Willa is Aunt Tillie's sister."

"She's the devil's seed!" Aunt Tillie howled. "I can't believe you invited that woman to my house!"

"Aunt Tillie, she asked." Mom couldn't stop fidgeting. "She was very pleasant on the phone. She said she wanted Rosemary to see Hemlock Cove – although she keeps referring to it as Walkerville – and I didn't see the harm."

"You mean you were spineless and refused to tell her where to stuff it," Aunt Tillie countered, furious as she finally managed to yank her shirt from Landon's grip. "I'm going to smite her to within an inch of her life."

"You'll do nothing of the sort," Mom argued, regaining some of her composure. "Aunt Willa and Rosemary are taking only one room. That's all we had. I hoped the idea of sharing a room would be enough to dissuade her, but it wasn't.

"It doesn't matter, though," she continued. "We have other guests at the inn. You cannot pick a fight with Aunt Willa when we have guests. I won't allow it."

Aunt Tillie rolled her eyes. She wasn't afraid of my mother. Well, she wasn't afraid of my mother most of the time. My mom is terrifying in her own right when she wants to dig in her heels. Aunt Tillie suddenly becomes judicious in picking her battles when that happens. I had a feeling she was going to pick this battle to win.

"What's going on?" Thistle asked, popping through the open doorway with her boyfriend Marcus close on her heels, the sun glinting off her purple hair. "What did Aunt Tillie do now?"

"Listen, fresh mouth, this has nothing to do with you, so you'd better shut it," Aunt Tillie snapped.

Thistle made a face. "Who slipped meth in your Cheerios this morning?"

"Aunt Tillie just found out that Aunt Willa and Rosemary are coming for a visit," I explained, leaning into Landon as he slipped an arm over my shoulders. He couldn't fathom why everyone was freaking out, but he knew when the Winchester witches were about to run off the rails and he was already preparing himself. "They're going to be here for ten days."

"Oh, gross," Thistle said. "Well, I take back what I just said. I'm with Aunt Tillie on this one."

Mom scowled. "Since when are you on Aunt Tillie's side? After she cursed you into the book, you vowed never to be on her side again."

"Things change," Thistle replied dryly. "I can't stand Rosemary. She's a righteous little snot."

"She's not a kid anymore," I reminded her. "She's probably a righteous big snot now."

LIFE'S A WITCH

"Who is Rosemary and why does that name sound familiar?" Marcus asked, his handsome face devoid of the horror infiltrating the rest of us.

"She's our second-cousin," Thistle explained. "Her mother, Nettie, is our mothers' cousin. Her grandmother is Aunt Tillie's sister. They're all real jerks. Aunt Tillie turned them into villains in her fairy tale world."

"Ah. Now I remember."

"Now, Thistle, we don't know that they're still jerks," Mom chided. "We haven't seen Rosemary since she was a girl."

"Yeah, at the summer camp from hell," Thistle said. "Do you remember what happened at that summer camp?"

"Yes, and we're not speaking about it," Mom hissed. "You're not helping matters."

"I remember what happened," Aunt Tillie said. "I told my sister I never wanted to see her stupid face again. In fact, I've told her that so many times I've lost count. Still, I was really firm that time. How dare she come back here!"

"You also cursed Rosemary with a spell that made her break out," Thistle said, smiling at the memory. "I loved that spell."

"Well, we'll do something worse this time," Aunt Tillie said, huffily climbing the steps. "I cannot believe you invited that woman into my house. Don't you remember what she tried to do?"

"I do remember," Mom said, choosing her words carefully. "I know you've never gotten along with Aunt Willa – and I don't blame you for hating her – but she's still family. Have you ever considered the possibility that she might want to make amends?"

"You're so naïve."

"Aunt Tillie, I'm sorry you're upset," Mom said, changing tactics. "We're adults now, though. Aunt Willa can't warp us to her way of thinking. I know you were worried about that back then.

"No matter what – not then or now – could Aunt Willa make us stop loving you," she continued. "You were always there for us. We're loyal to you."

"If you were loyal to me you wouldn't have invited that hag into my house," Aunt Tillie shot back. "Don't kid yourself. She's not coming back here to get to know you and your girls. I'm sure that's what she told you, but it's not true."

Mom bit her lip and I could tell that Aunt Tillie hit that particular nail on the head with a sledgehammer.

"She's not coming back because she cares about any of you," Aunt Tillie seethed. "She's coming back because she wants something."

"What?" Landon asked.

"To drive me crazy!" Aunt Tillie flounced into the inn, a little thought bubble filled with mayhem practically dancing over her head.

Landon glanced at me. "I think that's going to be a short trip."

"I think you're right," I muttered.

"**SO,** do you want to tell me what all the hoopla is about?"

Landon held my hand as we leisurely strolled back to the guesthouse after an uncomfortable dinner. Since most of the newly arrived guests heard all about Winchester dinner theater from earlier guests, they thought Aunt Tillie's attitude was part of the show. That was the only bright spot of an otherwise dismal meal.

"It's kind of a long story."

"We have all night, Bay," Landon replied. "I would like to know what I'm in for since these people are arriving before dinner tomorrow. I have a feeling they're going to ruin my weekend."

I frowned. That was another bombshell my mother dropped right before we left The Overlook. We were expected to be at the inn before breakfast the following morning to discuss how to welcome Aunt Willa and Rosemary with fake open arms. Apparently my mother and aunts were going all out to make them feel welcome.

"I don't really know Aunt Willa," I admitted. "I think I've seen her three times my entire life – and not one of those visits was pretty. She and Aunt Tillie truly hate each other. It's not like when Clove, Thistle and I swear that the others are dead to us when we're upset. This is true hate – actual malevolence."

"Is Willa older or younger?"

"She's the youngest in the family," I replied. "If you believe Aunt Tillie, that's why Aunt Willa acts entitled and is altogether unbearable."

"Do you believe that?"

I shrugged. "I don't remember her being nice," I answered. "She's kind of one of those relatives who lives in memory shadows. I remember her face … and I remember her being cold … but I really don't have distinctive memories of her."

"Why does Aunt Tillie hate her so much?"

"There are a lot of rumors regarding that," I said. "According to Aunt Tillie, her sister came out of the womb warped and depraved. Apparently Aunt Tillie and Aunt Willa always fought, and my grandmother was the buffer between them."

"I was under the impression that your grandmother and Aunt Tillie were close."

"They were," I said, stopping along the path that led to the guesthouse to stare at the sky. It was a beautiful night, even if the humidity from earlier remained. "My grandmother was the middle child, so she was kind of the peacekeeper. She and Aunt Tillie were close. I guess she refused to completely cut Aunt Willa out of her life like Aunt Tillie did, though. She was convinced that one day they would all be one happy family."

"That doesn't sound likely given what I've heard about Willa," Landon said. "When did things really go sour?"

"If you believe the family gossip – which I kind of do in this case – Aunt Willa went after Uncle Calvin when Aunt Tillie was dating him," I explained. "Apparently she threw herself at him, and Aunt Tillie caught her."

"And she's still alive?"

"I think it got ugly," I replied. "Aunt Willa left Walkerville – which is what Hemlock Cove used to be known as – right after graduation. She met some guy and married him. To this day I've never met him. She had one daughter named Nettie, and she spent most of her time south of us.

"When we were growing up, Aunt Tillie would tell us horrible

AMANDA M. LEE

stories about Aunt Willa," I continued. "We thought she was some sort of boogeyman until Mom set us straight and told us she was just a really terrible person and not some magical monster as Aunt Tillie painted her."

Landon snorted. "Aunt Tillie does have a way of making people see what she wants them to see."

"I think the real problem was that Aunt Willa showed up and tried to take Mom, Marnie and Twila away from Aunt Tillie after my grandmother died," I said. "Mom was already an adult and Marnie was really close to adulthood. When Aunt Willa realized she could never get her hands on them, she threatened to go after Twila."

Landon was taken aback. "She wanted to separate them right after their mother died?"

I nodded. "She threatened to take the matter to court, but Aunt Tillie warned her that Grandma tied up all of their inheritance in trusts that no one could touch. They didn't get the money until they were twenty-five.

"Aunt Willa thought Aunt Tillie was getting money for taking them in," I continued. "When she found out Aunt Tillie got the property instead and planned to use her own money to take care of everyone, she immediately backed down and left Twila with Aunt Tillie."

"So she just wanted the money?"

"That's what it seems like," I replied. "Through the years we saw Aunt Willa a few times. Aunt Tillie banished her from town the day she tried to take Twila. When she did show up, it was always uncomfortable."

"I'm surprised Aunt Tillie didn't curse her back then," Landon mused. "I don't understand why this woman would want to come back, knowing how everyone here feels about her."

"I'm sure she has an ulterior motive," I said. "We just have to watch her and see what it is."

"Tell me about Rosemary," Landon prodded. "You seem to really dislike her."

"I've only met her a few times, too," I answered. "She was a complete and total brat. We saw her at a few family reunions that were held away from the inn, and then Aunt Willa forced her on us one summer at camp."

"I went to summer camp once," Landon said. "I don't remember it being much fun even without horrible cousins to complicate things. All I remember are mosquitoes and sleeping in really dirty cabins."

"Rosemary teamed up with Lila," I explained. "They ... went after me because I was always such an easy target back then. I could see ghosts, and they thought I was being weird."

Landon brushed a stray strand of hair from my face. "I like that you're weird. You don't have anything to be ashamed about there. Stop worrying about stuff like that."

"Well, Aunt Willa doesn't like weird things and she certainly doesn't like any talk about us being witches," I supplied. "Aunt Tillie is going to be at her witchy worst, because she knows it will drive Aunt Willa crazy."

"I'm fine with that," Landon said, this thumb grazing my cheek as he studied me. "I hate to say it – and I'll probably deny it if you ever tell anyone – but I'm with Aunt Tillie. Why would your mother let these people come to the inn, knowing how everyone feels about them?"

"I don't know. I think ... I think my mother doesn't want to admit that some people are truly evil," I replied. "In her mind she probably thinks she can do the one thing my grandmother always wanted to do."

"Reunite her sisters?"

I nodded.

"Bay, sometimes people don't want to change," Landon said. "It sounds as if your Aunt Willa is one of those people. You need to be careful. If she really is up to something ... ."

"I know," I said, filling in the silence. "I wouldn't worry too much about Aunt Willa trying to pull a fast one, though. Aunt Tillie will be on her faster than you attack the plate of bacon at breakfast every morning."

Landon smirked. "Speaking of that ... ."

"Yes, Mom is cooking bacon tomorrow morning," I said. "Your weekend can start off with a cholesterol-fueled bang."

"That's good to know." Landon grabbed my chin and planted a huge kiss on me, taking me by surprise. "I missed you, my little witch. Let's go and enjoy the rest of the night together before Armageddon hits, shall we?"

His grin was too cute for words. "What did you have in mind?"

Landon slung an arm over my shoulder as we returned to our walk. "I'm so glad you asked. I've been dying to talk about how much I missed you for hours. I'm ready to show you."

Sometimes he's really good for my ego, and tonight was one of those times.

THREE

"I smell bacon," Landon said, grinning as we walked into The Overlook's kitchen the next morning.

"I'm just relieved it's not me," I muttered, my mind wandering back to one of Aunt Tillie's curses.

"Not me," Landon said, tickling my ribs. "That was the curse of my dreams."

It wasn't the curse of my dreams, but I couldn't help but giggle. He has a weird way of being able to make me smile – even if I'm expecting the world as I know it to end in a few hours.

"You two look happy," Mom said, lifting her eyes from the hissing frying pan and smiling at us. She's grown fond of Landon, mostly because she believes he's her only shot at marrying me off and possibly getting grandchildren one day. "I'm glad to see someone smiling."

"I'm just excited for bacon," Landon said, sneaking his hand under Marnie's elbow and grabbing a slice from the plate in front of her. Marnie swatted at him, but she didn't put a lot of effort into it. "Bacon makes everything better."

"I'm going to get you a slab of bacon for Christmas and call it a holiday," Mom grumbled, turning to me. "Are you going to give me crap today?"

I widened my eyes. "What did I do? You were just saying how happy I looked."

"I know you," Mom replied. "Rosemary terrorized you when you were a kid. You can't be happy about seeing her."

"No one is happy about seeing her," Landon supplied, reaching for another slice of bacon. This time Marnie caught him before he could steal his intended bounty. "I'll tell you right now, though, if she's mean to Bay I'm going to be mean to her."

Mom studied Landon, her face unreadable. After a moment, she shuffled closer to Marnie, grabbed two slices of bacon from the plate, and wordlessly handed them to Landon. "I'm pretty happy you're the one who stole my daughter's heart," she said. "Even when you argue with me, you always have her back. I like that about you."

Landon took the bacon and bowed. "You could reward me with a chocolate cake tomorrow if you really feel that way."

Mom smirked. "You have a way about you," she said, shaking her head. "Fine. We'll have chocolate cake tomorrow."

Landon winked at me, content in his victory. "Did you hear that? Your mom is making me cake."

"You're going to need that cake to put up with Aunt Willa and Rosemary," I said, breaking an end off one of his bacon slices and popping it into my mouth.

"I will share just about anything with you," Landon said, shooting me a look. "I draw the line at bacon."

I rolled my eyes. "Well, then maybe I draw the line at sharing my mom's chocolate cake."

"Oh, we both know that's not true," Landon replied, nonplussed. "You like it when I'm all sugared up, because then I have more energy for ... ."

Mom cleared her throat, causing Landon to straighten. The more time he spent around my family, the more comfortable he became. Sometimes he forgot himself.

"I was going to say that sugar gives me more energy for reading books and taking long walks under the moonlight," Landon said.

Now it was Mom's turn to roll her eyes. "Yes, well, I'll let that one slide today," she said. "I have enough on my plate. Speaking of that, where are Clove and Thistle?"

"They should be here any minute," I replied. "The guesthouse has one bathroom and six people stayed there last night."

"Yeah, we had to conserve water and shower together," Landon said, winking at my mom and hopping out of the way when she tried to swat him with her spatula. "The others should be down pretty soon."

"You have a smart mouth," Mom said, waving the spatula in Landon's face. "You're going to want to cut out the sex talk if you don't want to make Aunt Willa die of a heart attack."

"I don't really care what she thinks," Landon countered. "From what I understand, she's a horrible woman. I also understand that this … Rosemary … was mean to my blonde. I'm not going to put up with that. So if she's mean to Bay now, I'm going to say something. You've been forewarned."

"Landon, I understand that you want to stand up for Bay … ." Mom broke off, uncertain. "Actually, I don't know where I was going with that. Forget what I was about to say. I always want you to stand up for Bay. I would appreciate it, though, if you didn't do anything until Aunt Willa and Rosemary prove that they deserve it."

"I can live with that," Landon said, grabbing my hand. "Come on, Bay. Let's go see what Aunt Tillie is plotting. I need to know if I should pick up more fire extinguishers in town today."

We found Aunt Tillie sitting at the head of the dining room table, her gaze fixed on an empty space at the other end. I was pretty sure she was imagining Aunt Willa sitting there and wishing she had the strength to set someone ablaze with the power of her mind. That was one trick she hadn't yet mastered. Lightning was another story.

"What are you doing?" Landon asked, slipping into the seat next to her. We were early. The other guests were still upstairs. That was probably a good thing.

"I'm debating how I'm going to kill Willa," Aunt Tillie replied, not missing a beat. "What's painful but not messy?"

"You realize I'm with the FBI, right?"

"That's why I'm not going to involve you with my plan," Aunt Tillie said. "I'm not an idiot."

"Oh, well, good," Landon said, shooting me a reassuring wink. He wasn't worried about Aunt Tillie killing anyone. He was worried about her releasing unholy havoc on Hemlock Cove to prove her dominance, though.

"Aunt Tillie, can I ask you something?"

Aunt Tillie shifted her attention to me. "Don't worry, crybaby. I won't really kill her."

I scowled. I hated it when she called me that when I was younger. It was downright annoying as an adult. "That's not what I'm worried about."

Aunt Tillie waited.

"Did Grandma think Aunt Willa was a good person? Is that why she refused to cut her out of her life?"

"Your grandmother was a good person, and that's why she couldn't completely cut Willa out of her life," Aunt Tillie replied. "She ... had a heart of gold. She was the best of us all."

"Would she have changed her mind if she knew Aunt Willa tried to take Mom, Twila and Marnie away from you?"

"If she knew that she'd have burned Willa's house to the ground," Aunt Tillie answered. "Ginger could take a lot. She would not take anyone messing with her girls."

"Kind of like you, huh?"

"Oh, I'm meaner than Ginger ever dreamed of being," Aunt Tillie countered. "I loved your grandmother, but she had a weak imagination. I'm not encumbered by that little personality defect. When I kill Willa, it will be inventive."

"Like what?" Landon asked, clearly enjoying the game.

"Well, I was considering hedge clippers, but that will ruin the carpet if I do it inside, and you know how your mother feels about messes."

Landon patted the seat next to him to entice me to sit. "You don't want to do anything that leaves a body," he said. "Try to think of something involving fire."

"Don't encourage her," I warned, settling next to him. "If she thinks you're on her side, she's going to play up to her audience."

"I am on her side," Landon said. "I don't like anyone who was mean to you. That includes family members."

"You put up with Thistle," I reminded him.

"Yes, well ... that's sister stuff," Landon argued. "You guys fight like sisters, and that means low blows land every so often. I've learned to live with that."

Aunt Tillie snorted. "You're smarter than you look sometimes."

"Thank you ... I think." Landon shifted his gaze to me. "Do you have a lot of work to do today?"

"No."

"How about I drop you at the newspaper and then we get lunch?" he suggested. "I want to stop by to talk with Terry about a few things."

"It had better not be about my wine," Aunt Tillie interjected.

"No promises," Landon replied. "How does that sound, Bay?"

"It sounds good," I said. "I can finish all my stuff up in an hour or so. Brian wants to have a meeting about some new grand plan he has to boost circulation for The Whistler."

Brian Kelly owned the newspaper where I worked. Other than me, the only other regular staff included a layout person and photographer – and they were part-time. Since Brian's grandfather left a stipulation in his will that said he couldn't sell The Whistler, he was constantly devising ways to boost circulation and advertising to fatten his wallet.

"I don't like that guy," Landon muttered. "He keeps looking at you as if you're on the menu and he wants to order a la carte."

"Nice."

Landon squeezed my hand. "I can't help it if I feel territorial," he said. "You're mine, little witch."

"Ugh, you two are like a bad romance novel," Aunt Tillie muttered. "If I'm going to set anyone on fire, it's you two."

AMANDA M. LEE

"Oh, what a sweet sentiment," Thistle said, breezing into the room with Marcus, Clove and Sam on her heels. "What did I miss?"

"The fact that purple hair went out in the nineties," Aunt Tillie replied, gracing Thistle with a snarky smile.

"Ha, ha," Thistle intoned. "I thought we were working together this week since we have a mutual enemy. Has all of that gone away because you're crabby in the morning?"

"Sit your butt down," Aunt Tillie ordered. "We need to have a strategy session."

"Does anyone else think these guys are being overly dramatic?" Sam asked, taking his spot next to Clove at the table. He was the newest member of our little group, thanks to his romance with Clove. He was still getting used to our witchy ways. "These people can't be as bad as everyone makes them out to be."

"Have you ever seen *The Walking Dead*?" Aunt Tillie asked.

"Yes." Sam's face was neutral, but his eyes glowed with mirth.

"You know the zombies?"

"Are you saying that Aunt Willa and Rosemary are like zombies?" Sam asked. "If so, that means they're slow moving and we can take them."

"No, dumbass. I'm saying that they're like the cannibals who ate that guy's leg in front of him while he was still alive," Aunt Tillie countered. Of all the men in our lives, Sam was her least favorite. He'd grown in leaps and bounds in her estimation in recent months, but she wasn't exactly fond of him. "I would prefer zombies."

"Okay, I'll bite," Landon said. "How so?"

"Willa is a meat eater who doesn't care who she sacrifices as long she lives to tell the tale."

"You just described yourself," Landon pointed out.

"You're on my list," Aunt Tillie hissed, extending a warning finger in his direction. "You're right that I'll sacrifice those I don't care about to save myself. However, I'll also sacrifice them for the people I love. Willa isn't loyal to anyone ... but Satan."

I pursed my lips to keep from laughing. She was really wound up today. "Do you want to get together and plot with us at Hypnotic this afternoon?"

Landon shifted. "I thought we were having lunch."

"You can come plot with us," I offered. For some reason, I knew Aunt Tillie needed unfettered loyalty more than Landon needed a private lunch. She was feeling exposed. This was the best way I knew to give her the support she needed.

"That's a great idea," Aunt Tillie said, her eyes lighting up. "I'll steal cookies so we have something to eat."

"I'm going to have to take a pass," Marcus said. "I have stuff to do at the stable if I'm going to be ready for the expansion."

Thistle narrowed her eyes. "What stuff?" Marcus only recently announced his plan to expand Hemlock Cove's stables, and she was still getting used to the idea. Her biggest problem was that Marcus wouldn't let her take over the planning.

"Stuff that doesn't involve plotting," Marcus replied. "I love you. I don't want to get involved in this unless I have to, though."

Clove glanced at Sam. "What about you?"

"I'm going to withhold judgment until I actually meet these people," Sam replied. "I'm sure you understand that I need more to go on than Aunt Tillie's hatred before I can jump on the bandwagon."

Aunt Tillie scorched Sam with a hateful look. "You're never getting off my list. You know that, right?" She turned to Landon and arched an eyebrow. "What about you, Fed? Are you going to help or hinder me this week?"

"Oh, I'm in," Landon said.

Marcus shot him a surprised look. "You are?"

"I'm not risking getting cursed into another book," Landon replied. "Plus ... I already don't like these women on principle. I'm not as ... hopeful ... as the two of you. I have a feeling that Willa is coming here because she's up to something."

"What makes you think that?"

"Let's just say I think manipulation is part of the genetic makeup when it comes to the women in this family," Landon replied. "I know that Aunt Tillie won't let anyone purposely hurt Bay. Sure, she likes to do it as payback, but she stomps anyone else who tries. I'm siding with Aunt Tillie on this one."

"And you're off my list," Aunt Tillie said, beaming.

"Oh, screw it," Marcus said. "Count me in. If Landon thinks it's a good idea, who am I to argue?"

All eyes in the room turned expectantly to Sam.

"Oh, fine," Sam grumbled. "I'm only doing this so I can finally say I was part of the group, though."

"That's good," Landon said. "As the newest member of our group, that means you're responsible for lunch."

Sam frowned. "Now I have to buy lunch?"

"I want Olive Garden," Aunt Tillie said. "I want the seafood Alfredo and minestrone soup."

"And where am I supposed to get Olive Garden around here?"

"Traverse City is only an hour away," Aunt Tillie replied, blasé. "If you leave after breakfast you should have no problem picking up our lunch and getting back in time."

"Oh, well, this is just perfect," Sam muttered.

"Don't forget the breadsticks," Aunt Tillie said. "Make sure they're still warm."

"Being the newest member of this group sucks!"

FOUR

"I have a great new idea for the newspaper. You're going to kick yourself for not thinking of this yourself, Bay."

Brian Kelly sat behind his grandfather's desk, looking more like a boy playing publisher than the actual thing. When he first arrived in Hemlock Cove I found him annoying but tolerable. Now I mostly want to smack him in the head.

"And what's your new idea?"

Brian leaned forward, giving the impression that he was about to impart one of the world's greatest secrets. "We're going to do ... people features."

Oh, well, great. "Like what?"

"You know ... features on people." Brian held up his hands and shook them to emphasize his point. It still seemed like a lame idea to me.

"But features on people doing what?" I pressed. "Are there people in Hemlock Cove doing tricks I'm not aware of?"

Brian sighed. He hated my attitude. There was nothing he could do about it, though. His grandfather stipulated that I was to remain editor of The Whistler. If Brian tried to sell it – or fire me – I had the option of taking over the newspaper's ownership. That was the last thing Brian wanted.

"People features are a great way to draw readers in," Brian said, changing tactics. "They can be charming, funny, and if we do them right we can coax the business owners to buy ads."

He was so full of it I couldn't help but wonder how he didn't fall over more often due to the size of his ego. "And how does that work?"

"Are you purposely trying to be difficult?"

"No. I want to know how writing people features increases advertising."

Brian sighed, petulant and overdramatic. "If you do stories on people who have businesses, they're going to be excited and buy more copies of the paper," he said. "Once they do that, other people are going to realize they want a feature. Then they're going to buy more ads just so they can stop in and get a feature. Do you see how that works?"

Not even remotely. "I don't think it's going to work that way," I said, rolling my neck until it cracked. "Do you remember when you insisted on doing business features and we ran out of ideas within four months? Those didn't bring in extra advertising dollars."

Brian made a face. "I think that was your fault."

Of course he did. "I think that Hemlock Cove's advertising dollars are pretty well set," I countered. "Unless a new business comes to town – like the Dragonfly or the Dandridge – you have a set amount of dollars that are going to be spent. Most of the businesses here run a weekly ad already. Why do you think they're going to start running two?"

"Because ... ." Brian was stumped. It wasn't hard to do. "Because it will."

"Fine," I said, giving in. It would be easier to write three people features and let him find out for himself that it was for naught than argue with him. "Who do you want the first feature on?"

Brian was surprised by my capitulation. "Um ... let me think about it for a few days and get back to you."

"I can't wait," I said, getting to my feet. I stilled when I realized he was still staring at me. "Was there something else?"

"Are you still dating that FBI agent?"

Oh, good grief. "Yes," I said. "We're very happy."

"Okay," Brian said. "Well ... let me know when you break up."

"You'll be the first one I tell."

By the time I got back to my office I was debating the merits of letting Aunt Tillie loose on Brian – she hated him, too – when The Whistler's resident ghost, Edith, popped into view. I took an involuntary step back, my hand clutching the spot over my heart as I focused on her sharp features. "How many times have I told you not to do that?"

"If I could figure out a way to ring a bell before showing up I would do it," Edith sniffed.

I shut the door to my office, making sure prying ears couldn't overhear our conversation. Brian couldn't see or hear ghosts, so he would think I was talking to myself if I carried on a conversation in the open. I wasn't keen on him thinking I was crazy – er, well, crazier. He'd sat through too many meals at The Overlook to think anyone in my family was of sound mind. At least this way he wouldn't be able to hear our conversation – even if he happened by and saw my lips moving.

"What do you want?" I asked, turning my full attention to Edith. Since this week's edition of The Whistler was already out, and my meeting with Brian was over, all I needed to do to finish my day was plot with my family. It was a nice feeling.

"You're the only person who can see me, and that makes you the only person I have to talk with," Edith said dryly. "Why do you think I'm here?"

Edith died long before I joined The Whistler staff. I had a feeling she was even less pleasant in life than she was in death. She had to be somewhat friendly to me. If she wasn't, she would have absolutely no one to talk with. The only other people in Hemlock Cove who can see and hear her are Sam and Aunt Tillie. Speaking of that ... .

"You knew my Aunt Tillie way back when, right?"

Edith seemed surprised by the question. "Are you trying to torture me?"

I didn't bother hiding my smirk. Edith's history with Aunt Tillie was almost as tempestuous as Aunt Willa's. "No. It's just ... did you know my Aunt Willa?"

"I went to school with Willa and Tillie," Edith replied. "They were nothing alike."

I wasn't sure how to take that. "Does that mean you liked Aunt Willa?"

"Oh, definitely," Edith said. "She was pleasant, and she was the only Winchester girl who tried to follow the rules."

It didn't surprise me that Edith preferred Aunt Willa to Aunt Tillie. Edith was a prim and proper woman with a belief system that bordered on the offensive at times. Oh, who am I kidding? The woman is a bigot who idles at unpleasant. I still feel sorry for her, because she has no one else to talk with.

"Did Aunt Tillie and Aunt Willa ever get along?"

Edith furrowed her ethereal brow. "Not that I recall," she answered. "Ginger and Tillie were thick as thieves. Tillie and Willa hated each other. Ginger seemed to ... tolerate Willa. She tried to get along with her – or at least it seemed that way to me. They weren't tight, though. Not like three sisters should be."

"Do you know why?"

"Tillie is evil." Edith answered without taking a moment to even consider the question.

"You were dead by the time my grandmother died," I said. "You were still hanging around here, though. Do you remember anyone talking about Aunt Willa trying to get custody of Twila?"

"No," Edith replied. "I do remember everyone being sad. Unlike Tillie, Ginger was beloved. She was a good mother. She would've been a great grandmother for you girls. Much better than ... Tillie."

"Aunt Tillie was a great grandmother to us," I countered, loyalty taking over. "We had a lot of fun with her. She wasn't perfect, but no one is."

"I'm not going to fight with you about Tillie," Edith said. "I am curious as to why you're asking about Willa, though."

"She's coming to town. She'll be here tonight. Aunt Tillie is ... upset."

Edith snorted. "In other words you're about to bear witness to World War III, and you're worried," she said. "I would be, too. I once saw Tillie and Willa come to blows in the town square."

"You did?"

"I don't know what it was about, but whatever it was had both of them screeching like angry cats and scratching each other," Edith said. "Ginger rushed in and played peacekeeper – like she always did – and when the dust settled they were still facing off. I remember – and it's funny the things you remember from your youth – but Tillie declared that there was room for only one of them in this town. I guess she won."

"I guess she did," I said. "I still don't understand why Aunt Willa is coming."

"Maybe she wants to make amends."

"I've only met her a few times, but nothing makes me think that's her goal," I replied. I shook myself out of my reverie. "Anyway, I probably won't be back until Monday. I have to go to Hypnotic and plan Aunt Willa's demise with everyone else. If you get bored, you should come out to The Overlook to see the show."

It was an empty gesture. Edith was uncomfortable leaving The Whistler. She'd ventured out a few times, but she almost always retreated to the place she knew best.

"I'll consider it."

"**SO**, what do we want to do to Willa first?" Aunt Tillie asked shortly before noon, rubbing her hands together as she sat on Hypnotic's couch. She loved being the center of attention. She also loved plotting. If it wasn't so hot and humid outside, I would almost believe it was Christmas for her.

"Shouldn't we wait for Sam?" Clove asked, worrying her bottom

AMANDA M. LEE

lip with her teeth as she glanced toward the door. "He drove all the way to Traverse City to get you Olive Garden. It doesn't seem fair to cut him out of the planning."

Aunt Tillie rolled her eyes as Landon and I exchanged an amused look. "We're going to be planning for ten days. He'll have his turn. Don't worry about that."

Clove sighed, resigned. "Okay. What's your big plan?"

"Well, I was thinking I would do the 'Drunk as a Skunk' curse to start things off," Aunt Tillie suggested.

Thistle and I shook our heads in unison.

"You can't do that one," Thistle said. "Mom will know it was you."

"What's the 'Drunk as a Skunk' curse?" Marcus asked.

"It essentially makes Aunt Willa act drunk and do stupid things," I explained.

"Was that the spell she cast at the Dragonfly's soft opening?" Landon asked, narrowing his eyes. He wasn't a fan of that spell, mostly because everyone got out of hand and started fighting.

"Yes."

"We're not doing that one," Landon said. "I don't like how upset Bay and Thistle got."

"When did you become the boss?" Aunt Tillie challenged.

"When you decided to start plotting in front of me," Landon replied, unruffled. "If I remember correctly, you, Marcus and Thistle ended up sharing a bed that night. How well did that work out for you?"

"Pretty well," Aunt Tillie shot back. "Marcus felt me up."

"I did not!" Marcus was horrified.

Thistle patted his knee. "She's only messing with you."

"She's doing a good job of it."

Landon snickered. "Can't you come up with something that's embarrassing but not so destructive that it will tip off Winnie, Marnie and Twila that you're responsible?"

"What's the fun in that?" Aunt Tillie's face was blank.

Landon sighed. "Can't you … I don't know … curse her to be nice?"

Aunt Tillie stilled. "I … huh."

"Oh, that might be fun," Thistle said. "You could make it so she can say only nice things."

"I like that idea," Clove said. "Although … ."

"I knew you would be the one to be a baby about this," Aunt Tillie muttered. "What's your problem now?"

"I don't have a problem," Clove protested. She was always the first to get nervous right before a big spell. "I think if Aunt Willa is a B-I-T-C-H, we should definitely curse her with that spell."

Landon glanced over his shoulder. "Who are you spelling for?"

"She doesn't like to swear," Thistle replied. "She has a Mary Sue complex."

"I do not." Clove crossed her arms over her chest. "I just don't think it's necessary to be crass."

"Well, I'm going to side with Clove on this one," Landon said. "Not about the spelling thing; that's weird. I do think you should have a plan in place for Willa if she's going to be a … pain. However, I would prefer you didn't cast the spell until we feel her out."

"I prefer going on the offensive before she hits town," Aunt Tillie countered.

"I know you do," Landon said. "Don't you want to know what she's doing here first, though?"

"What do you mean?"

"She's coming for a reason," Landon said. "I agree with you that no matter why she pretends she's here, she has ulterior motives. If you cast a nice spell on her, she might not tip her hand to what that is. I, for one, want to know what she's up to."

"You have a devious mind," Aunt Tillie said. "I like that. Still, I want to make sure we're prepared. We should come up with a list of spells and make sure we have all of the ingredients we need from the store before we go."

"You know we don't keep any of the hard herbs here," Thistle said. "If you want the big dogs, you'll have to cut them from your own greenhouse."

"Fine," Aunt Tillie said, rolling her eyes. "We need a list, though."

"Let's get to it," Thistle said, grabbing a notebook from the end table. "Why doesn't everyone shout out their favorite spells and I'll write them all down. Then, when we have everything nice and tidy, we can cross off things we don't like."

"I like the bacon spell," Landon announced.

I made an exasperated sound in the back of my throat. "Do you really want Aunt Willa to go around smelling like bacon? You know she's not going to find it funny if you lick her face."

Landon scowled. "That's disgusting. I want you to smell like bacon again."

"Well, you're the only one."

"I want you guys to smell like bacon again, too," Marcus admitted, averting his eyes when Thistle glared at him.

"No," I argued. "I hate that spell."

"I'll make them smell like bacon again when this is all over with if you guys help me this week," Aunt Tillie offered.

"How is that a reward for us?" Thistle challenged.

"I didn't say it was a reward for you, fresh mouth," Aunt Tillie replied. "I just think the boys should earn a fun day for themselves if they help me."

"I'm starting to like being on Aunt Tillie's side," Landon said, slinging an arm over my shoulders. "Let's start the list. The faster we win, the faster I get to lick Bay's face."

I opened my mouth, a harsh retort on my lips, but was cut short by Sam's arrival. He had two huge bags of food and a nasty look on his face.

"Hi, honey," Clove said, hopping to her feet and scampering to his side. "Thank you so much for doing this."

"Did you guys start without me?" Sam was angry. "I drove two hours to get you people lunch and you started without me!"

"Welcome to the group," Landon said. "The good news is that we also negotiated a day for Aunt Tillie to curse the girls so they smell like bacon when this is all over."

Sam brightened considerably. "Well, then I guess it was worth it."

Landon winked at me. "It will be totally worth it. Now, if I could only find a way to add tomato and bread to the spell, things would be perfect."

I shook my head. "You're sick."

"Oh, you haven't seen anything yet."

FIVE

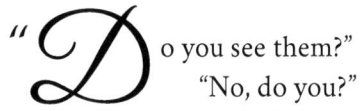

"Do you see them?"

"No, do you?"

"Would I have asked if you saw them if I saw them?"

Thistle rolled her eyes as we stood in the doorway between the library and main foyer. Mom, Marnie and Twila fluttered about, exchanging nervous whispers and pacing grooves into the hardwood floors. Everyone was on edge waiting for Aunt Willa and Rosemary's big arrival. I had no idea where Aunt Tillie was. Wherever she was dealing with her edginess, she was not inside the inn. We checked – eight times – and could not find her. She was probably out taking the edge off in her pot field, which was going to be a whole other issue when she finally did make her presence known.

"Stop hovering in the doorway," Landon ordered, reclining on the couch as he flipped through this week's edition of The Whistler. "Haven't you heard that expression about a watched pot never boiling?"

"Have you ever watched Aunt Tillie boil something?" Thistle challenged. "She can make a pot boil with the power of her mind."

Landon glanced at me. "Is that true?"

I shrugged. "She can also control the weather and make pigeons poop on the cars of her enemies."

Landon snorted. "That's probably more information than I needed." He patted the spot next to him on the couch. "Come on, Bay. Have a drink and relax."

"You, too, Thistle," Marcus instructed, pouring two glasses of wine and handing one to each of us.

I reluctantly joined Landon on the couch while Thistle perched on the arm of Marcus's chair. Nobody wanted to talk about Aunt Willa's arrival, yet it was all we could think about.

"Where is Clove?" Thistle asked, shifting her eyes so she could scan the hallway. "She was supposed to be here twenty minutes ago."

"She was waiting for Sam at the guesthouse," I replied. "I think his nose was out of joint about lunch and plotting without him."

"That's not why she's waiting for him," Landon countered. "Sure, he was ticked about lunch, but she wants a few minutes alone so they can cuddle without you two making fun of her."

"Cuddle?"

Landon tweaked my nose. "What would you call it? Would you prefer I said they were down there getting to third base?"

Mom poked her head in the library. "No sex talk tonight, mister!"

Sometimes she has supersonic hearing, I swear. "Are you eavesdropping on us?"

Mom ignored the question and backed out of the library to resume her pacing.

"I don't think she trusts me sometimes," Landon said.

"And you have such a trustworthy face," I teased, tugging on his cheek. "I just want to kiss it."

"I guess I can tolerate that," Landon said, leaning in and planting a big smack on my lips. I was surprised when he jerked his head away a moment later. When I looked up, I realized why. Mom had a hunk of his hair in her hand.

"There will be none of that," Mom warned. "Aunt Willa doesn't like it when people show affection."

Landon pulled his head back so that Mom lost her grip. "Can

someone explain to me again exactly why we care what this woman thinks?"

Mom crossed her arms over her chest. "Because she's family."

"Aunt Tillie is family and we don't care what she thinks," Thistle said.

"Speaking of Aunt Tillie … ." Mom narrowed her eyes, her mind clearly busy. "Has anyone seen Aunt Tillie since breakfast?"

Uh-oh. That was a loaded question.

"No," Thistle lied, taking a hard decision away from me. "She's probably down at her greenhouse. Isn't Belinda here today? Aunt Tillie prefers spending time with Annie rather than us as it is. Leave her down there."

Belinda and Annie were the newest members of our extended family. After discovering Annie disheveled and dazed walking along the road, we took care of her for two days before we found her mother unconscious in a ditch after a car crash. After Belinda's recovery, Mom gave her a job – they really did need an extra pair of hands – and Belinda and Annie were living in the attic room until they could get on their feet financially.

Belinda was a godsend to our mothers, and Annie ingratiated herself to just about everyone, including Aunt Tillie. No one was more surprised than me that Aunt Tillie seemed to enjoy Annie's presence. She took the girl with her everywhere when she was around – which was often now that school was out – and Annie loved working in the greenhouse with Aunt Tillie. Landon put his foot down about Annie working in the pot field, but I had a feeling Aunt Tillie was getting around his ultimatum by only letting Annie work out there when she was sure Landon was stuck in Traverse City for the day.

"Belinda dressed Annie up to meet Aunt Willa," Mom replied. "I hope Aunt Tillie isn't letting her get dirty."

"Yes, because that would be the real shame of the evening," Landon deadpanned. "Ignore the horrible people insulting everyone, because there's a child who got dirty after having a good time."

Mom scorched him with a look. "Why are you being so difficult? You don't even know Aunt Willa and Rosemary."

"Technically, that's not true," Landon countered. "They were in the fairy tale book."

"That wasn't really them."

"Are you sure? Because the characters Aunt Tillie based on you seemed a lot like you," Landon said. "Right now, for instance. I'm expecting you to try to behead me at any moment."

I pursed my lips. Landon was still upset about being cursed into the book and he was clearly unhappy with the idea of putting on a show for people he disliked.

"Landon, I know you want to protect Bay, and I applaud that," Mom said, choosing her words carefully. "I think you're brave and loyal. I even like your hair, despite all the things Aunt Tillie says about it."

Landon preened.

"You still need to shut up and act like a proper gentleman tonight," Mom continued. "Suck it up. You're not a child. You're an FBI agent, for crying out loud. You have to deal with people you dislike all the time. Stop being a pain."

Landon ran his tongue over his teeth as he decided how to respond. "Fine," he said finally. "I will be on my best behavior. If either one of them says one word to anyone in this family, though … ."

"Then you can beat your chest and go all caveman on them," Mom said, cutting him off. "You're a representative of this family tonight. You too, Marcus. That means you have to be pleasant to our guests … and Aunt Willa and Rosemary are technically paying guests."

"I've got twenty bucks that says they find a way not to pay their bill," Thistle said.

Mom swiveled to focus on her niece. "Couldn't you have picked a less … vibrant … color for you hair this month? Aunt Willa is going to have a heart attack when she sees that purple."

Thistle's short-cropped hair changed more frequently than Aunt Tillie's plans for world domination. I barely noticed when she changed her color these days.

"Now you're making me wish I had dyed it eight different colors,"

AMANDA M. LEE

Thistle shot back. "I didn't know potential heart attacks were an option. Darn. I missed out on a golden opportunity there."

"You all are going to give me an ulcer," Mom said, pressing her hand to her stomach. Aunt Willa's imminent arrival had managed to unnerve her. It was a disturbing sight.

"We'll all behave, Mom," I said. "I promise."

"Can you guarantee your Aunt Tillie is going to behave?"

"I can guarantee that she ... probably won't kill anyone," I replied, although I wasn't sure that was true. "That's the best I can do."

"Oh, whatever," Mom said. "I ... ."

Whatever she was about to say died on her lips when Twila poked her riotous red head into the library. "They're here."

AUNT WILLA LOOKED DIFFERENTLY than she did in the fairy tale world. Deep lines pulled at the corners of her eyes, and her hair, which was more gray than anything else, was pulled back in a severe bun. She dressed in an expensive suit that was completely impractical for a week in Hemlock Cove, and the smile she flashed at Mom was disingenuous.

What? I swear I'm keeping an open mind.

"It's so good to see you, Winnie," Aunt Willa said, pulling Mom in for a stiff hug.

Marnie and Twila lined up behind their sister, ready for their turn in front of the firing squad. By the time Aunt Willa turned to Thistle and me she looked bored with the whole witch and wardrobe show.

"You must be ... Bay," Aunt Willa said, glancing over her shoulder so she could see Rosemary give her a cursory nod. "You've grown into a ... lovely ... girl."

She said "lovely" like I would spit out "pus boil." I smiled regardless. "Thank you."

"And Thistle ... ." Aunt Willa looked her up and down. "You look like your mother."

Thistle and I exchanged bemused looks. Aunt Willa didn't even try to muster a compliment on that one.

"How are you, Bay?" Rosemary asked, stepping up behind her grandmother.

Rosemary's long hair was curled into spiral waves, stiff with too much hairspray, and her face was as pinched and unpleasant as I remembered from childhood.

"I'm good," I replied. "How are you?"

"Well, I'm a lawyer," Rosemary replied. "I make more than sixty-thousand dollars a year. I have benefits and four paid weeks of vacation."

What a weird way to introduce yourself to someone after almost fifteen years of separation. "Congratulations?"

"Yes, I'm doing quite well." Rosemary obviously missed my discomfort as she shifted her eyes to Landon. "And you are?"

"Oh, I'm sorry," I said, regaining my faulty faculties. "This is Landon Michaels. He's … ."

"Let me guess," Rosemary interrupted. "Are you the … gardener?"

Landon narrowed his eyes. "I'm the FBI agent."

"Oh, no," Aunt Willa said, her hand flying to her chest. "I hope something horrible hasn't happened. Are you here to arrest Tillie? I'm sure whatever she did was a mistake."

Mom chuckled hoarsely. "No, Aunt Willa. He's not here to arrest anyone," she explained. "He's Bay's boyfriend."

"Boyfriend?" Rosemary arched a perfectly sculpted eyebrow. "You're with Bay?"

Landon moved closer to me and slipped an arm around my waist. I could tell he was already tired of Aunt Willa and Rosemary's feigned perfection. "I am," he said. "It's a tough job, but I'm up to the task."

"Well, that's nice," Aunt Willa said. "I … can you really be an FBI agent with hair that long?"

Landon maintained he needed his hair long in case he had to go undercover again. That's how we met, and his hair was one of the things I noticed on initial introduction. He hadn't gone undercover in more than a year, though, and I was starting to think he liked it long because he knew it added to his sex appeal.

"There aren't any rules about hair length in the bureau," Landon replied. "My boss is fine with it."

"Oh, well, that's nice," Aunt Willa said, dismissing Landon and turning to Marcus. "And who are you?"

"This is Marcus," Thistle supplied. "He owns the stable in town. He's my boyfriend."

"He has long hair, too."

"I can say with certainty that the horses don't mind," Marcus quipped. No one laughed so he snapped his mouth shut. He probably wouldn't open it again for the rest of the night.

"And where is Clove?" Aunt Willa asked. "She's the one who is missing, right? I would've thought she'd want to be here to greet me."

"She's down at the guesthouse waiting for her boyfriend," Thistle answered. "She'll be here soon."

"And what does her boyfriend do?" Rosemary asked. "Is he with the FBI, too?"

I already wanted to smack her. Even as a child she was surly and mean. Those characteristics were even more unappealing on an adult. "He owns the Dandridge," I said. "It's a local lighthouse. He's been renovating it to turn it into a haunted attraction. It's a big job. That's probably why he's late."

Without anyone left to focus her attention on, Aunt Willa finally brought up the one person we were all terrified for her to interact with. "And where is my sister?"

"We think she's down in the greenhouse with Annie," Thistle said. "She'll be back in time for dinner."

"I don't remember a greenhouse on the property," Aunt Willa said, wrinkling her nose. "Is that new?"

"We had it constructed in the spring as a gift for Aunt Tillie," Mom explained. "She loves it."

"And who is Annie?"

"She's ... ." Mom broke off, unsure how to respond.

"She's the daughter of a woman who works here," Landon said, taking the onus of the conversation off Mom. "She's a sweet girl, and she's taken a shine to Aunt Tillie."

"Yes, well, Tillie always had a way with children," Aunt Willa sniffed. "She was a big child herself, and that's why children liked her. They never understood that rules were important to growing up, because Tillie never instilled that in them."

I frowned. Aunt Tillie did have more in common with children – including perfected hissy fits and tantrums – but I didn't like the way Aunt Willa talked about my great-aunt. If anyone was going to talk bad about the woman, it would be one of us.

"She's good with Annie," I supplied. "They enjoy hanging out. I'm sure she'll be up here shortly."

"Oh, I'm sure she will, too," Aunt Willa said, offering me a patronizing pat on the head as she moved past me. "I'd love to take a look around and see everything you've done here."

"I ... of course," Mom said, glancing at Marnie and Twila. "I'm sure that Bay and Thistle can show you around while we put the finishing touches on dinner."

"I'd rather be hit by Aunt Tillie's plow," Thistle muttered.

"I'd rather drive the plow and run away," Landon added.

"Did you two say something?" Aunt Willa asked.

"No," Mom said, drawing Aunt Willa's attention back to her. "They would all be thrilled to show you around the property."

That was news to the four of us.

"Well, let's start with the greenhouse," Aunt Willa suggested.

"I don't think ... ." I shot Mom a worried look.

"Aunt Tillie doesn't allow anyone in the greenhouse unless she specifically invites them," Marcus said, shifting uncomfortably. I was surprised he braved adding to the conversation again after his joke fell flat. "Last time I checked, Bay and Thistle were banned."

"Banned?" Aunt Willa made a face. "She banned you from her greenhouse?"

"To be fair, we did keep searching it and one of the guys we went to high school with hid money he stole from the bank in there. She wasn't happy."

"Ah ... ." Aunt Willa clearly had no idea how to respond to that. "I want to see the greenhouse, though."

"That will be happening over my dead body," Aunt Tillie said, appearing in the doorway, Annie at her side. "I would rather die a thousand deaths than let you anywhere near my greenhouse."

Landon leaned back, amused as he lowered his mouth to my ear so only I could hear what he was about to say. "And so it begins."

SIX

"Tillie."

"Willa."

That was the end of the conversation.

"Aunt Tillie, we were wondering where you were," Mom said, attempting to break the uncomfortable pall settling over the room. "We figured you were down in your greenhouse."

"We were," Annie said, her eyes sparkling. "Aunt Tillie taught me how to ... ."

"No one needs to hear about that," Aunt Tillie said, patting Annie's head. "Our gardening time is private."

"I bet," Landon muttered.

Annie's eyes lit up when they landed on Marcus. "Marcus!" She hurried across the room and threw herself at him, giggling as he caught her mid-jump and hoisted her up. "I'm so glad you're here. I haven't seen you in days and I thought I would just die if you didn't come around soon."

I smirked. Annie developed a crush on Marcus not long after we found her. She absolutely loved him. He played the part well, doting on her and feigning interest in every story and excited utterance.

"There's no need to die," Marcus said. "I've been busy at the stable.

I'll try to remember that your life is in constant peril and stop by more often. I was here last night, but you weren't. I thought I would die of disappointment."

"Mom made me go to the reading group at the library," Annie said, making a face.

"That's good for you," Landon interjected. "Reading is a lot of fun."

"You have to say that because you're 'The Man,'" Annie said. She'd picked up a few of Aunt Tillie's favorite phrases over the past few weeks. "'The Man' is always trying to take the fun out of life."

Landon scowled and shot a dark look in Aunt Tillie's direction. "Will you stop telling her things like that?"

Aunt Tillie shrugged. "I can't lie to the girl. She looks up to me."

"I agree with Landon on this one," Marcus said, risking Aunt Tillie's wrath in the process. "You should read as much as you can. It's a good habit."

"Yes, but all the kids there were babies," Annie explained. "I like hanging out with you guys more. You're not babies. Well … except for Clove sometimes. Aunt Tillie says she whines like a baby."

"Well, I see I arrived just in time," Clove said, walking into the room with Sam at her side.

"I said you whined like a baby some of the time," Aunt Tillie said. "I just told them – and now I'll tell you – that I promised not to lie to her. What would you have me do?"

"I'm not sure this is a conversation we should be having now," Mom said, nervously clasping her hands. Everyone ignored her.

"Stop telling her things that alienate us from her," Landon suggested. He would never admit it, but I knew his nose was a little out of joint because Annie had a crush on Marcus instead of him.

"I don't think you're an alien," Annie said, her expressive face plaintive. "I'm just scared of you because everyone knows 'The Man' wants to take Aunt Tillie down."

"Okay," Mom said, moving forward to take Annie from Marcus's arms. "I think you should come with us while we cook dinner."

"I want to stay with Marcus," Annie whined.

"Marcus and everyone else are going to show Aunt Willa around while we make dinner," Mom said. "Would you like to meet Aunt Willa?"

Aunt Willa plastered what she probably supposed was a friendly smile on her face. She looked like a deranged clown on the lam from the circus police. "I've heard all about you," she said. "You're a very pretty little girl."

Annie wrinkled her nose. "Aunt Tillie says you're the Devil and we should never be tempted by the Devil."

"Oh, dear Goddess," Mom muttered, clutching Annie tighter to her chest.

"Take Annie and go," I said, taking pity on her. "We'll ... handle this."

Mom didn't have to be told twice. She kept Annie pressed to her chest as she scampered into the kitchen. Marnie and Twila looked dubious about leaving us, but their self-preservation instincts kicked in and they wordlessly followed their sister. That left the absolute worst people in the inn to deal with ... well, the worst people in the inn.

"She's a lovely child," Aunt Willa said, her eyes resting on Aunt Tillie's scornful face. "You said her mother works here?"

"They live in one of the rooms on the attic floor," Thistle explained. "Annie's mother was in a car accident not long ago. She's still recovering. We took care of Annie while she was in the hospital, and then our moms hired her here because they needed help."

"Yes, well, this place is certainly impressive," Aunt Willa said, glancing around the lobby. "It doesn't look anything like the old homestead."

"The original house is still part of the design," Clove offered. "Our moms and Aunt Tillie still live in that part of the building."

"Well, I can't wait to see that."

"We have a no-assholes policy," Aunt Tillie said. "You don't pass muster."

Landon coughed into his hand to hide his laughter, causing Aunt Willa and Rosemary to shoot him twin looks of dislike. He wouldn't make their "favorite people" list anytime soon.

"We should start," I said, glancing around. "Perhaps Landon, Marcus and Sam should help Aunt Tillie get ready for dinner while we're conducting the tour."

"Oh, great," Landon muttered. "I'm never going to get my bacon curse if you make me babysit her."

"It's either one bout of terror or the other," I shot back. "Do you want the enemy you know or the one that crawls in your sleeping bag when you're camping and injects poisonous venom into your butt?"

"It's good to see your head is in the right place for this," Landon said, pressing a quick kiss to my forehead before turning to Aunt Tillie. "Do you want to spend some time with me?"

"Is that my only choice?" Aunt Tillie was nonplussed.

"It's your best choice," Thistle said, dejectedly moving to my side. "We'll get Aunt Willa and Rosemary settled in their room and give them a tour. Hopefully when we're done dinner will be ready."

And then we can stuff food in our face as fast as humanly possible and retreat to the guesthouse, I silently added. "I think that's a plan," I said.

"**WHAT** IS THAT SMELL?" Rosemary wrinkled her nose as she sat at the dining room table forty minutes later.

"It's called food," Landon replied, his irritation showing.

I sat in the chair next to him, instinctively squeezing his hand. He glanced at me a moment, his eyes hard, and then his expression softened.

"I'm sorry I left you with Aunt Tillie," I whispered. "I thought you would prefer her to Aunt Willa."

"I'm not angry with you, Bay," Landon replied. "I'm just … tired."

"I'll give you a massage when we get back to the guesthouse," I offered. It was a lame bribe, but I didn't have much else to barter.

"I'll only accept that deal if you're naked."

"Don't talk about naked massages at dinner," Aunt Tillie instructed from her chair at the head of the table. Mom wisely seated Aunt Willa and Rosemary in the middle so Aunt Tillie wouldn't be tempted to

LIFE'S A WITCH

stare anyone down during the meal. Instead, Clove and Sam moved from their regular spots, and Clove had to face off with Aunt Tillie throughout the meal.

The big worry of the evening was legitimate inn guests. My mother has a hard and fast rule: You are not to act up in front of paying customers. We've broken that rule so many times we've become known for our dinner theater. I worried this meal would switch us from the comedy category to horror.

Everyone at the table swiveled their faces in Aunt Tillie's direction, assuming the show was about to start. My cheeks burned as my mother scorched me with a look that could've set an iceberg on fire.

"So, Bay, how did you and Landon meet?" Rosemary asked, trying to steer the conversation to a safer topic.

"Oh, well … ." I glanced at Landon, unsure.

"I was undercover on a case and I met her at a local corn maze," Landon answered for me. "She was the prettiest woman in the field, and I couldn't take my eyes off of her."

He's charming when he wants to be.

"How did you really meet?" Rosemary pressed.

Landon rolled his neck until it cracked. "That is how we met."

"Oh." Rosemary looked disappointed. Of course, given her face, that could've been her happy expression for all I knew. "I thought it would be under more exciting circumstances."

"Like?"

"Like … I don't know," Rosemary said, shrugging. "I thought maybe you arrested her or something."

Landon opened his mouth to say something I knew would make my mother melt down, but he didn't get a chance to respond, because Mom appeared and started dishing pot roast, potatoes and fresh corn onto his plate.

"Landon and Bay have been inseparable for months now," Mom said, pasting a fake smile on her face. "We're very fond of him."

"I only like him some of the time," Aunt Tillie announced. "Right now would be one of those times."

Mom narrowed her eyes. "Why? Where were you this afternoon that you suddenly like Landon?"

Aunt Tillie ignored her. "Generally my motto is that the only good cop is a dead one – I have that in common with N.W.A."

"What's N.W.A.?" Rosemary asked, confused.

"Don't answer that," Landon ordered.

"I happen to like Landon right now, though, so I'm giving that up as my motto," Aunt Tillie said.

"Why do you like Landon now?" Aunt Willa asked, addressing Aunt Tillie directly for the first time since their uncomfortable meeting in the foyer.

"Anyone is better than you," Aunt Tillie replied. "Where's my dinner? If I'm going to get indigestion at least I should get dinner first."

"I'm going to kill you," Mom hissed as she dished a heaping slab of pot roast onto Aunt Tillie's plate. "You shove that food in your mouth and behave."

"That's what she used to tell me when I was a kid," I said, going for levity. "It works better with cake."

The guests laughed while Aunt Willa and Rosemary looked annoyed.

"And what do you do, Bay?" Rosemary asked. I had no idea why she kept returning the focus to me. We were the same age, so I was expected to entertain her on the rare occasions we were in the same place while growing up. It was never fun, and I knew now would be no different.

"I'm editor at The Whistler."

Aunt Willa snorted. "I can't believe that newspaper is still in business. Is it as pathetic as it used to be?"

Landon stiffened next to me, annoyed on my behalf. "It's a weekly newspaper in a small town," he said. "Bay does an amazing job, considering what she has to work with."

"I'm sure she does," Aunt Willa said.

Mom must have sensed the tension growing to "red alert" levels

LIFE'S A WITCH

and decided to change topics. "How is your dinner, Aunt Willa? Is the pot roast good?"

"You set a lovely table."

I narrowed my eyes as my heart rolled and my foot itched to kick someone in their bony behind. No matter what you say about my mother and aunts, their cooking is beyond reproach. Aunt Willa was intent on being as obnoxious as possible ... and I was pretty much at my limit.

"The pot roast is fantastic as usual," Sam said, flinching when Aunt Willa turned her attention to him.

"And you own a lighthouse?" Aunt Willa asked.

Sam sighed. "I do."

"Is there much money in that?"

"There's more than enough for me to live on," Sam replied. "I haven't been in town all that long. I love the atmosphere and people, though. I wanted to stay, and I thought the Dandridge was a great opportunity. Plus, I met Clove. I think it was a good move."

Clove beamed. "He's done amazing things out there."

"Clove has helped a great deal," Sam said, patting her hand. "She put in all of my gardens."

"And what do you do, Clove?"

Clove swallowed when the conversation shifted to her. "I own a magic shop downtown with Thistle. It's called Hypnotic."

"A magic shop?" Rosemary chortled. "Do you read tarot cards and palms, too?"

"We do a little of everything," Thistle replied. "In case you haven't noticed, Hemlock Cove is a magically-branded town. People come here because they like the fantastical and supernatural. That's what we offer."

"And you make a living doing that?"

"We do well. Thank you."

"If you do so well, why are you all living in the guesthouse on the family property?" Aunt Willa asked. "I would think you'd want to strike out on your own."

"That guesthouse is just sitting there," Mom said, annoyance flashing in her eyes. "It's perfect for the three of them until they decide to change things on their own. There's no reason they should move if they don't want to."

"Why wouldn't they want to?" Rosemary asked. "Aren't children supposed to want to get away from their mothers and ... great-aunts?"

"In your case I think that would be a given," Landon said.

"What did you say?" Aunt Willa asked.

"He said you're a witch with a B," Aunt Tillie replied, spearing a hunk of pot roast and popping it into her mouth.

"I love the show," one of the guests enthused. She was a middle-aged woman and her eyes sparkled as she glanced around the table. "Do you guys perform at every meal?"

"Only if you're lucky," Thistle answered, reaching for a slice of bread. "You picked a good week to be here, if that's your thing, though."

"Yay!" The woman clapped her hands.

"You know what, Tillie?" Aunt Willa gripped her knife so tightly her knuckles whitened. "You haven't changed a bit since we were children. You were awful then and you're still awful."

"I can live with that," Aunt Tillie said.

"Yes, but can everyone else?" Aunt Willa asked. "Look around. These people hate you."

"I think you have Aunt Tillie confused with you," Thistle said.

"Thistle," Mom barked. "You're being rude to your aunt."

"So what?" Thistle tossed her napkin on the table and pushed back her chair. "I'm sorry, Winnie. I know this farce is important to you. It's not important to me, though. I don't know these people. I don't want to know them. I just ... it's summer. We're supposed to be having fun. This isn't my idea of fun."

Mom glanced to me for help, but Thistle's words were greater motivation than my mother's silent pleading.

"I'm with Thistle," I said, tossing my own napkin on the table and glancing at Landon. "I know you love pot roast, but ... ."

"The pizza is on me," Landon said, hopping to his feet. He sent an apologetic look in Mom's direction. "I really did try."

"No, you didn't," Mom replied, folding her hands into her lap.

I focused on Aunt Tillie. "Do you want to come with us?"

Her answered surprised me. "Of course not," she said. "I can't torture Willa if I'm not here. I'm powerful, but that would suck the fun right out of my night."

Oh, well, I should've seen that coming. "Just try to keep yourself from burning the house down," I said, moving from the table and stopping at my mother's side. "We'll stop by for breakfast, but if things aren't better … ."

"Just go," Mom ordered. "I can't even look at you right now."

SEVEN

"What are you thinking about," Landon murmured the next morning, tugging me closer to him as he situated the covers more snugly around us. "I can hear your mind working from here."

I generally hate mornings – except when I get to wake up next to Landon. He's always warm and cuddly. "I'm thinking that my mother is probably really upset."

Landon sighed. "Bay, I love your mother, but ... you can't live your life on her terms," he said. "Those women are horrible. You can see on their faces that they're here to stir up trouble."

"That's what worries me."

"You're worried that they're up to something? Join the club. I know they're up to something. Until they make their intentions known, though, we're in the dark. Being nice to those women isn't going to propel them to tell us what they want. Being nice to them only hurts us."

"You really hate them, don't you?" I asked, running my finger down his cheek.

"I really hate anyone who goes after you," Landon replied. "In case you missed it, I think you're pretty great. I love you. You make me smile and I enjoy watching you laugh."

"That's pretty sweet."

"I have my moments."

"It's also schmaltzy," I said. "I didn't know you were that schmaltzy."

"I think you make me schmaltzy," Landon said, tickling my ribs. "Don't let your head get too big, though. You're also a pain in the ass, and your family gives me heartburn."

I sobered. "I'm sorry about all of this," I said. "You came here for a relaxing weekend, and it's been anything but relaxing. We have only two days left together before you have to leave again."

"I don't like leaving either," Landon said. "I don't really have a choice. I've been trying to get over here at least one day during the week, too. That's how much I miss you."

"What we really need is a case here in Hemlock Cove. Then you could stay and work at the same time."

Landon grinned. "Please don't go out and kill someone simply because you want me close," he said. "As flattering as that would be, I would prefer not having to lock you up."

"I'll consider it. You're pretty cute, though. It might be worth a murder to keep you around."

Landon rolled on top of me, pressing his lips to mine to let me know what he had in mind. He pulled back long enough to study me for a moment. "Are we going up to the inn for breakfast?"

"Do you want to try to subsist on the crumbs in the toaster? That's all we have for food."

"Fine. We'll go up there. Breakfast had better be good, though."

"Isn't it always?" I asked.

"Generally," Landon said. "I'm going to need something to entice me to put up with those horrible people, though."

"I gave you a naked massage last night."

"And that was a nice start," Landon said. "Now I want to give you a naked massage."

"I guess I can live with that."

"That's good," Landon said, moving his mouth to my neck. "This would be so much better if you smelled and tasted like bacon, though."

Wait ... was that an insult?

"I CAN'T BELIEVE Thistle and Marcus abandoned us," I muttered, entering The Overlook through the back door an hour later. "Thistle said she actually would rather eat toast crumbs than risk breakfast up here."

"Clove was the smart one," Landon said. "She spent the night at the Dandridge, so she has a ready-made excuse for not being at breakfast."

"Yeah, she lucked out there."

"I'm just glad the inn is still standing," Landon said. "Do you think we cut it close enough to mealtime to avoid an uncomfortable meeting with your mother in the kitchen?"

"Probably not."

The back of the inn serves as private quarters for my mother and aunts. It's accessible only through the kitchen, and guests wouldn't dare enter. I wasn't surprised to find Aunt Tillie sitting on the couch watching a morning news program. Her outfit did surprise me – although at this point nothing she wears should give me pause.

"What are you doing?" Landon asked.

Aunt Tillie, her combat helmet firmly in place, glanced up. "I'm deciding whether the world is going to end today."

"Oh, well, I'm glad you're not taking this to extremes or anything," I said, smirking. "Where did you get those pants, by the way? I thought you gave up yoga pants."

"These are not yoga pants," Aunt Tillie countered. "They're active wear."

"That's the same thing."

"No, it's not," Aunt Tillie argued. "Yoga pants can be used only for yoga. I read it online somewhere. Active pants can be worn anywhere you want to be active."

"I see," I said, pursing my lips to keep from laughing. Her "active pants" had zombie faces on them. I looked a little closer and realized they also had faces of *The Walking Dead* heroes. That was her favorite show these days – she fancied herself the Daryl of our group – and she was biding her time until it came back on the air. "Is there a reason you're wearing zombies on your active pants?"

"They fit my mood."

"Are you saying you're one of the walking dead or that you're going to make Willa and Rosemary part of that tribe?" Landon asked. "I can't hang around for breakfast if you're going to kill someone."

"He needs to give me time to hide the body," Aunt Tillie said, winking.

"That's exactly what I was thinking," Landon said, widening his eyes to comical proportions.

I shifted my eyes to the kitchen door, my heart flopping. "Have you seen Mom this morning?"

"Are you asking whether she's going to make you one of the walking dead?"

"I ... ."

Aunt Tillie shook her head. "Your mother understands why you guys took off last night, even if she can't admit it right now," she said. "She doesn't blame you. She's not thrilled that you left her holding the bag – and by bag I mean that Willa has all the appeal of a bag of cat guts – but she doesn't blame you for leaving."

That didn't sound at all like my mother. "Did anything happen after we left?"

"It was a perfectly normal meal."

That could mean anything. "What did you do?"

"I didn't do anything," Aunt Tillie protested. "I was on my best behavior."

Landon barked out a laugh. "She did something," he said. "Let's go in and find out what it is. I want to eat as fast as possible and get out of here."

"What do you want to do after breakfast?"

"Isn't this town having a festival? In fact, isn't this town always having a festival?"

I nodded. "We'll go to the festival," he said. "I'll win you another stuffed animal. I think that story of no guy ever winning you a stuffed animal at a carnival is pathetic and now I want to win you one at every festival. We can eat junk food until we throw up. Then we won't want to eat dinner, and we'll have a handy excuse to live like monks for the rest of the night."

"I see you have this all figured out."

"He's a pervert. Of course he has it all figured out," Aunt Tillie supplied.

Landon glared at her. "You're starting to bug me."

"Then I haven't been doing my job correctly," Aunt Tillie shot back, climbing off the couch and shuffling toward the kitchen. "I should've passed the 'start' mark yesterday. Come on, pervert. I'm sure they have bacon, and you have a busy day planned."

Landon watched her go, his face unreadable.

"I kind of like that you're a pervert," I offered.

He fought to keep a straight face ... and ultimately lost. "What do you think your mother is going to say about those pants she's wearing?"

"I think my mother is already overloaded. The pants might do her in."

"Well, come on," Landon said, grabbing my hand. "I need to see Willa's face when she sees those pants."

He wasn't the only one.

We were the last to arrive in the dining room, and Mom scorched me with a look – which I decided to ignore – as the rest of the guests happily chatted. Aunt Willa was another story. She and Rosemary were quiet and composed, but there was a definite air of tension in the room as they stared at Aunt Tillie's ensemble.

"Good morning everyone," Landon said, taking his usual spot next to Aunt Tillie.

I sat next to him, offering Twila and Marnie tight smiles while trying to avoid eye contact with my mother.

"How was your night, Bay?" Rosemary asked.

"I slept well. Thank you. How was your night, Rosemary?"

"The bed was lumpy."

I darted a worried look in my mother's direction and saw the clenching of her jaw. All the mattresses at the inn were less than a year old. I'd slept on two of them and knew the beds were comfortable. "That's too bad," I said. "Other than that, how was your night?"

"I guess you didn't hear what happened last night," Aunt Willa interjected. "You ran off and missed the big show."

Uh-oh. "What big show?"

"It doesn't matter," Mom said.

Something told me that wasn't true. Something also told me that if Mom told the story yelling might be involved. "Okay." I grabbed the platter of pancakes and held them so Landon could dish some onto our plates. "What is everyone doing today?"

"We're going to the festival," Marnie replied. "Aunt Willa and Rosemary want to see the town and Hypnotic. We're going to make a day of it. What are you guys doing?"

Landon made a face, his plans going up in smoke. "We haven't decided yet," he said. "We might just hang around the guesthouse."

"I thought you were going to the festival?" Aunt Tillie teased. "Wasn't there some bold talk of winning stuffed animals for Bay?"

"Things change. Move along." Landon used his best no-nonsense tone, but Aunt Tillie wasn't about to be dissuaded.

"No. You said you were going to the fair to get sick on junk food so you could avoid dinner tonight."

So much for us being allies. "What did you do last night that has everyone so upset?"

"I didn't do anything," Aunt Tillie challenged, crossing her arms over her chest. "Why do you always assume I've done something?"

"Because we know you," Landon replied, nonplussed. "You've obviously done something. I've seen happier people at natural disaster sites."

"I think we should all go to the festival together," Mom announced, taking me by surprise.

"I think that's a terrible idea," Landon said.

"Yeah, I'm not going to the festival," Aunt Tillie said. "The people in town give me gas."

Most of the guests snickered.

"I wasn't talking about you," Mom clarified. "I think that the rest of us should go as a family, though. How does that sound?"

"I'm pretty sure I'm going to be sick," I answered, knowing I was digging myself deeper but unable stop myself. "I feel a plague coming on."

"I think I'm going to be sick with her," Landon added. "We'll probably be bed ridden."

"Pervert," Aunt Tillie muttered.

"You're not sick," Mom said. "Everyone is going." Now she used her no-nonsense tone.

"Mom ... ."

"Don't even bother arguing, Bay," Mom replied. "After last night, you owe me."

"She doesn't owe you anything," Landon countered. "If she doesn't want to go ... ."

"Don't push me," Mom warned.

"Don't push me," Landon shot back. "I ... ."

The sound of someone clearing his throat by the main dining room door caused everyone to turn in that direction, killing the potential argument. Chief Terry, Hemlock Cove's top cop, shuffled uncomfortably as he watched the scene.

"I'm sorry to interrupt," he said.

"You're not interrupting," Mom replied, hopping to her feet. "Have a seat. The pancakes are still warm."

"So is the bacon," Marnie said, lifting the plate. My mother and aunts were locked in a never-ending competition to see who could win Chief Terry's affection. I have no idea what would happen if one of them ever actually took first place.

Landon reached around me and grabbed three slices from the plate, earning a dark look from Marnie. "Have a seat," he said. "You too can enjoy our breakfast from hell for the low, low price of being someone who doesn't want to kill me."

"I'm not sure what that means, but I'm not here on a social call," Chief Terry said.

Landon shifted in his chair, his sarcastic mirth turning to worry. "What's wrong?"

"I'm glad you're in town this weekend. We found a body."

"What kind of body?"

"A dead one, pervert," Aunt Tillie supplied.

Landon wagged a threatening finger in her face. "I'm going to make those active wear pants come true if you're not careful."

Aunt Tillie rolled her eyes. "Promises, promises."

"Who died?" I asked.

"I'm not at liberty to say just yet," Chief Terry replied. "I need Landon to go out to the scene with me."

Landon and I exchanged a look. "I guess I'm on the job," he said. "I would worry you did this, but I know where you've been the last twenty-four hours."

"Ha, ha."

He brushed a quick kiss against my cheek and stood, grabbing his bacon for the trip. "Can you drive? My truck is at the guesthouse."

"Sure," Chief Terry said. "I'm sorry for ruining your day."

"Oh, you haven't ruined our day," Mom said, her voice full of faux sugar. "Now Bay doesn't have an excuse to ditch the festival."

My heart sank as my stomach rolled.

"Actually she does," Landon said, causing hope to flare. "I need her to come to the scene with me."

Aunt Willa frowned. "You're taking Bay to see a dead body? That doesn't sound very sanitary."

"I need her to … look things over and tell us what she sees," Landon explained.

"Why?" Rosemary was confused.

"Because I need her with me," Landon replied, glancing at Chief Terry for support. "You don't care if she comes, do you?"

Chief Terry shrugged. He knew something was going on, and even though he wasn't sure what it was, he clearly wasn't in the mood to argue. "The more the merrier."

"Oh, darn," I said, standing and gracing my mother with a rueful smile. "I guess I'm going to miss out on the festival. What a bummer."

She couldn't argue with Landon and Chief Terry about the necessity of my presence at the scene without tipping Aunt Willa and Rosemary about why they wanted me there.

"Fine," Mom said, giving in. "This isn't over, though. We will have a talk about this."

"I can't wait."

EIGHT

"Does anyone want to tell me what was going on at breakfast?" Chief Terry asked, navigating his Dodge Durango from The Overlook's driveway and heading out of town. "Things seemed tense."

"Oh, no. That's how they always are," I replied from the back seat.

"No one needs your sarcastic tone, missy," Chief Terry warned, although his eyes twinkled as they met mine in the rearview mirror. He never stayed angry with me.

"It's … a long story," I said, adjusting my attitude. It wasn't Chief Terry's fault my mother wanted to kill me.

"We have twenty minutes until we get to Hollow Creek," Chief Terry replied. "Spill."

"My Aunt Willa is in town," I started. "She brought Rosemary."

Chief Terry furrowed his brow. "Rosemary? Isn't she the cousin who terrorized you at camp that one summer?"

"How do you know that?" Landon asked, surprised.

"I know everything about Bay," Chief Terry replied. "She had a rough childhood sometimes. That Rosemary teamed up with Lila. I remember that because she was upset. I don't like it when she's upset. I'm a softie where she's concerned. Why are they here?"

"We have no idea," Landon replied. "They're clearly up to something ... and they haven't said a pleasant thing since they arrived. Aunt Tillie is planning mayhem, and Winnie is struggling to hold things together."

"How are you handling it, Bay?" Chief Terry was always sympathetic and kind.

"I'm not the same kid I was back then," I reassured him. "Rosemary can't get to me like she used to. I'm more ... self-confident ... now."

"That's because you have a handsome boyfriend who carries a gun," Landon interjected.

Chief Terry snickered. Even though he fought Landon's interested in me for a long time, he was resigned to the fact that we are a couple now. In fact, he'd grown fond of Landon ... although he probably would never admit it. "Yes, Bay. You're popular now because you're dating an FBI agent."

I rolled my eyes. "It's not that ... although you are studly and handsome, sweetie," I said. "For several years there, when I was younger, I couldn't seem to find footing. Everyone thought I was weird, and Lila was always out to get me. Sometimes it felt as though I was suffocating."

"And that's why you left town and moved south," Chief Terry supplied. "I remember."

"And then I found out about a different kind of suffocating," I muttered, my mind wandering back to my years in southeastern Michigan. When I was a teenager, the idea of fleeing to a big city where no one knew about the Winchester witches seemed an attainable dream. The reality was different, and once I returned to Hemlock Cove I knew I was home to stay.

"You needed that time to find yourself," Chief Terry said. "You came back a much happier person. I know you didn't like it down there, but it was good for you. By the time you came back, you could hold your own and didn't need Thistle to fight your battles."

"Thanks for the pep talk!"

Chief Terry rolled his eyes. "You know what I mean, Bay," he said. "You've always been my favorite ... mostly because Thistle was mean and Clove used to cry on a dime to manipulate me. I used to worry about you, though."

"Well, you don't need to worry about her now," Landon said. "That's my job."

"Whatever," Chief Terry muttered. "Tell me about Willa. I don't remember anything good about her."

"As far as I can tell, there's nothing good to remember about her," I replied. "She knows exactly how to get under Aunt Tillie's skin. Granted, that's not hard to do, but she seems to get off causing emotional upheaval.

"So far she's gotten in digs about Mom's food, the beds at the inn, Landon's hair, Sam's job and Aunt Tillie's parenting skills," I continued. "She seems to be on a mission to make us all miserable."

"Why did Winnie allow her to stay?"

I shrugged. "I've been asking myself that very question for two days now," I answered. "The only thing I can come up with is that my grandmother wanted peace in the family, and this is a way for my mother to do what she couldn't."

"Your grandmother was a good woman," Chief Terry said. "She was easy to get along with. Tillie and Willa were the exact opposite. They are older than me, but my father told me some stories about the two of them."

"Like what?" Landon prodded.

"I'm getting this all secondhand from stuff my father told me, so take it with a grain of salt. Apparently Willa went after Calvin at some point," Chief Terry replied. "Everyone in town knew Calvin Hoffman was head-over-heels for Tillie. That didn't stop Willa from going after him out of spite."

That didn't surprise me.

"There was some hair pulling and threatened curses," Chief Terry continued. "They screamed at each other in the middle of a festival dance, and Tillie swore up and down she would turn Willa's hair green and make her teeth fall out."

"Wait a second," Landon interjected. "Calvin's last name was Hoffman. Why isn't Aunt Tillie's last name Hoffman?"

"Aunt Tillie claims there's power in names," I answered. "She never changed her last name. My mother and aunts changed theirs briefly, but after the divorces they all changed them back."

"Why don't any of you guys have your fathers' names?"

That was a good question. "When we were born we had hyphenated last names," I explained. "Aunt Tillie insisted we would be unprotected if we didn't keep the Winchester name. I think that was a power play. It doesn't really matter now. I'm Bay Winchester. I don't really remember having a different last name. When our mothers returned to their maiden names they also switched ours."

"Didn't your fathers put up a fight about that?"

"Have you seen our fathers put up a fight about anything?" I challenged.

Landon waited a beat, letting me rein in my temper before continuing. "I take it things aren't any better between you and your father since we cast that truth spell on his guests."

"It's fine," I said. "I ran into him in town three days ago and he was perfectly ... pleasant."

"Is that code for something?"

"Landon, it's fine," I said, too weary to analyze my troubled relationship with my father. "I can only deal with one family crisis at a time. Aunt Willa and Rosemary win right now."

"Well, you might think that's the end of the conversation, but it's not," Landon said. "If you don't want to talk about it right now, I'll let it go. I'm going to bring it up again, though. Prepare yourself."

"I'm working to tamp down my excitement even as we speak."

Landon turned his attention to Chief Terry. "Tell me about the body."

"Our best guess is that it's a teenager," Chief Terry replied. "We don't have an identification yet. He's been in the water for some time. The medical examiner should be there when we arrive. It looks as though he was stabbed, though."

"Have any local kids been reported missing?"

"No. That's troublesome. What's more troublesome is that he was dumped at Hollow Creek."

"Isn't Hollow Creek where I found you guys searching for buried treasure last year?" Landon asked me. "You were all out there pretending you were on a picnic, but then you found the body in the cave. That's the same place, right?"

I nodded, smiling at the memory. That was long before we hooked up. He was suspicious of us that day. I didn't blame him.

"I know what you're thinking about," Landon said. "I knew you guys were up to something, and I was dying to know what it was. I think that's when I knew I was a goner where you were concerned. I couldn't stop myself from thinking about you."

"You know I'm in the same vehicle with you guys, right?" Chief Terry asked, scowling. "She's still eight with pigtails where I'm concerned."

"It's not as though we did anything," Landon countered. "Bay, Clove and Thistle were out there searching, and they were all terrible liars."

"Oh, you're so smitten," Chief Terry taunted.

Landon was nonplussed. "I'm not going to deny it," he said. "Back then I was just trying to figure her out."

"And how is that going for you?"

"It gets easier every day," Landon replied, leaning forward when he caught the telltale swirl of emergency vehicle lights. "I take it we're almost there."

"Yeah," Chief Terry replied. "Bay, if you see anyone's ghost, keep quiet about it. Make sure you're careful. There are going to be a lot of people out here who won't understand why you're here. I think we should lie and say you two were together and she would've been stranded if we didn't bring her along. I can't control this scene with county people here."

"That's a good idea," Landon said.

Chief Terry parked and Landon hopped out first, opening my door and grabbing my hand. "Stick close to me," he whispered. "I have to look at the body. If you see something … ."

"I'll be careful," I promised.

Landon squeezed the back of my neck with his free hand. "I love you, Bay. Even when we fight – and we're still going to talk about your father – even then, though, I still love you."

"I love you, too," I murmured.

Landon planted a quick kiss on my forehead and then released my hand. He was on official business now. You don't hold your girlfriend's hand at a crime scene. I wordlessly followed him, cringing when I saw the county medical examiner poking the body with a gloved finger. Chief Terry wasn't exaggerating when he said the body had been in the water for some time. The smell was pungent from twenty feet away, and the bloated carcass barely resembled anything human.

I turned away. There was nothing for me there. If I was going to help, it would be in another area. I was careful as I moved around the scene, watching where I stepped to make sure I didn't contaminate evidence.

I drew a few strange looks before Chief Terry made a big show about explaining my presence. After that, I was largely ignored. Most of the foliage was thick and I avoided stepping in any of it. I kept an eye on Landon, who impassively knelt next to the body and carried on a conversation with the medical examiner. I had no idea how he managed to do his job – and do it well – when I was often overtaken by the plight of human misery. In Landon's mind he needed to know the "hows" and the "whys." In my mind I was stuck on the "what ifs" and "what could've beens."

I trudged down to the water, rolling my neck as I took in the scene. Even though I'd always liked Hollow Creek, I rarely visited the location. It was out of the way. It was a fun picnic spot when we were younger, but each generation took it over and made it their own. Teenagers partied on the banks during the summer, while adults gravitated to the multitude of other lakes and streams.

I was studying the murky water when something caught my attention out of the corner of my eye. I moved closer, leaning down for a better look. When I realized what I was staring at, I straightened.

"Landon!"

Landon jerked his head in my direction, surprised. "What's wrong?"

"There's a wallet in the water here."

Landon and Chief Terry moved toward me, Landon gently nudging me out of the way with his hip – making sure to keep his glove-covered hands from touching me – and stared in the direction I pointed.

"Get a bag," Landon instructed.

Chief Terry retrieved an evidence bag as Landon dug into the water. He pulled the sopping wallet out and opened it, digging through it to retrieve a driver's license. "Does anyone know a Nathaniel Jamison?"

Chief Terry and I exchanged a look.

"He graduated from Hemlock Cove High School two years ago," I said. "He's a local boy. He's not a teenager, though. He should be at least twenty by now."

"We can't be sure the body is Nathaniel," Chief Terry cautioned. "Not yet, at least."

"If it is, it might explain a few things," Landon said. "Most people don't report a college kid missing if he's not under regular parental supervision. His parents might not know he's missing."

"He only has a mother in town," Chief Terry replied. "Patty Jamison. She was a pretty attentive mother, as I remember. His parents divorced years ago, and his father left town. I'm not sure how much he sees his kids."

"He has a sister, right?" I asked. "I think her name is Chloe."

"Yeah, she's still in high school," Chief Terry said. "I think she'll be a senior this year."

"If he's home on summer break, wouldn't his mother and sister know he's missing?" I asked.

"I guess we'll have to ask them," Chief Terry said, his face grim. "The quickest way to find out if that's Nathaniel is to find out when he was last seen. We can feel Patty out about the wallet first. Hopefully news about the body won't have spread to town yet. This place is pretty isolated."

"I guess that's our next stop," Landon agreed, lowering his voice. "Have you seen anything else out here?"

"If he's a ghost, he's not here now," I replied. "That doesn't necessarily mean he's not stuck here. He could be home ... or still trying to control his reality. Now isn't the time to try to find him. There are too many people watching."

"I agree with that," Landon said. "If it becomes necessary, I'll bring you out here later so we can look around when it's only the two of us."

"You're just looking for an excuse to get out of another uncomfortable evening with my family," I said, going for levity. Given the body on the riverbank, though, I immediately regretted my words.

"It's okay," Landon said, as if reading my mind. "Let's head back to town. There's nothing more we can do out here. We need answers, and the only way we're going to get them is by talking to friends and family."

"Yeah," Chief Terry said, blowing out a frustrated sigh. "Let's go. Whatever happened out here was terrible, but our answers are back in town."

From his perspective, he made sense. Something inside of me told me there was more to discover at Hollow Creek, though. Unfortunately there was absolutely nothing we could do about that right now.

NINE

"Are you sure you want us to leave you here?" Landon asked, glancing around the quiet high school parking lot worriedly. "We can take you back to the inn before we question Nathaniel's mother. I wish we could take you with us, but it's unprofessional, and I don't want to leave you in the Durango for hours if we're going to be in there for a bit. You might die of heat exhaustion."

"Are you saying you don't want to lock me in the car like a dog?"

Landon smirked. "You know what I mean," he said. "Chief Terry doesn't mind taking you back to the inn."

"If I go back to the inn I'll be stuck going on an afternoon outing with Aunt Willa and Rosemary," I reminded him. "I'd much rather be marooned here."

Landon didn't look convinced. "What are you going to do? It's summer. School is out."

"Yes, but summer school is in," I countered. "There are bound to be a few kids forced to take classes, and there's a basketball court on the other side of the building. The boys spend hours there every day. Maybe some of them can give us some insight into what Nathaniel was doing."

"We don't know that it's Nathaniel yet," Landon cautioned.

"I know that," I replied. "Odds are it is him, though. I'm not going to tell them he's dead. I'm only going to feel them out for what's going on at Hollow Creek these days."

"That's not a bad idea," said Chief Terry, leaning against the front of the Durango. After leaving Hollow Creek we drove into town. Neither Landon nor Chief Terry could come up with a legitimate excuse to bring me when they questioned Patty Jamison. That's when I suggested they drop me off at the high school. "Teenage kids are less likely to open up to law enforcement officials. A pretty blonde is another story."

"Yes, I love it when you suggest using my girlfriend's looks to entice other men," Landon muttered.

"They're not men," I reminded him. "They're teenage boys. I think I can handle teenage boys. Besides, most of the teenage boys here have a very high opinion of Aunt Tillie. That can work to my advantage for a change."

"Do I even want to know why teenage boys like Aunt Tillie?"

"I don't," Chief Terry said, nonplussed. "If I know why they like her I'll have to arrest her."

"She doesn't sell them pot, does she?" Landon asked, his face twisting as he contemplated the ramifications. "Wait ... I don't want to know."

"She doesn't sell them pot," I said. "Actually, she doesn't like sharing, so the pot is all hers. They know about the wine and pot, though, and they think they might be able to snow her into sharing. She encourages that ... even though she has no intention of giving them what they want.

"Plus, well, ever since the teenage boys found out Aunt Tillie was teaching the teenage girls how to fire guns they've been trying to get on her good side so she won't talk badly about them when she's holding one of her clinics," I said.

Landon narrowed his eyes. "I told her she couldn't teach those girls to fire weapons," he said. "Are you telling me she's still doing it?"

Uh-oh. "I'm telling you that Aunt Tillie has a way with teenagers that can't be measured or fathomed," I replied.

Landon made a disgusted sound in the back of his throat. "Okay. I guess you're safe here in the middle of the day," he said finally.

He was too cute for words sometimes, especially when he became protective and territorial. Yes, I know that sends a bad message. Sue me. He's adorable. "You realize I've been taking care of myself for a long time, right?"

"I realize that I would be mighty sad if you weren't around," Landon countered, leaning over to give me a quick kiss.

"Ugh. I'm officially grossed out by you two," Chief Terry complained. "It's like watching a small child kiss a perverted older man."

"Why does everyone think I'm a pervert?" Landon was annoyed.

"I think it's probably your hair," I teased, squeezing his hand. "Call me when you're done so we can meet for lunch and compare notes."

"We're meeting in town, right?" Landon pressed. "I do not want to risk going back out to the inn with your mother displaying all the tell-tale signs of having a major freakout in the next few days."

"We're definitely meeting in town," I said. "I only want to talk to a few of the kids to see what they know about Hollow Creek. It's always been a party place for the kids during the summer, but I'm kind of curious what kind of parties go on out there these days."

"I'll call you when we're done," Landon said, giving me another quick kiss.

"Stop kissing her," Chief Terry ordered, climbing into his Durango. "It's gross."

"Get over it," Landon shot back.

Sometimes I think they should be filmed for a reality show. I watched them leave, waving until they pulled out of the parking lot, and then headed in the direction of the school.

Hemlock Cove is tiny. Each graduating class has only about fifty students. That means students of various ages hang out in the same place, so I wasn't surprised to find ten boys playing basketball behind the high school when I rounded the corner.

I scanned the faces, hoping for one I recognized. The only familiar one belonged to Dakota Evans. He was one of the boys making regular stops at The Overlook. He was as good a place to start as any. I was about to head in his direction when I noticed a dark figure detach from a nearby tree and move toward me.

I narrowed my eyes, the sun making it difficult to focus. Jim Welby was almost on top of me before I realized who he was. "Hey, Bay."

"Hey, Jim." We'd gone to high school together, although he was a year older. He was always nice, but I had the feeling he believed every whispered rumor about Aunt Tillie and lived in fear of anyone bearing the Winchester name. "What are you doing up here?"

"I'm handling one of the summer school classes," Jim replied, gracing me with a smile. "The pay is nice, and I'm saving up to buy a big-screen television."

"Well, at least you have a goal," I said, laughing. "Are you taking a break?"

"When I decided to become a teacher I fancied myself changing lives and helping kids learn the important lessons in life," Jim replied. "In truth, I'm basically acting as a glorified babysitter and trying to figure out a way to stop the kids from smoking pot in the bathrooms between classes."

I snickered. "Some things never change, huh?"

"It was more fun when I was the one smoking the pot," Jim said. "My kids are in reading chapters right now – which means they're really making plans for what they're going to do tonight and staring at the girls' legs because it's shorts season."

"I didn't even know they had summer school on weekends," I admitted.

"There are two choices," Jim explained. "They can go two hours a day Monday through Wednesday or they can go six hours on Saturday. Believe it or not, some of them opt to put everything on one day – even if it ruins their weekend – because it's easier."

"That's the choice I would make," I said. "Other than that, how is it going?"

"It's going pretty well," Jim answered. "How are things with you? I see you around quite a bit, although I don't bother you because that FBI guy is usually with you."

"Landon," I said. "Yeah, he's here almost every weekend."

"You guys seem close."

"We are," I said, briefly wondering whether Jim was trying to feel me out for a specific reason. "How about you? Dating anyone?"

"Not really," Jim replied. "Hemlock Cove's dating pool is fairly limited – especially when all the good ones are taken by FBI studs."

My cheeks burned and I decided to change the subject. "Did you know Nathaniel Jamison very well?"

Jim shrugged off the conversational shift. "Fairly well," he said. "He graduated two years ago. He was smart, but didn't apply himself. He was much more interested in sports than anything else. Why do you ask?"

I ignored the question. "Was he good in sports?"

"He was good by Hemlock Cove's standards," Jim replied. "He was the starting quarterback. He pitched for the baseball team. He was a fairly decent wrestler, too. I think Nathaniel's problem was that he thought being good by Hemlock Cove's athletic standards meant he was good by other people's standards, too."

"What do you mean?"

"Well, I heard he tried out for the football team at Central Michigan University – that's where he goes to school now – but he didn't even make it off of the practice field the first day," Jim answered. "Nathaniel was an alpha jock. He got his self-worth from being an athlete. I think that's how he got girls, too. I don't think the change in his social status was something he expected."

"You're saying he was popular with the girls here because he was an athlete, but he was just another kid at Central," I said. "Have you heard anything about him recently?"

"He's been hanging around playing basketball," Jim said. "I think he's been working some of the farms for money, too. That's what I heard anyway. Why are you asking?"

I bit my lip. "I can't really say," I said. "Not yet, at least."

"Does this have something to do with your FBI boyfriend?"

"He has a name," I replied, smiling. "I really can't say yet. Thanks for the information, though."

After chatting with Jim a few more minutes I left him to return to his class and moved toward the boys on the court. Dakota was the first to acknowledge my presence.

"Hello, Ms. Winchester."

He always was a smarmy little thing. "Hi, Dakota." I glanced at the rest of the boys. "How are you guys doing today?"

"We didn't do anything," one of the younger boys said. Upon closer inspection, I recognized his freckles. He was Chuck Johnson's son.

"You're Charlie Junior, aren't you?"

Charlie widened his eyes and nodded. "You're not here because Ms. Tillie sent you, are you?"

"Why would Aunt Tillie send me?"

"She hates all the boys in town ... except for me," Dakota said, puffing out his chest. "She loves me."

"Trust me. She doesn't love you," I countered. "If she's nice to you, it's because you're bribing her or she wants something from you."

Dakota made a face. "You don't know. Ms. Tillie could like me."

It was doubtful, but stranger things had happened. "I need to ask you guys a few questions," I said. "What can you tell me about what goes on at Hollow Creek these days?"

Dakota exchanged a look with one of the blond boys to my right. "Why do you want to know?"

"Why don't you want to tell me?" I challenged.

"Maybe we don't trust you," the blond boy said. "You do date that FBI guy."

"Ms. Tillie says that he's working undercover to bust us all," Charlie added, clapping his hands over his mouth when he realized what he said. He had a lot in common with his father, including the inability to control what came out of his mouth.

"Aunt Tillie lies," I said. "You guys should know that. Didn't she tell all the girls in your school that you were only after their virtue?"

"That wasn't a lie," Dakota said. "We are horny beasts."

I narrowed my eyes. I was really starting to dislike him. "I'll tell Aunt Tillie you didn't help me. Is that what you want?" Aunt Tillie's reputation was a double-edged sword. I was hoping to use the pointy end on Dakota.

"Fine," Dakota huffed. "Hollow Creek is still the party place in the summer. You're too old, but I'm sure you might get some takers if you sniff around and everyone is really drunk."

"I'd take her," one of the other boys offered.

"The FBI dude carries a gun," Charlie said. "He'll shoot your thing off if you're not careful. That's what Ms. Tillie says."

"Don't worry about the FBI dude," I said. "I only want to know what's going on at Hollow Creek. Do you guys go up there every weekend?"

"Pretty much," Dakota said. "Now we can't because we know you're going to send your boyfriend out there to arrest us, though."

"Landon doesn't care that you guys are drinking along the creek bank," I said. "That's outside the purview of the FBI."

"Not when he's 'The Man,'" Charlie whispered to another boy.

"When was the last time you guys saw Nathaniel Jamison?" I asked, tamping down the urge to smack Charlie.

Dakota's eyebrows flew up. "Nathaniel? Is that why you're here? That dude is trouble."

"How so?"

Dakota shrugged. "He's turned into a real tool. He's always talking about being underappreciated. He's also been looking for ways to make money, and keeps calling us high school babies."

"If you're high school babies, why does he hang around with you?"

Dakota shrugged. "You'll have to ask him."

"When was the last time you saw him?"

Dakota's gaze bounced between the boys. "I think it's been a few days," he said, dribbling the basketball. "It might even be a week. I'm not sure."

"Have you been down to Hollow Creek during that time?"

"We usually go Fridays and Saturdays," Dakota replied. "But now that 'The Man' will be staking the place out we'll have to find a different spot."

I rolled my eyes. "Okay. Thanks." I turned to leave and then stilled.

"One more thing," I said, swiveling back to face the boys. "What else does Aunt Tillie tell you guys about Landon?"

"She said he can't control the gun in his pants or his hand," Charlie answered, ignoring the groans from the other boys. "She also says he's 'The Man' and 'The Man' is going to bring us all down if we're not careful."

"Thanks, Charlie," I said. "I'm glad to see you inherited your lack of filter from your father."

"Mom also says I have his tendency to be a jackass, and I'll make some woman miserable one day."

I can see that.

TEN

"Hey, sweetie," Landon said, dropping a kiss on my forehead before sitting next to me at the diner table. I'd been nursing an iced tea for a half hour waiting for his arrival.

"Hi, sweetie," Chief Terry mocked, kissing my forehead for good measure before sitting on the other side of me.

Landon scowled. "Keep it up," he said. "It's not going to be funny when I pound you."

Chief Terry didn't look worried. "Don't make me laugh."

"How did things go?" I asked, sipping my iced tea.

"It's Nathaniel," Landon replied. "He's been missing for days. His mother wasn't sure he was actually missing because he's been all over the place and spending nights with old buddies since he got back to town. He never apprised her of his location, so she didn't report him missing."

"Are you sure it's him?"

"The clothing description matches and Frank Tobin is over there with the dental records right now," Chief Terry said. "It's him, though."

"How did his mother take it?" I asked, my heart rolling. I didn't know Patty Jamison well, but no one deserved to lose a child.

AMANDA M. LEE

"She was ... upset," Landon said. "She kept it together, though. I think she was in shock. She'll probably hold it together through the funeral and then break down afterward. I've seen it before."

"That's too bad," I said. "She seems like a nice woman."

"Do you know her well?" Chief Terry asked.

I shook my head. "She's come into the newspaper office a few times to place garage sale ads," I answered. "I can't really remember ever talking to her otherwise."

"She's never been a problem," Chief Terry said.

"What about Nathaniel?"

"He got in a few scrapes when he was in high school. Nothing big," Chief Terry replied. "I think I busted him drinking down at Hollow Creek a few times, too. Most of those things just ended with warnings and calls to his mother, though."

"What about you?" Landon asked. "Did you come up with anything?"

"Well, I ran into Jim Welby behind the school," I answered. "He's teaching summer school this year. He said that Nathaniel had problems adjusting to the realities of college because he wasn't a stud on campus at Central."

"Meaning?"

"Meaning that he was used to girls falling at his feet because he was a jock in Hemlock Cove," I said. "Apparently he didn't realize that being good at football in Hemlock Cove wasn't the same as being good at football everywhere else."

"I hate to say it, but I've seen that from more than one kid around here," Chief Terry said. "Hemlock Cove is small enough that even a modicum of athletic talent can put you on top. That popularity fades, though. Did Welby say anything else?"

"Just that he's seen me around with Landon and was wondering if we were still together."

"See," Landon said. "I told you she would get hit on."

"Jim Welby is harmless," Chief Terry said. "He's a nice guy. You don't have anything to worry about."

"You don't," I agreed, patting Landon's knee. "No matter how big my ego grew after talking to Jim, the teenage boys put me in my place and told me that if I was thinking of hanging around Hollow Creek I might be able to pick up a guy if he was really drunk."

Chief Terry made a face. "What is that supposed to mean?"

"They said I was old."

Landon barked out a coarse laugh. "Oh, my poor girl," he said. "Did they hurt your feelings? It's okay. I don't think you look old."

I rolled my eyes. "They had a few things to say about you, too. Do you want to hear?"

"I guess," Landon said. "Wait … does this involve them hitting on you?"

"They're teenage boys," I countered. "To them I look like their mothers."

"Okay, go ahead," Landon said, grinning at my discomfort. "I'm just glad you don't look like my mother."

"Apparently Aunt Tillie has been explaining a few things to them," I said. "Dakota Evans, for example, really does believe he's a horny beast, and he's perfectly fine with Aunt Tillie telling all the girls that he's only after their virtue."

"Now that kid is a pain," Chief Terry interjected. "I keep expecting to get a call about him being a date rapist or something."

"He's full of himself," I agreed. "He thinks Aunt Tillie likes him, though. I have to remember to ask her about him."

"Well, I definitely don't like him," Landon said dryly.

"Little Charlie Johnson Jr. inherited his father's inability to think before he speaks," I said. "He was a fountain of useless information."

"He makes me laugh," Chief Terry said. "He told me last week that I couldn't search his car without a search warrant but not to worry because there was nothing in it anyway."

"He's … scattered," I said. "He's mostly trying to fit in with the other boys. He did tell me that Aunt Tillie is warning all of them that 'The Man' – meaning Landon – is going to arrest them if they're not careful."

"Hey, if they're afraid of me, that's a good thing," Landon said.

"She also told them you can't handle the gun in your pants let alone the one in your hand."

Chief Terry let loose with a hearty guffaw, slapping the table as Landon scowled. "Oh, I love Tillie sometimes!"

"I'm going to make those stupid active wear pants of hers come true if she's not careful," Landon muttered.

"Oh, don't worry. I think you handle your guns fine," I soothed. "Of course, I'm old. What do I know?"

"I think the lesson we've learned here is that teenage boys are evil," Landon said. "Did they tell you anything else?"

"Well, finally I threatened them with Aunt Tillie's wrath if they didn't 'fess up about what was going on at Hollow Creek," I said. "They said that they're partying out there most weekends – although now they can't because they're sure I'll alert 'The Man' and he'll want to go out there and shut them down."

"Yes, I've always loved breaking up keggers," Landon deadpanned.

"They said that they haven't seen Nathaniel in days, but they have been down to Hollow Creek in that time," I added. "I don't know how they missed a body in the water if they were down there last night. They said they go Fridays and Saturdays. I didn't tell anyone why I was asking, although I'm guessing word is going to spread pretty quickly."

"Is that it?" Landon asked.

"Oh, when one of the boys said he would take me even if he wasn't drunk if I went to Hollow Creek, Charlie said that you would shoot his thing off, because that's what Aunt Tillie told him. I think that's it."

"Well, at least the little mouth got something right," Landon said, leaning back in his chair. "So basically we have a college kid who never got in any big trouble who was struggling as he tried to adjust to college life because he was used to being the big man on a tiny high school campus. None of that gives us any indication how he ended up stabbed eight times and floating in Hollow Creek."

"He was stabbed eight times?" I knit my eyebrows together. "That sounds like overkill."

"I see you've been watching cop shows again," Chief Terry teased.

"Am I wrong?"

"No," Landon answered. "Whoever killed Nathaniel wanted to make sure he was dead. That doesn't mean it was premeditated, though. It could've been a heat-of-the-moment thing. Now is when the real investigating starts."

"See, I knew you were more than just looks and a mishandled gun," I said.

Landon tickled my ribs. "You're lucky you're cute."

"And I'm ready to throw up again," Chief Terry said, turning his attention to the waitress as she approached. "Can you get me a bucket to puke in?"

Holly Warner was spending her last summer in Hemlock Cove before leaving for college. She was young, giggly and clearly knew how to handle herself when faced with an uncomfortable situation. "You haven't even tried the fish of the day yet," she scolded. "How can you already be sick?"

"These two," Chief Terry replied, jerking his thumb in our direction. "They're giving me indigestion."

"Hi, Holly," I greeted her warmly. "How is your last summer in town?"

"It's not technically my last summer," Holly explained. "The tips here are too good during summers because of all the tourists, so I plan on coming back every year to pad my wallet for the school year."

"That's good to know," I said. "What's on special today?"

Holly recited the specials like a pro, and after we ordered she left to fill our drink requests.

"She seems nice," Landon said, causing me to elbow him. Holly was built for a runway if she wanted – and a stripper pole if she was ever so inclined – and she'd turned quite a few heads in Hemlock Cove during the past year. "Ow! I didn't mean anything by it. Did you forget I like them old?"

I elbowed him again, but this time he was expecting it and managed to shift his body to avoid the blow.

"You two need to knock that off," Chief Terry ordered. "I feel like

I'm chaperoning a high school dance and I need to separate you for getting handsy."

"Yes, I remember you separating Tyler Ridgeway and me at the spring dance when you chaperoned my senior year," I said. "Good times."

Landon grinned. "Did you go around with a ruler to make sure everyone was six inches apart?"

"I'll have you know I didn't even want to chaperone that dance," Chief Terry countered. "Winnie conned me into it."

"Yes, and then she and my aunts spent the entire night trying to see who could dance with you the most," I said. Holly returned with our drinks and I stopped her before she could wander away again. "Hey, did you spend much time with Nathaniel Jamison?"

Holly seemed surprised by the question. "Nathaniel? Not really. He was older than me, so he was out of my league when we were in school. After he came back the past two summers, I realized I was out of his league."

"That's very true," I said, marveling at Holly's self-confidence. "What do you know about him?"

"I know he's been hanging out with all the potheads down at Hollow Creek," Holly replied. "Why?"

Chief Terry arched an eyebrow. "Potheads?"

"Yeah, that's where all the burnouts group together," Holly explained. "They go out to the creek to get stoned and drunk. They usually build a bonfire and then a couple people go at it in the woods. Typical stuff."

"I didn't know they were smoking pot out there," Chief Terry said, conflicted. "I thought they were just tossing back a few beers."

"Just so you're aware, smoking pot out there isn't new," I said. "We used to do it out there, too."

"Hey! You're supposed to be my little angel," Chief Terry warned. "I don't want to hear about the rampant pot smoking you did as a teenager."

"I wouldn't call it 'rampant,'" I argued. "You can probably let it go now, though. It was a decade ago. I think the statute of limitations has passed."

"That's probably why you look so old," Landon said sagely. "All that smoke ruined your skin."

"You're on my list," I snapped.

"You're on my list," Landon countered. "I'm going to punish you with my ... ."

"Don't finish that sentence," Chief Terry snapped, turning back to an amused Holly. "Was Nathaniel hanging out at Hollow Creek all the time, or just some of the time?"

"You know I'm not really part of the Hollow Creek crowd, right?" Holly asked. "Everything I know comes from rumors."

"That's okay," Landon said. "We don't suspect you of anything. You can be straight with us."

"Okay, here's the situation," Holly said, leaning in and lowering her voice. "Hemlock Cove is a small town. There's no theater ... or bookstore ... or even a dedicated coffee shop where younger people can hang out. All anyone really does is get drunk and have sex in a field."

"That's true of most small towns I think," I said.

Holly nodded. "You're either a goody-goody if you don't do those things or one of the popular kids if you do," she said. "I fall in the goody-goody crowd. I'm fine with that. That doesn't mean I don't hear about the other crowd. They seem to get off on people thinking they're badass.

"Nathaniel liked to think he was a badass when he graduated," she continued. "I guess for Hemlock Cove standards, he was. That's not saying much, though. Malcolm Theed told me that Nathaniel realized he wasn't very cool when he got to Central. Everyone was out-partying him, so he decided to up his reputation."

"How did he do that?"

"He started drinking more ... and he started smoking more pot," Holly replied. "The problem is that those things cost money. The cost of living in Hemlock Cove isn't very high and I don't think Nathaniel realized that his mother didn't make a lot of money until he was faced with the fact that it took everything she had to put him in college.

Malcolm said that Nathaniel wanted his mother to give him more money, but she told him to get a job."

"How did that go over?" Chief Terry asked.

"Not well. Nathaniel doesn't have much of a work ethic."

"Jim told me that Nathaniel was picking up extra work at some of the area farms," I offered. "He didn't say which ones, but I'm sure it wouldn't be hard to find out."

"That's a good idea," Chief Terry said. "Maybe we can get a feel for who he was hanging out with and what kind of worker he was. If Holly is right, it doesn't sound like he wanted to work."

"There's one other thing," Holly hedged, chewing on her bottom lip.

"It's okay," Landon prodded. "We're not here to kill the messenger, and we're not interested in telling anyone where we got our information."

"It was pretty well known that Nathaniel didn't like to work and yet ... well ... he was seen flashing big wads of money around town this summer," Holly said. "A lot of people thought he was doing it for show, but I could never figure out where he was getting the money."

"If his mother wasn't giving it to him and he wasn't earning it, that means he could've been getting it through other methods," Landon said, rubbing the back of his neck. "Maybe illegal methods."

"Maybe drugs," I suggested.

"There's those cop shows again," Chief Terry said. "Well ... that's interesting. I don't know what to think about that yet."

"Can I ask why you want to know about Nathaniel?" Holly asked.

"We found a body down at Hollow Creek today," Chief Terry replied, resigned. It was only a matter of time before the information became public. "We're pretty sure it's Nathaniel, although we're waiting for final confirmation now."

Holly's blue eyes widened. "He's dead?"

"He was murdered," Chief Terry clarified. "I want you to spread the word that no one is to go out partying alone. I know you're not into that scene, but gossip in this town spreads like wildfire. Until we know who killed Nathaniel, it's not safe for anyone to be running around alone. Can you do that for me?"

Holly nodded.

"That's good," Chief Terry said. "This town is about to blow up with conspiracy theories, and I'd rather not worry about the younger set getting into trouble if I can help it."

"I'll take care of it," Holly said, her eyes stormy. "I can't believe he's really dead. Now I kind of feel bad about calling him a dirtbag."

"Don't worry about things like that," I said. "You can't go back in time. You can only look forward – and you have a bright future ahead of you. Try to think about that."

"That's good advice," Landon said. "You should listen to her. She's old and full of wisdom."

"I'm never telling you anything again," I muttered.

"Is that because you're old and you're starting to forget things?" Landon didn't even bother to hide his smirk.

"You're definitely on my list."

ELEVEN

I left Chief Terry and Landon to their investigation and walked to Hypnotic after lunch. They offered to take me back to the inn, but I had another idea. When I entered the store, both of my cousins looked frazzled.

"What's wrong?"

Thistle scowled. "I blame you for what just happened."

"That seems fair," I replied, nonplussed. "What just happened?"

"Aunt Willa and Rosemary stopped by to the see the store," Clove volunteered from her spot behind the counter.

Uh-oh. "How did that go?"

Thistle dramatically threw herself on the couch in the middle of the store, exhaling heavily. If her scene was to be believed, whatever happened was right out of a cheesy soap opera.

"That bad, huh?"

"It was awful," Clove said.

I shoved Thistle's legs off the couch so I could sit and focus on Clove. "I'm dying to hear all about it. Just for the record, though, I think you guys deserve it for sticking me with breakfast duty alone this morning."

Thistle narrowed her eyes. "I'm going to make you eat dirt if you don't shut up."

I ignored her and kept my eyes trained on Clove. "What happened?"

"Well, they made their grand entrance," Clove replied, prancing out from behind the counter to reenact it for me. "They told us it was a quaint store."

"They kept using that word," Thistle said. "Quaint. What a quaint store. What a quaint table. What quaint candles. What a quaint cash register." Her imitation of Aunt Willa was pretty impressive given the fact that we'd only shared one meal with the woman. "I wanted to shove my quaint fist in her obnoxious face."

"I'm surprised they even wanted to come here," I said. "I wouldn't think a magic shop would pique their interest."

"Oh, they don't like magic," Clove said. "Rosemary informed me that Wicca is something sexually adventurous teenagers immersed themselves in because they can't control their sexual urges. She read it online, so it must be true."

"Oh, well, that explains it," I said, trying to swallow my smirk.

"Then she told me that the herbs we offered – all of which couldn't conjure a fly on a hot summer day, mind you – were gateway items for the eradication of God in our society," Clove supplied.

"I'd like to shove my fist in her gateway and choke her to death," Thistle muttered.

"I can see you're handling this well." I patted Thistle's knee. "Did you yell at them?"

"I held my tongue because Winnie looked as if she was about to explode," Thistle replied. "I'm genuinely worried she's going to have a heart attack if she keeps this all bottled up."

"Well, she's ticked off at me," I offered. "I was supposed to go to the festival, but a body was found down at Hollow Creek. I went with Landon and Chief Terry instead. I'm sure I'll hear about that tonight."

"What body?" Clove asked.

"Nathaniel Jamison. He was stabbed eight times."

Thistle lifted her eyebrows. "That's some serious overkill."

"That's what I said," I replied. "Then Chief Terry accused me of watching too many cop shows."

Thistle snorted. "Everything we need to know we learned from HBO," she said. "How long has he been dead?"

"They're waiting for a time of death from the medical examiner," I said. "He was in the water for days and his body was ... not good."

Clove wrinkled her nose. "That's awful. I don't know too much about him. Do they have any suspects?"

I told them about my afternoon, stopping while Thistle laughed about me being old, and then fixed a bright smile on my face. "I'm actually hoping one of you can loan me your car."

"Where is your car?"

"It's up at the inn," I answered. "Chief Terry drove, and he and Landon are off doing ... body stuff."

"Gross," Clove said. "You can take my car. I'll ride home with Thistle."

"What are you going to do?" Thistle asked.

"I'm going to stop by the Jamison house and offer my condolences."

"And you're going to see if you can find Nathaniel's ghost," Thistle finished. "I take it he wasn't out at Hollow Creek."

"No."

"Well, at least you have a reason to miss any meals you don't want to attend," Thistle said. "Is Landon sticking around this week?"

The thought hadn't even occurred to me. "I don't know. I hope so."

"Well, either way, Winnie informed us that everyone is expected at dinner tonight, and if we try to come up with an excuse she's going to let Aunt Tillie curse us to her heart's content," Thistle said. "Since Aunt Tillie is on our side right now, I'm not sure how much of a threat that is. I'm not sure I'm willing to risk it, though. Aunt Tillie goes power mad when she has approval to do whatever she wants."

"I only wish we knew Aunt Willa's endgame," I admitted. "She clearly wants something. If we knew what it was ... ."

"We still wouldn't be able to do anything about it," Thistle finished.

"We're pawns in this one. Aunt Willa's plan revolves around our mothers and Aunt Tillie. All we can do is offer support."

I narrowed my eyes. That didn't sound like the cousin I knew and loved ... well, most of the time.

"And by offer support I mean that I'm going to punch both of them before the week is out," Thistle added. "I can pretty much guarantee it."

"Well, I'm looking forward to that," I said. "I guess I'll see you guys for dinner. Wish me ghosts."

THE JAMISONS LIVED on a quiet street on the east side of town. The houses are small but well kept, and their lawn was immaculate. Everyone in Hemlock Cove works overtime to keep the town pretty. When your entire income rides on tourists, you don't have much of a choice.

I parked across the street from the house, second thoughts getting the better of me as I exited Clove's car. This was a private time, and Patty Jamison was going through one of the worst things imaginable. I didn't want to intrude on her grief.

I leaned against the car and studied the house. In truth, I didn't want to talk to Patty. I hoped Nathaniel was hanging around his old stomping grounds. Most people pass on when they die. The exception is a particularly violent death or when they pass on before realizing what's happening. Nathaniel's death was definitely violent. Whether he realized what happened and tried to cling to this world, though, was anyone's guess.

"Can I help you?"

I jumped when I heard the voice, turning swiftly to find a teenage girl studying me from the sidewalk. She had a bag from the diner in her hand and a weary look on her face. Her eyes were puffy, which told me she'd been crying. I recognized her without that observation, though. It was Chloe Jamison.

"Hi Chloe," I said, keeping my voice even. "How are ... ?" I broke off. That was an incredibly lame question, given the circumstances. "Do you need anything?"

"You're the lady from the newspaper, right?" Chloe asked, stepping closer. "You're Bay Winchester."

"I am," I acknowledged. "I heard about your brother. I wanted to stop by and ... ." And what? Talk to his ghost? I didn't think Chloe would understand that particular admission. "I wanted to see if you and your mom needed anything."

"You're here looking for a story, aren't you?" Chloe asked, her green eyes suspicious as she pushed her brown hair away from her face.

"No, Chloe, I'm not looking for a story," I said. "We'll do a story on your brother's death, but that's not why I'm here today."

"Why are you here?"

There was no good way to answer that question. She would be suspicious no matter what. "Honestly? I was looking for some information about Nathaniel and I was planning to talk to your neighbors." That was a lie, but it was the only thing I could think to tell her.

"What kind of information?"

"I ... well, I've heard a few things about Nathaniel," I admitted. "When you're trying to solve a murder, you need to know about the victim. I honestly did not mean to come here and bother you. I know you and your mom are grieving."

Chloe snorted, the sound taking me by surprise. "My mother is making lists and I'm getting food. Nathaniel was missing for days and we didn't even know it. I'm not sure we're technically grieving."

"He was your brother."

"And he's dead." Chloe's words were harsh and I could tell she was putting on a brave front. "Go ahead and ask your questions."

I pursed my lips. She was making this too easy. Still, I wasn't one to pass up a prime opportunity. "Do you know where your brother was working?"

"He was doing odd jobs out at the Peterson farm three days a week, and he helped at the fruit market two days a week."

That was interesting. "Do you know how much time he was spending at Hollow Creek?"

"He went there every weekend," Chloe replied. "There's nothing better to do in this hick town, so that's what he did."

"Did you go out there with him?"

"I went a few times," Chloe said. "I wasn't really into the beer and pot scene, though, so he told me I couldn't go with him again. He said I was too young. I thought that was pretty funny because he was a college guy hanging out with high school kids. But it doesn't really matter now, does it?"

She was bitter. Her words were harsh, but she was clearly struggling. I tried not to take her tone to heart. "Your brother was seen flashing a big wad of money," I said, trying a different tactic. If she thought I was trying to cast aspersions on Nathaniel she might let something slip. "People don't think he had much of a work ethic, so they're curious where he got the money."

I expected Chloe to stand up for her brother. I got exactly the opposite. "Nathaniel had no work ethic," she said. "He didn't think he should have to work. He was always looking for the easiest way to make money. He put in hours at the Peterson place, but I wouldn't call him a good employee."

"What would you call him?"

"A drug dealer."

I stilled, surprised. Even if she believed that, volunteering information of that sort to a news reporter was never a good idea. "Your brother was dealing drugs?"

"He had no marketable skills. What else was he supposed to do?"

"Where did he get the pot?" I asked, going for the obvious question first.

"There are plenty of small dealers around here," Chloe answered, shuffling in front of me. "That's how Nathaniel got his start. He bought ounces and broke them down into dime bags and sold them so he could make enough money to smoke his share without going broke."

She knew a lot about her brother's drug business. I couldn't help but find that suspicious. "He still needed to get his hands on product," I prodded. "Where was he getting it?"

Chloe shrugged. "He never told me that."

That didn't mean she didn't know. "I know a lot of people in the rural areas have small fields," I said, choosing my words carefully. "Was he getting it from one of them?"

Chloe snorted. "Isn't your aunt one of the people with her own pot field? It's not exactly a secret. Everyone knows it's out there, although no one can seem to find it."

"If they can't find it, how do they know it's out there?" I challenged.

"Because your aunt tells everyone she has a pot field," Chloe replied. "She thinks it makes her look tough. The problem is, everyone is afraid of her because the whole town thinks you guys are witches."

I swallowed hard. The big family secret wasn't really a secret. Most people didn't have the gall to accuse us outright, though. "What do you think?"

"I think you guys play into the town's mystique to keep all of your businesses afloat," Chloe replied, not missing a beat. "You guys just pretend to be witches, right?"

"You got us," I said, my heart rate slowing.

"You know people have been trying to find your aunt's pot field for years, right?" Chloe asked.

"I've seen people loitering around the property," I confirmed. Aunt Tillie's pot field was magically cloaked, so it was nearly impossible to find. "I wouldn't worry about that. I can guarantee they won't find anything."

"Is that because there's nothing to find or it's too well hidden?"

"They won't find anything," I said, skirting the question.

"My brother went out there looking last week," Chloe mused. "Whatever was going on with him, he was desperate to make more money. He figured he could steal some product from your aunt and she would never know because she's so old."

"I'm not sure that's how Aunt Tillie sees it," I said, briefly wondering how this conversation had gotten so far off course. "It doesn't matter. Your brother never would've left our property with what he was looking for. Out of curiosity's sake, though, how do you know all of this?"

"Nathaniel liked to brag," Chloe replied. "He didn't like to work and he didn't like to study, but he was good at bragging."

"Chloe, was your brother in trouble because of the dealing?" I asked. "If he owed money to someone … ."

Chloe cut me off. "My brother would never tell me anything about stuff like that," she said. "If he thought it made him look like a big man, he would tell me. Otherwise he pretty much ignored me."

And that's what hurt her the most, I realized. She always thought she would earn her brother's respect – even if the man who was supposed to give the respect deserved none in return. Now she would never get the chance.

"I'm sorry for your loss, Chloe," I said, meaning every word. "You should probably get that food in to your mom."

"Are you going to tell your aunt that my brother was trying to steal her pot?"

That was a good question. "I'm going to discuss the situation with her," I said. "She'll probably be tickled to know that everyone is town is spreading gossip about her." That sounded reasonable, right?

Chloe snickered. "I think she knows everyone in town gossips about her," she said. "I think she likes it."

Unfortunately, she was right. "Take care of yourself, Chloe," I said. "Take care of your mom, too. It's going to be sad for a little bit, but you guys will be able to work past this."

"I'm already past it," Chloe said. "I can't change it, so there's no reason to dwell on it. If you have more questions you can stop by again. Otherwise … I guess I'll see you around."

I watched Chloe walk up to the house, conflicted. She was putting on a brave face because she didn't know what else to do. What would happen when that bravado failed her? I could only hope someone would be there to help her pick up the pieces.

TWELVE

"Bay!" I headed straight for Aunt Tillie's field when I got back to the inn, playing a hunch that she would be hiding out there to avoid Aunt Willa's prying eyes. I was right. Unfortunately, she wasn't alone.

Annie raced toward me, her face flushed and her eyes excited. I caught her as she hopped up and threw her arms around my neck.

"We're taking care of the oregano," Annie said. "It needs to be watered just right so it doesn't get ... um ... seedy."

I ran my tongue over my teeth as I worked to rein in my temper. Landon would have a fit if he found out about this. "I see," I said, lifting my eyes until they found Aunt Tillie's. She'd changed from her combat helmet to her garden hat – although I wasn't sure it was much of an improvement – and she still wore her zombie active wear.

"Annie, I thought everyone agreed that you wouldn't come out to the oregano field anymore," I reminded her. "You're only supposed to help Aunt Tillie in the greenhouse."

"But she said I could," Annie protested.

"Yes, but ... ." How do you explain matters of the law to an eight-year-old? "You really shouldn't be out here."

I lowered Annie to the ground, keeping her hand in mine as I trudged toward Aunt Tillie. I was almost at her side when Marcus popped up in the space behind her, taking me by surprise.

"I didn't know you were here," I said, nudging Annie in Marcus's direction. "I'm glad, though. Do you think you could take Annie up to the inn and get her something to drink?"

His worried gaze bounced between Aunt Tillie and me. "Um ... ."

Marcus was one of the few people Aunt Tillie never got angry with. He volunteered his time to help with her gardening – ostensibly because she taught him important techniques – and they rarely squabbled. I think he's afraid she'll do something awful to him if he doesn't help. In reality, I think Aunt Tillie is too fond of him to ever do anything truly terrible to him.

"It's okay, Marcus," Aunt Tillie said. "We're almost done here anyway. I think Captain Killjoy is about to rain on our parade, and I don't want Annie to get in trouble because of it."

"Because Bay is a tattletale, right?" Annie asked, causing me to scowl. "That's what Aunt Tillie said."

"I'm not a tattletale," I countered. "I'm ... ."

"Sleeping with 'The Man,'" Aunt Tillie finished.

"Stop saying things like that in front of her," I hissed.

"I don't want to go," Annie said. "We've only been out here for a few minutes."

The red glow of her cheeks told me differently. "I think you should go inside," I said. "Marcus will get you some lemonade."

"Then can I come back?"

"Then you can go to the greenhouse and work on another project with Aunt Tillie," I suggested. "That will be just as much fun."

"I prefer working with the oregano," Annie griped, although she took Marcus's proffered hand and trudged out of the garden area.

Once they were gone I unleashed my wrath on Aunt Tillie. "You can't keep bringing her out here," I snapped. "Do you have any idea what kind of trouble this could cause?"

Aunt Tillie was nonplussed. "What trouble? It's not like I'm letting her smoke anything."

"Oh, well, that makes everything okay."

"You're so sarcastic," Aunt Tillie muttered, returning to her hoe. "Whose body did they find out at Hollow Creek?"

She was trying to change the subject. I wasn't done on the Annie front yet, but this gave me the opportunity to ask her about Nathaniel and get a straight answer before I laid down the law regarding the field. "It was Nathaniel Jamison."

Aunt Tillie furrowed her brow. "That's Patty's kid, right?"

"Yes," I replied. "He was stabbed eight times and dumped in the creek. He was there for a few days."

"Yuck." Aunt Tillie shook her head. "I'll bet he was a sight."

"I tried not to look at him."

"At least he wasn't a zombie," Aunt Tillie said. "Then he really would've been gross."

I rolled my neck until it cracked. "Aunt Tillie, did you know that a bunch of high school kids have been coming out to the property to find your pot field?"

"How do you know that?"

So she did know. Wait … of course she knew. She's Aunt Tillie. She might be in her eighties, but nothing gets past her. "They can't find it, right? Nathaniel's sister said he was dealing, and he came out here trying to find product because he needed extra money. If someone manages to get their hands on your … ."

"It's magically warded," Aunt Tillie interrupted. "I'm not an idiot."

I wasn't so sure, and for once it had nothing to do with her clothing choices. "Has anyone tripped the wards?"

Aunt Tillie let loose with a long-suffering sigh. "If you must know, busybody, someone was tromping around out here about a week and a half ago. The wards held. No one saw anything."

"And yet everyone in town knows the field exists," I challenged. "They say you're bragging about it. That's not a good thing."

"Who says I'm bragging about it?"

"That doesn't matter," I replied. "Your name came up so many times today I lost count."

"I'm very popular in certain circles." Aunt Tillie puffed out her chest. "I'm a legend."

"Yes, well, Charlie Johnson Jr. is telling people that Landon is going to shoot their things off if they're not careful. He said you told him that."

"That kid has a huge mouth," Aunt Tillie grumbled. "I knew it was a mistake to tell him anything."

"Dakota Evans said that he's your favorite and insinuated you're going to help him unleash his special brand of romance on the unsuspecting girls of Hemlock Cove."

Aunt Tillie snorted. "That boy couldn't find his own penis with both hands and a magnifying glass. Don't worry about him. He's all talk."

I shuddered at the unintentional visual. "They all say you've warned them about 'The Man' and his plans for them," I challenged.

"Are you telling me Landon wouldn't arrest them if he caught them doing something illegal?" Aunt Tillie retorted. "You can't get angry with me for telling the truth."

"Aunt Tillie, you need to be very careful right now," I warned. "Chloe said Nathaniel was dealing drugs. That's bound to be what Chief Terry and Landon focus on once I tell them what she said."

"So ... don't tell them."

"A boy is dead," I snapped. "I have to tell them. I wouldn't lie about something like this. It's too important. We both know that if Nathaniel was dealing it probably has something to do with his death."

"Not necessarily," Aunt Tillie argued. "He was stabbed eight times. That's overkill. A drug dealer would simply cap him in the head."

Apparently we all watch too much television. "That's not the point," I said, although I couldn't argue with her logic. I'd been thinking the same thing. "You need to shut this down until it all blows over."

"Shut what down?"

"This!" I gestured emphatically at the small field.

Aunt Tillie blew a loud raspberry. "I need this for my glaucoma," she said. "It's medicinal."

"You don't have glaucoma."

"Are you a doctor?" Aunt Tillie was getting shrill.

"Aunt Tillie, we have so much going on right now," I pleaded, trying a different tactic. "We have a dead boy who was probably out here looking for pot less than a week before his death. If I found that out in less than an hour, what do you think Landon and Chief Terry will discover?"

"They're not going to find my field," Aunt Tillie replied. "I added special wards so no members of the fuzz can ever find it. If they try, they get diarrhea."

That was a horrible thought. "I ... seriously?"

Aunt Tillie nodded. "If you got diarrhea every time you thought about something, wouldn't you stop thinking about it?"

That was both diabolical and disgusting. It also wasn't the point. "What if Aunt Willa finds it?"

"A little relaxation might do that shrew some good," Aunt Tillie said. "Is she back at the inn yet?"

"I have no idea. I came straight here. She did go to Hypnotic, by the way. It didn't go well."

"Nothing she does goes well," Aunt Tillie countered. "She's a horrible person."

"So why is she here?"

"How am I supposed to know?"

"You have to have an idea," I pressed. "You know her better than anyone."

"That's not saying much. I've never understood that woman."

I groaned, pinching the bridge of my nose to ward off an oncoming headache. "You're impossible. You know that, right?"

"I'm getting T-shirts made up that announce it to the world."

"Please, if you could just ... for a few days ... let this place go, I would really appreciate it." I was practically begging. I didn't like it, but I also didn't know what else to do.

Aunt Tillie sighed. "Fine. I won't work in my garden, and I'll strengthen the wards. Are you happy?"

"I'm happier," I clarified. "Hopefully people will stay away given what's going on with Nathaniel. I'm worried the opposite will be true, but I honestly don't know what to do about that."

"You're in a real tizzy today," Aunt Tillie said. "I blame Willa."

I smirked, Thistle's words from earlier in the afternoon echoing through my mind. Thistle was going to turn out like Aunt Tillie. I just knew it. "I blame her, too," I said. "I'm worried about what kind of damage she's going to do to Mom and her self-esteem before this is all said and done. Can't you do something to get rid of Aunt Willa?"

"Murder is illegal."

"I didn't say kill her," I spat. "Can't you cast a spell to banish her?"

"I could, but I'm not ready to do that yet," Aunt Tillie admitted. "Your boyfriend was right the other day – although if you tell him I said that, I'll curse you so you smell like bacon for a month."

"What was he right about?"

"Willa has something specific in mind," Aunt Tillie replied. "I shouldn't care. It's not as if she has power over me. I can't help but wonder what it is, though.

"She picked this time to come here because whatever she's plotting is going to happen soon," she continued. "She wants to feel us out. She wants to watch us interact. She wants to unnerve us. Then she's going to lower the boom."

"If that's true, then she has big plans, and I'm not sure that's good for any of us," I said. "Why not get rid of her now?"

"Because I want to play with her first."

And there it was. Aunt Tillie was readying a game of her own. "What do you have planned?"

"You were there when I did my planning," Aunt Tillie said, averting her eyes.

"Yes, but you've obviously come up with something else on your own," I pressed. "What is it?"

"You're not privy to everything in my life, Bay," Aunt Tillie shot back. "You're my niece and I love you ... some of the time. That doesn't mean you're my keeper. I'm my own keeper."

"Fine," I said, giving in. "Just keep from making things worse for everyone in this family."

"I can't promise that."

Crap. She really was up to something. Whatever it was held the potential to be both legendary and awful. "When this blows up in your face, don't come crying to me for help," I warned. "Make sure you keep Annie out of this pot field, too. Landon is going to freak if he finds out she was out here again."

"Landon needs to chill out," Aunt Tillie said. "If anyone was ever in dire need of some relaxation medication … ."

"Don't you dare suggest that to him," I ordered. "Also, you need to stop telling Annie that he's something to fear. It's not true, and it hurts Landon's feelings when she says those things to him."

Aunt Tillie stilled. "I didn't mean to hurt his feelings. Most of the time I only talk about that stuff because it's funny. I forget how much she picks up. I'll try to be better about that."

"That's not all," I added. "If she's afraid of him, what happens if she's in trouble and he's the only one there to help?"

"What trouble is she going to get in?"

"The trouble that always finds this family," I answered. "I know you mean well – and believe it or not, I know you like Landon, despite the things you say – but she shouldn't be afraid of anyone in this house. Not if they can help her if things go bad one day."

"I … ."

"Just think about it," I said, cutting off Aunt Tillie before she could come up with an excuse. "What if there was another car accident and Landon found her? What would happen if she wouldn't go to him?"

"Fine," Aunt Tillie said, blowing out a frustrated sigh. "You bring up a good point. I'll handle the Landon situation."

"Thank you."

"I think he's more upset that she has a crush on Marcus than anything else," Aunt Tillie grumbled.

"There is that, too," I conceded. "That doesn't change the fact that he's a good man and doesn't deserve to have Annie fear him."

"I'll take care of it," Aunt Tillie repeated. "If he tries to take my pot field, though, all bets are off."

"I would expect nothing less."

THIRTEEN

"I figured you'd be hiding in here."

Landon let himself into the library a few hours later, lifting my legs so he could settle next to me on the couch.

"Did you find anything?" I asked.

Landon ignored the question. "Where's my kiss?"

I scrunched up my face and leaned over to give him what he asked for, smirking as he made a loud smacking sound. "Better?"

"Much better," Landon said, resting his head against the back of the couch. "As for your question – not much. We found out that Nathaniel wasn't well liked and he had a chip on his shoulder. None of that leads to any suspects. What about you?"

I pursed my lips, causing Landon to narrow his eyes.

"You found something, didn't you?" Landon pressed. "Spill, little witch." He tickled my ribs.

"I wish you wouldn't call me that," I said, gasping as I tried to keep from laughing.

"Why not? I think it's cute and endearing."

"I think it often sounds like you want to put a B in front of it and call me something else," I countered.

Landon grinned. "Not generally, although I'd be lying if I said that wasn't true occasionally," he said. "Tell me what you found."

I blew out a weary sigh. "Well, I went to the Jamison house," I said. "I didn't plan to talk to the family. I was hoping to run into Nathaniel."

"I figured as much. Was he there?"

"I have no idea," I replied. "I didn't really get a chance to look for him, because his sister caught me on the street."

"That can't be good," Landon said, his face sobering. "What did you tell her?"

"I told her I was stopping by to talk to neighbors," I answered. "I'm not sure she believed me, but she put on an act that she's not upset and her brother was the world's biggest butthead. Now, I don't deny that her brother sounds like a butthead, but I think she's still upset."

"Kids that age are hard to read," Landon mused. "They want to be cool above all else, so they take on different personas so people can't see they're hurting. Did she tell you anything else?"

"She told me a few other things," I said, resigned that lying was out of the question. "She said her brother was selling drugs. She didn't know where he got his product, but apparently he boasted about moving pot. I didn't press her too much on whether he was selling anything else, because I didn't think it was my place.

"She also said he was a poor worker and he took her to a few parties at Hollow Creek before deciding she was too young to hang out there and rescinding the invitation," I continued. "She seemed ... lost."

Landon rubbed the back of his neck as he considered what I told him. "How easy is it to get pot around here?"

I shrugged. "I haven't tried since I was in high school, but I'll bet if I was motivated I could find some."

"Yes, but you have a great-aunt growing her own little field right on your property," Landon said, making a face. "You wouldn't have to look too hard."

"I wasn't including Aunt Tillie in that scenario," I countered. "She's not known as a sharer. If I was looking for product I probably wouldn't even consider her."

"That doesn't mean someone else wouldn't," Landon said. "I don't suppose you've talked about this with her, have you?"

I shifted uncomfortably, drawing my eyes away from Landon and staring at the bookshelf across the room.

"You know, Bay, if you keep stuff like this from me it's going to cause problems," Landon said, his voice even. "I know you want to tell me. I also know you're loyal to Aunt Tillie. I don't know what to tell you on that front. You have to make a choice, though."

"I already made the choice," I said, forcing my eyes back to his. "I just ... she's my aunt."

"I know she is," Landon said sympathetically. "Sweetie, I don't want to put you in this position. Maybe ... ."

"I have more to tell you," I said, cutting him off. "I just don't want to get in a fight."

"Well, that's not my first choice of evening activities either."

"Are you staying in town now that there's a murder?"

Landon jolted at my conversational shift. "Will it make you feel better if I say yes?"

I nodded.

"I decided to stay before this conversation," Landon said. "I called my boss earlier and told him what was going on. He made fun of me for being whipped, and then officially tasked me here until the murder's solved."

"Are you going to stay even if we fight?"

"Bay, you're killing me here," Landon grumbled. "We're not going to fight. Okay? Just tell me what you need to tell me, and we'll go from there."

He was trying to soothe me, but I didn't think he could keep his "no-fight" promise. "Chloe told me that Nathaniel tried to steal pot from Aunt Tillie's field about a week and a half ago because he needed more product," I said. "I questioned Aunt Tillie about it and she said someone tried to get past the wards ... but couldn't.

"I made her promise to stay out of the field while this is going on and strengthen the wards," I continued, hurrying through all of the information. It was like ripping off a Band-Aid. "She agreed. She also said she cursed law enforcement with diarrhea when they try to find her pot field, and promised to make sure Annie doesn't have the wrong idea about you."

Whew. I felt better. I risked a glance at Landon and found his face rigid.

"That's a lot of information, Bay," Landon said. "Thank you for having her talk to Annie. I don't like that the kid is afraid of me. The diarrhea was an overshare. As for the pot field ... well ... I'm not surprised that kids try to find it. I probably would've done the same thing at their age."

I waited for him to explode. It didn't happen. "That's it?"

"You know I try really hard to be a reasonable man," Landon said, a small smile playing at the corner of his mouth. "I don't actually like yelling at people. I especially don't like yelling at you."

"I think sometimes you like to yell," I countered.

"Maybe sometimes," Landon conceded. "I don't like yelling at you, though. I do have a good time yelling at Aunt Tillie, and Thistle on occasion. I'd be lying if I said otherwise."

"What are you going to do about the pot field?"

"Nothing," Landon replied, nonplussed. "There's nothing I can do about it right now. I can't technically prove it's there, and I really don't want to write in a report that I know where a pot field might be, but my magical girlfriend and her family are hiding it. I've opted to ... let that go."

"Thank you."

"I'm not doing it for you," Landon clarified. "I'm doing it for us. It's tense enough around here without taking on the pot fight."

He wasn't wrong. I opened my mouth but stilled when I saw a small figure hovering in the doorway. Annie, her eyes wide, stepped into view.

"What's wrong?" I asked.

"Aunt Tillie said I should be nicer to Landon," Annie said. "She said that I take what she says too ... um ... ." She searched for the right word.

"Literally?" I suggested.

Annie nodded. "I want Landon to know I'm not afraid of him even though he is 'The Man,'" she said.

"Thank you," Landon said, shaking his head as he smirked. "You know I would never do anything purposely to hurt you, right?"

"I know," Annie said. "You just want to take all of the oregano away from Aunt Tillie. She told me to make sure you never find out I was out there helping her again today." Annie realized what she said only when it was too late to haul it back. Instead, she clapped her hand over her mouth. "Oops!"

Landon shifted his gaze to me. "Did you forget something in your retelling of the afternoon?"

Well, there goes our fight-free weekend. Crap.

"HOW WAS YOUR DAY?" Mom asked, her face drawn as she sat across the table from me a half hour later.

"It was delightful," I replied, fighting off my own bout of aggravation. "I went to Hollow Creek and saw a dead body. Then I talked to a grieving teenage girl. Then I ... hung out with Aunt Tillie."

Landon made a growling noise in the back of his throat.

"Who died?" Marnie asked.

"Nathaniel Jamison."

"Patty Jamison's boy?" Mom asked, her expression softening. "That's awful. He was ... young."

"He was definitely young," I agreed.

"How did he die?" one of the guests asked. Everyone was interested in the conversation, even though Nathaniel's case was the last thing I wanted to talk about.

"He was ... ."

"Stabbed eight times and tossed in the creek," Aunt Tillie replied. "Don't worry. He wasn't bitten. He won't come back as a zombie."

"Thank you, Aunt Tillie," I seethed.

"You're welcome."

Landon rolled his neck until it cracked, leaning back in his chair as he stared Aunt Tillie down. After Annie's bombshell about being in the "oregano" field with Aunt Tillie all afternoon, he was largely quiet. He wasn't yelling ... but he wasn't really talking, either.

"Did you see Patty?" Mom asked.

I dragged my gaze from Landon and shook my head. "I stopped over there to ... offer my condolences ... but I ran into Chloe instead."

"How is she?"

"She's a teenager," I replied. "She was stoic and a little chatty."

"We should put a care package together," Marnie suggested.

"Definitely," Twila agreed, bobbing her head. "We'll bake some pies and make a casserole so they have food. The last thing they need to be thinking about now is cooking something."

"We can drop it off tomorrow morning," Mom murmured.

"Well, I think this is just awful," Aunt Willa announced.

"I think that goes without saying," Aunt Tillie said. "A young man was stabbed to death. It's not exactly as though you're wowing us with your insight."

Aunt Willa narrowed her eyes. "I was talking about the rampant crime in Hemlock Cove," she snapped. "In my day, we didn't have boys being stabbed and dropped in the creek."

"That's because they hadn't invented knives yet," Thistle said dryly, fingering her own knife. "Now you'd probably be lucky if someone didn't drop you in the creek."

"Thistle!" Mom scorched my cousin with a dark look.

Thistle rolled her eyes. "Don't mind me. I'll just be over here with my quaint dinner ... and my quaint murder fantasies."

"Don't make me come over there," Mom warned.

"What are the police doing about this?" Aunt Willa asked, turning to Landon.

"We're investigating," Landon replied, stabbing a piece of chicken and tossing it in his mouth.

"It's very early in the investigation," I explained. "They have to talk to people before they can magically solve the case."

"I know who did it," Aunt Tillie said.

"If you say it was zombies I'll strangle you," I threatened.

"Of course it wasn't zombies," Aunt Tillie scoffed. "Have you listened to one thing I said? It can't be zombies. He wasn't bitten."

"Who do you think it was?" Mom asked, fear flitting across her face.

"I think it was another teenager," Aunt Tillie replied. "They're always hanging around down at Hollow Creek."

"Well, that narrows the suspect pool to about four hundred kids," I muttered.

"When did you come up with this epiphany?" Landon challenged, swiveling to face Aunt Tillie. "Was it before or after you had Annie help you with your … gardening?"

"I thought people weren't allowed in the greenhouse," Aunt Willa interjected. "If a child can see it, surely I can see it."

"We weren't in the greenhouse," Annie said from her spot between Thistle and Belinda. "We were in the oregano field."

"Oregano?" Aunt Willa furrowed her brow. "I didn't know you had an oregano field."

"That's because it's not oregano," Thistle offered.

"You know what, Annie? I think now would be a good time to take you into the kitchen to finish your dinner," Belinda said, grabbing Annie's plate and motioning for the girl to follow.

"I don't want to eat in there," Annie complained. "Marcus and Aunt Tillie are out here … and Aunt Tillie said I have to be nice to Landon because I've been being mean to him. She says he's going to cry if I'm not careful."

Landon scowled. "I am not going to cry."

"I may cry," I offered. Everyone ignored me.

"Why would you need a whole field of oregano?" Aunt Willa asked. "Are you opening a pizza parlor? Is that your next great business adventure?"

"Shut up, Willa," Aunt Tillie ordered. "You're being a pain in the ass."

"Don't talk to me that way, Tillie," Aunt Willa demanded. "You're being a … horrible person."

"You always were quick with a comeback," Aunt Tillie deadpanned.

"I told you not to take Annie out to that field with you," Landon said. He bordered on the verge of screaming. I could feel it.

"You're not the boss of me," Aunt Tillie sniffed.

"What's the big deal with oregano?" Rosemary asked. "Is it some cash crop no one is supposed to know about? Is everyone dying to try oregano around here?"

"Only if they want the munchies," Thistle replied, causing several of the guests to snicker as they realized what she was talking about.

"I'm not supposed to touch the oregano because it will make me sick," Annie announced, reminding everyone she was still in the room. "I have to wear gloves and never eat any brownies Aunt Tillie bakes. I took an oath."

Thistle burst out laughing as Clove bit her bottom lip. Marcus and Sam stared at their plates while the guests chortled. My mother looked as though she was about to commit a murder – although I had no idea whether Aunt Tillie or Thistle was the intended victim. Marnie and Twila fixated on the wall on the opposite side of the table. And Aunt Willa? Well, it took her a little bit, but she finally realized what everyone was referring to.

"Omigod! Are you growing pot on the family property? That's illegal!"

"Why don't you say it a little louder," Aunt Tillie deadpanned. "I don't think the county cops can hear you until you hit the register that dogs can pick up."

"I'm really pissed off," Landon said, his eyes still fixed on Aunt Tillie. "I asked you to do one thing. One stinking thing. You can't even do that."

"Is Landon going to kill Aunt Tillie?" Annie asked Marcus.

"I have no idea," Marcus replied, tapping the edge of her plate as Belinda returned it to the table. It was too late to head off an argument. Even though Belinda was new to our family ways, she'd picked that little tidbit up early. "Eat your dinner."

"I don't want Aunt Tillie to die," Annie sniffed.

"Aunt Tillie will never die," Thistle supplied. "Evil never dies. Don't worry about that."

"You're on my list, missy," Aunt Tillie warned, wagging her finger to get Thistle's attention. "You've been off for two straight weeks. How does it feel to be back on my list?"

"It feels like I need some oregano," Thistle replied, causing every guest at the table – check that, every guest we weren't related to – to chuckle.

"This is the best dinner scene yet," one of the guests whispered.

"You know what? I'm going to arrest you," Landon said. "Yeah, I said it. I'm going to arrest you and charge you with manufacturing pot. Now you're on my list. How do you like that?"

"You have no proof of anything," Aunt Tillie countered. "I already promised Bay that I would stop taking Annie there. What more do you want from me?"

"I want you to stop growing pot!" Landon exploded.

"It's oregano," Annie corrected. "You plant things in a pot. You don't plant the pot."

I rubbed my forehead worriedly. "Maybe we should call it a night."

"Not yet," Landon said, refusing to back down as Aunt Tillie tried to stare a hole through him. "You listen to me. You'd better hope I don't find that field. If I do, I'll burn it. Do you understand me?"

"I think you're getting too big for your britches."

"Oh, stuff it," Landon muttered, grabbing my hand. "Come on. I don't care if we have to eat toaster crumbs. I can't take another second of this."

I hurried to keep up with him, my heart flopping as we scampered through the house. "Are you okay?" I asked as we neared the back door. "Are you going to yell at me now?"

Landon turned quickly, but instead of the ire I expected his eyes sparkled. "I feel so much better now that I yelled at her," he said. "Come on. I'll take you to town for dinner."

I stilled, surprised. "That's it?"

"I think it's this family," Landon admitted. "I don't feel normal now until I yell at someone. I can't yell at you. I can yell at Aunt Tillie and not worry about hurting her feelings. Man, it's as if a weight has been lifted from my shoulders."

"I ... are you sure?"

"Come on," Landon said, tugging on my hand. "If you're good, I'll buy you ice cream after dinner."

I'm pretty sure we've been a bad influence on him.

FOURTEEN

"What are you going to do today?" I asked Landon the next morning as he dropped me in front of The Whistler. Instead of braving breakfast at the inn, we drove into town early to eat at the diner. He was still in a good mood, although I couldn't fathom how we'd managed to completely corrupt him in such a short amount of time.

"Ask questions, investigate ... you know, the usual stuff," Landon replied. "What are you going to do?"

"I'm going to get some stuff ready for our festival spread," I said. "I also have to figure out where we're going to put Nathaniel's story in this week's paper. We don't go to print until Thursday for Friday, but Brian hates it when murder and festivals overlap."

Landon snickered. "Well, he's a tool. How are you going to get back out to the inn? I'm not sure what time I'll be done today."

"Thistle and Clove are working. I can catch a ride with them."

"Are you going to investigate Nathaniel's case?"

"I don't know," I said. "If something comes up I won't ignore it. I wasn't planning to get involved, though. If his ghost was hanging around, that would be a different story. So far, that doesn't seem to be the case. I'm not sure what help I'd be."

"I think you sell yourself short sometimes," Landon said, brushing a strand of hair from my face. "You always manage to help."

"I think you're being awfully charming this morning."

"I'm charming every morning," Landon countered. "You're the crabby one in the morning."

"You're crabby in the morning, too."

"Fine," Landon conceded. "I wasn't crabby this morning, though."

"No, you were grabby," I teased.

"You say that like it's a bad thing." He leaned in and planted a smoldering kiss on my lips. "What do you want to do about dinner tonight?"

"I don't know. Why don't we decide that when we're sure about your schedule?"

"I can live with that," Landon said. "I'll text you when I know what's going on."

I moved to climb out of his truck, but he grabbed my arm to still me. "Is something wrong? Are you finally going to yell at me?"

Landon blew out an exasperated sigh. "I need you to do something for me, Bay."

"What? You've probably earned whatever favor you're about to ask for."

"I have earned it," Landon agreed. "I need you to stop worrying that I'm going to storm out of the inn and you're never going to see me again."

"I ... what?" My voice sounded squeaky.

"Sweetie, you're terrified that I'm going to take off one day after an argument," Landon said, choosing his words carefully. "I see it on your face, and I don't like it. I know I've earned some of this because of the way I left when you told me about being a witch. I was confused then. I didn't know what to do.

"I accept who you are and what you can do," he continued. "I'm not going to leave after a fight. I promise. You can fight with me without fear of that."

"I ...."

Landon shushed me with a look. "I'm not done," he said. "I love you. I'm not going anywhere. I need you to believe that. That's what I need you to do for me."

I pursed my lips, my mind rolling. He was getting better and better about expressing his feelings. I felt guilty for thinking the worst of him. "In my head I know you're not going to leave," I explained. "My heart worries because it can't help itself. Part of me still wonders why you'd put up with the craziness that surrounds my family."

"Your family is part of the package, and you're the package I want," Landon replied. "Believe it or not, no matter how crazy they are, I love your family, too."

"You love Thistle and Aunt Tillie?" I was understandably dubious.

"I love you," Landon said. "I do love them, too. It's in a different way ... and there are times I want to smack them both silly ... but that's how a family works. I like the craziness of your family. Even when I don't like it, I still kind of like it. So, please, stop worrying about stuff that's never going to happen. Will you do that for me?"

I nodded, and Landon leaned over to kiss me again, holding me close for a second.

"I love you, too," I murmured.

"Of course you do," Landon said, his smile mischievous when he pulled away. "I'm handsome and I'm a catch."

"And modest, too," I said, reaching for the door handle. "I ... oh, crap. What is he doing here?"

Landon followed my gaze, scowling when his eyes landed on my father. He was at the other end of the lot, leaning against his car as he watched us. Landon killed the engine and pocketed his keys, opening his door and hopping out before I realized it.

"You're not going to yell at him, are you?" I asked, hurrying around the front of his truck.

"I haven't decided yet," Landon replied. "If fighting with Aunt Tillie made me feel better, just think what fighting with your father will do for my happiness."

"What do you think he wants?" I asked, falling into step with Landon as we closed the distance.

AMANDA M. LEE

"He probably wants to make up with you. If he wants something else, though, I'm ready to fight."

That didn't make me feel better. Still, I plastered a smile on my face as we approached. "Hi, Dad."

"Bay," Dad replied, pushing away from his car. "Landon. How are you guys?"

"We're good," I replied, keeping my voice even. "Did you need something?"

"I came to talk to you," Dad said, his eyes flashing momentarily as they bounced to Landon before returning to me. "I wanted to apologize for what happened at the Dragonfly. I might have overreacted."

My relationship with my father is one of those tricky issues I can't seem to reconcile. After separating from my mother when I was a kid, he left for the southern part of the state. We spoke sporadically by phone and visited occasionally, but he was uncomfortable with my family and the witchiness surrounding it.

When he and my uncles returned to town to start their own competing inn, things got tense. Everyone tried to find common footing, but Aunt Tillie constantly worked against them, and she had no problem bringing magic into the mix when it fit her plans.

A few weeks earlier we conducted a locator spell to find a robber who murdered a bank teller. It led to the Dragonfly. As part of our investigation, we cast a truth spell that caused a lot of old wounds to be ripped open. When Dad found out we cast a spell on his guests he was angry – and rightfully so – and he'd kept his distance since.

I was used to fighting with family. That's the way of the world in the Winchester household. When we fight, though, we're forced to make up due to proximity. I hadn't seen my father – other than a brief public encounter – in almost three weeks.

"We shouldn't have cast a spell on your guests," I offered, hoping I sounded conciliatory. "We should've at least asked you before we did it."

"That would've been nice."

"If it's any consolation, we were hoping to do it without you knowing," I admitted.

Dad made a face. "That makes it worse, Bay," he said. "We're trying to build a family here. It's not the family you're used to, but we would still like this to work. I said some unkind things when you were at the inn. I'd like to make it up to you."

"What did you have in mind?"

"Well, we were hoping to have a family dinner tonight," Dad replied. "Our group is leaving early this afternoon, so we'll have the dining room to ourselves. Warren and Teddy are at Hypnotic now, inviting your cousins. I'm not sure you'll all be up for it, but ... ."

"We're in," Landon interjected, cutting him off.

Dad was surprised. "You are? Just like that?"

"We're in," I agreed, mentally rubbing my hands together because we'd been handed a ready-made excuse to get out of another excruciating meal with Aunt Willa and Rosemary. "We want everyone to make up, too."

"See, this worries me," Dad admitted. "Usually we have to trick you ... or browbeat you ... or outright guilt you to get you out to the Dragonfly. Why are you giving in so easily?"

"Because I'm really looking forward to it," I lied.

"Okay." Dad didn't look convinced. "Can you be there at seven?"

"We're thrilled to accept your invitation," Landon said.

I WAS PONDERING my brief conversation with Dad in the front of the office an hour later – Edith nattering on at my side about the horrible death and how things like that only happen now because people slip meth in drinking water – when the bell over the front door jangled.

"I'm sorry. We're not open for business today," I called over my shoulder, not turning around. "If you need to place an ad, someone will be in tomorrow."

"I'm here to see where you work."

I froze when I heard the voice, my stomach inadvertently flipping. I forced a smile as I turned, fixing Rosemary with what I hoped was a welcoming look and swallowed hard before speaking. "I ... how did you know I was here?"

"Well, Grandma insisted on seeing the guesthouse because she was dying to know where you guys hide out all the time," Rosemary answered. "When we went down there, though, it was empty. Well, except for the mess."

I racked my brain, trying to remember what state we left the guesthouse in. Clove spent the night with Sam at the Dandridge, but the rest of us drowned our family sorrows with chocolate martinis. I was pretty sure we hadn't even bothered to throw the empty bottles in the trash can.

"We're not big on cleaning," I said.

"Perhaps you should get a maid."

I made a face, forcing my attention to remain on Rosemary even as Edith circled her with intent eyes. "Is this Willa's granddaughter?"

There was no way I could answer without making Rosemary think I was even more batshit crazy than she already did. "Is there something you're looking for, Rosemary?"

"I only wanted to see where you work," Rosemary replied, moving through the front office. "It's not very large, is it?"

"It's big enough for what we have to do."

"After working for a real newspaper down south, it must've been disappointing to have to come back up here because you couldn't hack it in the real world."

"She's definitely related to Willa," Edith said.

"I came back home because I love the area," I said. "I happen to enjoy working at The Whistler."

"I'm sure you do," Rosemary said. "What's not to love about living on your family's property?"

I narrowed my eyes. "Don't you live with your grandmother?"

"That's because she needs my help," Rosemary sniffed. "It's not the same situation at all."

"Whatever," I muttered. "Go ahead and look around. There's nothing here to interest you."

"I don't think that's true," Rosemary countered. "It's very quaint … but homey."

Now I understood what Thistle meant about the word "quaint." I ignored Rosemary as I continued searching through the files. I'd pulled the graduation records from two years earlier so I could look at the spread. I wanted to see whether Nathaniel was in any of the photographs. I was even more interested in finding out who he hung out with.

I was lost in thought, trying to pretend Rosemary wasn't touching everything in sight as she made small sighing noises while roaming the area, and almost managed to put her out of my mind until Brian strolled toward me. "Hey, Bay. What do you plan on doing with this murder out at Hollow Creek?"

"I plan on writing a story."

"Ha, ha," Brian said. "What kind of story?"

"I was thinking of turning it into a fairy tale." I didn't bother to look up. Brian wasn't even my least favorite person in the office right now. That was almost mind-boggling.

"People in town are saying it's tied to drugs," Brian said. "Have you uncovered anything like that?"

"I've heard about the drugs, but I don't have any proof yet."

"It's terrible that so many kids throw their lives away because of drugs," Rosemary chimed in.

Brian swiveled quickly. "I'm so sorry. I didn't even see you standing there. I wasn't aware Bay was doing an interview."

"I'm not doing an interview," I replied. "That's my second-cousin, Rosemary. She stopped by to the see the office." And give me a migraine, I silently added.

"Rosemary, it's so nice to meet you," Brian said, moving toward her so he could shake her hand. "I just love meeting members of Bay's family. I'm Brian Kelly. I own The Whistler."

"How nice," Rosemary said, returning Brian's smile. "I wasn't aware that anyone but Bay worked here."

"I wasn't aware Brian even worked," I muttered, causing Edith to snicker.

"So, how are you related to Bay?" Brian asked, ignoring my dig. "Are you a relative on her mother's side?"

"I am."

"Oh, that's ... ." Brian searched for the appropriate word.

"You don't have to put on a show, Brian," I said. "Rosemary likes my family – and especially Aunt Tillie – even less than you do. I'm sure you'll have plenty to talk about, if you're so inclined."

Brian scorched me with a dark look. "I'll have you know that I adore Aunt Tillie."

"Uh-huh."

"Don't you dare tell her that I don't," Brian ordered. In truth, Aunt Tillie terrified him. I didn't blame him. On a normal day Aunt Tillie merely dislikes people. Every day she genuinely hates Brian.

"I don't think you'll come up in conversation," I said, focusing on Nathaniel's two-dimensional face when I found him in a photo. I didn't recognize either of the boys flanking him. This endeavor looked to be a dead end. "I'm not seeing Aunt Tillie tonight, so you're safe."

"You're not coming to dinner?" a petulant Rosemary asked. "That's not a very nice way to show your extended family that you want to spend time with them."

"Then I guess I'm doing things correctly," I replied. "If you must know, though, I'm going to the Dragonfly to have dinner with my father. Clove and Thistle will be there, too. You're on your own with Aunt Tillie tonight."

"That's a frightening thought," Brian muttered.

"I think she's going senile," Rosemary suggested.

I rolled my eyes. "I think you guys have a lot in common and should go talk about it ... elsewhere," I suggested. "Brian can show you all around town, Rosemary. He loves festivals."

"Really?" Rosemary smiled. "I'd love that."

"Well then, that's what we'll do," Brian said, puffing out his chest. "It would be my great pleasure to show you around."

And it would be my great pleasure for both of them to make themselves scarce for the remainder of the afternoon. Brian Kelly had finally done something right. Who knew he was even capable of it?

FIFTEEN

"I'm so glad you could make it," Dad said, ushering us inside the Dragonfly a few minutes before seven. "I was starting to worry you'd find an excuse not to come."

"It's my fault," Landon replied, placing his hand at the small of my back as he urged me forward. "I was working with Chief Terry. We had to question some people today on the Jamison death. It took longer than I thought."

"I heard about that," Dad said, leading us into the dining room where everyone else was already seated. "That's a shame. Do you have any leads?"

"It's kind of a tough thing to unravel," Landon admitted, pulling my chair out so I could sit between my father and him, while nodding in greeting to everyone else. "There are a lot of stories out there about Nathaniel and what he was up to, yet we can't find anyone who actually admits to spending time with the kid."

"I pulled the graduation spread from two years ago looking for friends, but I didn't recognize either of the kids standing next to him," I said. "I'm not sure how many people are still around from that graduating class."

"I think Toby Jenkins was a member of that class," Thistle offered.

"I saw him at the festival today. He was running the booth for his parents. It was right next to our booth."

"I'll try talking to him tomorrow," Landon said.

The table lapsed into uncomfortable silence.

"So, um, we really want to apologize to you guys for overreacting about what happened," Dad said, his finger tracing a circular pattern on the napkin in front of him. "While we don't think what you guys did was right, we know our reaction was definitely wrong. We're very sorry, and we want another chance."

"Listen, this is hard on all of us," I said. "We're used to doing things one specific way with our mothers. We sometimes forget that other people don't do things the same way."

"And you guys left because of the way our mothers did things," Thistle added. Of all of us, she was the most bitter about her father leaving. She could hold a grudge longer than … well, just about anyone, other than Aunt Tillie.

"Thistle, we did not leave because we didn't like the way your mothers did things," Uncle Teddy clarified. "We left because … things weren't working out. We didn't want to make things worse by staying. It's our fault for not explaining things better to you guys when you were kids."

Landon slipped his arm around my back, rubbing a lazy pattern against my neck as he leaned back in his chair. "This isn't any of my business, but that's never stopped me from getting involved before," he said. "Do you guys regret leaving the way you did?"

Dad met Landon's even gaze, his face unreadable. They were having growing pains of their own. It was hard for Dad to see me with Landon. I thought it was because he didn't like him. In truth – and it was something he admitted while under the spell – he was really worried Landon would die on the job and break my heart. We all held beliefs about each other, and it seemed most of them weren't based in actual truth.

"I regret most of it," Dad replied. "Winnie and I were fighting a lot. She's your mother, and you have your own relationship with her.

From my perspective, though, she was bossy and refused to back down."

I snorted. That was my relationship with her at times, too.

"That doesn't mean I didn't love her," Dad continued. "Part of me will always love her. We had some good years in there. You probably only remember the bad parts, but there were fun times, too."

I didn't particularly remember the good or bad times, but I didn't think now was the time to admit that. After he left, I tried to push back all memories of him because it bothered me to dwell on things I couldn't change. He was here now, though. "I think we've all been trying really hard to walk on eggshells around each other," I said, glancing at Landon. "Someone reminded me today that a real relationship doesn't work if you're trying to avoid a fight."

Thistle laughed. "Oh, good grief," she said. "I take it you and Landon had a talk about last night's massive family freakout."

"It wasn't really about that," I countered. "What he said makes sense, though. We're too worried about fighting. We need to agree that fighting is part of our relationship and move on."

"I think we're all a little worried that if we tell you what we're really feeling you guys will take off again," Clove admitted. "It's hard for us, because ... well ... we know we can yell and scream at our mothers and it will be fine. We're not as sure about that with you."

"Because they never left, and we did," Uncle Warren supplied. "I get that, and I see where it's a real fear for you guys. I'm not sure how to fix it, though. We have a business. We've decided to make our lives here. I don't know what else to tell you."

"Maybe you don't need to fix it," Landon suggested. "You can't tell people you're not going to leave and have them automatically believe it. You have to prove it to them." He squeezed the back of my neck to reassure me. "They don't know what you're thinking and feeling any more than you know what they're thinking and feeling. You might want to consider a weekly meal to get to know one another again. They're not kids any longer. You have to get to know them as adults."

"That's actually a good idea," Teddy mused, rubbing his chin.

"It's also probably not wise to constantly fixate on the big stuff,"

Landon added. "Try bonding over the little stuff, and work your way up to the big stuff."

"You're smarter than you look," Dad quipped.

"That's impossible, because I look like a genius," Landon countered, causing everyone at the table to laugh.

Things were more relaxed after that. Everyone doled Teddy's special seafood Alfredo onto their plates and focused on mundane conversational topics. Well, at least our fathers thought they were mundane.

"What's going on at The Overlook these days?" Warren asked.

Thistle, Clove and I groaned in unison, causing our fathers to raise their eyebrows.

"That doesn't sound good," Dad said. "What's up?"

"Did you ever meet Aunt Willa?"

Dad frowned. "Once," he answered. "There was a big Winchester family reunion, and I met her there. She and Tillie got in a screaming match, and the day pretty much ended before it began. Why?"

"She's in town with Rosemary," Thistle replied, making her disgusted face. "They're evil."

"I'm surprised," Warren said. "There was no love between Tillie and Willa. Ginger kept them together, from what I understand. Tillie and Willa were happy to go their separate ways once she died."

"Did you know that Aunt Willa tried to get custody of Mom?" Thistle asked Teddy. "Did Mom ever mention that when you were married?"

Teddy furrowed his brow. "Now that you mention it, she did bring it up once," he said. "I didn't remember until just now. We were drinking one night, and she was talking about Ginger and how hard it was for all of them when she died.

"In actuality, she was trying to explain why they were all so loyal to Tillie," he continued. "I'm sure you can imagine how rough your great-aunt was on us when we started dating. I didn't understand why everyone was loyal to her given the way she acted."

"What did she say?"

"Well, let me think," Teddy muttered. "I was drunk that night, too.

Twila said something about Willa wanting all three of them. I think Winnie was already of legal age, though, and Marnie was very close. That left only Twila up for grabs, and she was terrified Willa would get custody."

"I can't imagine any judge taking teenagers from someone if they didn't want to go," Landon said. "I know Aunt Tillie has a certain reputation, but I don't think anyone could ever argue that she doesn't love her nieces. She drives me crazy, but I've never doubted that."

"You haven't been around to hear all the stories about Tillie, though," Dad countered. "I know this will blow your mind, but she's actually tame compared to how she used to act."

"That's terrifying," Sam said.

Teddy chuckled. "At her core, Tillie is a good woman," he said. "She's also set in her ways and bossy."

"Bossy is an understatement," Warren said. "She picked out Marnie's wedding dress when it came time. Marnie didn't like it, but Tillie won that argument ... as she always does."

"If I remember the story correctly, Tillie explained to Willa that even if she took Twila, there would be no money in it for her," Teddy said. "Tillie took over your grandmother's part of the land, but every cent Ginger put away went to the three girls."

"The land must be worth a pretty penny now," Marcus said. "Land values in Hemlock Cove keeping rising thanks to the tourist trade. I wonder how much it was worth back then."

"I have no idea," Teddy replied.

"The better question is how Willa got cut out of the family property in the first place," Landon said. "I'd guess that property – given its size and location in the township – has to be worth a high six figures now. It could be worth more than that."

"I doubt that's what it was worth back then," Warren cautioned. "You weren't around Hemlock Cove when it was Walkerville. For a time there, when the industrial base dried up, this was just a small town struggling to survive."

"The rebranding did wonders for it," Dad said. "Property is at a premium here. We spent almost three-hundred grand when we bought this place."

Thistle choked on her wine. "You've got to be kidding me! This place was a dump when you bought it."

"It was also the cheapest parcel in the area," Teddy said. "I'll bet that Tillie and Ginger bought Willa's share of the property after their parents died. Back then they probably didn't have to give her much to make her go away."

"And I'll bet Willa is bitter about it," Landon added. "Given how popular the inn is, that business is probably worth seven figures now that I know what you guys spent on this place."

"I still don't understand what Aunt Willa hopes to do by coming here," Clove said. "She's obviously not interested in making up with Aunt Tillie. They can't stand each other."

"Aunt Willa makes Aunt Tillie look cuddly," Thistle said.

"Whatever Willa is doing here, she's obviously not ready to make her intentions known," Landon said. "We all have to be ready when she does, because when it happens, Aunt Tillie will turn herself into a tornado to make sure she gets what she wants."

"Everyone should be ready to duck and cover," Dad said.

"That's the way we live our lives as it is," I replied. "This is merely going to be a different storm."

SIXTEEN

"This was a terrible idea," Thistle announced three hours later as we trudged through the heavy foliage that led to Hollow Creek. "I can't believe we agreed to this."

"It was your idea," Marcus gently reminded her.

After numerous glasses of wine – and a lively dinner conversation that didn't unravel into an argument for a pleasant change – Thistle suggested everyone take a trip to Hollow Creek to look for Nathaniel's ghost once we left the Dragonfly. She was always gung-ho for adventures when she was drunk. She was going to regret it in the morning.

Sam and Clove begged off, both claiming early mornings as they headed in the direction of the Dandridge. That left Marcus and Thistle to ride with us. It still felt weird to be on an adventure without Clove constantly whining about how much trouble we were going to get into. She and Sam were spending almost all of their nights at the Dandridge now. I don't know why, but the realization gave me pause.

"Do you think Clove and Sam are going to move in together?"

Landon, his fingers linked with mine, glanced over. "Where did that come from?"

"I was just thinking how Clove wasn't here for the adventure," I replied. "She wouldn't have wanted to come anyway. We would've had to threaten and tease her to get her to come. She hates wandering around the woods in the dark."

"She hates wandering around in the woods during the day, too," Thistle said.

"They barely spend nights at the guesthouse now," I said, "maybe once every two weeks or so. I don't think she's been there more than one night this week."

"I don't know," Landon replied, scanning the ground to make sure we didn't trip. "Would that bother you?"

That was an interesting question. I'd lived with my cousins for so long another arrangement seemed strange. "I don't know," I said. "It's not as though we wouldn't see her if it happened. It's just ... weird."

Landon and Marcus exchanged a pointed look, which wasn't lost on me. Something unsaid passed between them, but I couldn't figure out what.

"You know you guys can't live together forever, right?" Landon asked, grabbing me around the waist to help me over a fallen tree. Unlike Thistle, I had only two glasses of wine at dinner. I wasn't drunk, and it wasn't necessary, but it was still a cute move.

"I know that," I said. "I didn't expect to live together as long as we have. It's just ... ."

"No one expected Clove to be the first one to move out," Thistle supplied, cursing under her breath when she slammed her foot into a hidden root. "This was a terrible idea!"

"Is that what's bugging you?" Landon asked, his face barely visible in the darkness. "Are you upset Clove might be moving out, or are you upset because she's the first to consider it?"

"I don't know," I replied honestly. "I don't think I'm upset. In fact, if she moved out that means the guesthouse would be a little less crowded. It just occurred to me that I think it's going to happen."

"I think it's probably going to happen, too," Landon said, clutching my hand tighter. "I also think it's probably a good thing you guys don't spend so much time together. You get on each other's nerves as it is."

"Says you," Thistle sputtered. "I don't get on anyone's nerves."

Marcus, Landon and I snorted in unison.

"You're officially drunk," Landon said.

The sound of partying filled our ears as we approached Hollow Creek, causing us to slow our pace and strain to listen. We made out the typical party sounds of whoops and yells that usually accompany teenage alcohol consumption.

"Are they supposed to be out here?" Marcus asked, tugging Thistle closer to his side. "Isn't this a crime scene?"

"We couldn't keep it cordoned off," Landon replied. "It's too big, and it's state land. We had it for twenty-four hours, and then we had to open it back up."

"What do you want to do?" I asked.

Landon smirked. "I kind of want to put a scare into them."

"That sounds fun," Thistle enthused. "Let's do that."

Landon led the way, keeping me behind him as Marcus herded Thistle ahead of him and brought up the rear. When we pushed through the trees, no one noticed us right away. Then Charlie Johnson Jr., a red plastic cup gripped in his hand as he glanced in our direction, handled things in a mature and serene matter.

"Cops! It's the cops! Run for your lives!"

The kids broke out into screams and scattered, some racing into the water – even though there was nowhere to go once they got there – and others fleeing into the woods. Landon reached out and snagged Charlie by the back of his shirt before he could run.

"Where do you think you're going?"

"I wasn't going anywhere," Charlie whined. "I was just … ."

"Screaming like a girl?" Landon suggested.

"No. I … ."

Landon ignored him. "Everyone stop screaming and stay where you are," he bellowed. "If you make me run after you, I'll arrest you and you'll never get a job as an adult."

"That's not true," I whispered.

"Shh." Landon winked at me. "Who's in charge of this little shindig?"

No one stepped forward, which wasn't surprising.

Landon yanked on Charlie's collar. "Are you in charge?"

"No," Charlie protested, his eyes widening. "Dakota did it!" He pointed toward the boy trying to hide in the shadows on the other side of the bonfire. "He's the one."

"You're nothing if not predictable, Charlie," I said.

Landon smirked. "Are you the one who said I was going to shoot someone's thing off if they looked at my girl?"

Charlie was too afraid to answer.

"That's probably the one smart thing you've ever said," Landon said, releasing Charlie and focusing on Dakota. "Do you want to come over here, please?"

Dakota reluctantly shuffled forward, puffing out his chest in a show of false bravado for his peers. "What?"

"Did you throw this party?"

"It's a party," Dakota replied. "Who cares how it started?"

"That's not an answer," Landon challenged.

"Why do you want to know?" Dakota wasn't going down without a fight.

"Because I want to know who the idiot is who decided to arrange a party where someone you all knew recently died," Landon replied, not missing a beat. "I want to find that idiot and shake his hand. Really, guys. This was a great idea."

"We were having a wake," Charlie squeaked.

"This doesn't look like any wake I've ever been to," I said.

"That's 'cause you're old."

I had no idea who said it, but I lifted my head and scanned the crowd anyway. Next to me, Landon shook with silent laughter as he tried to keep himself together.

"That is not funny," I hissed.

"Oh, I like that my girlfriend is part of the Geritol crowd," Landon said, forcing his face back to stern before addressing the teenagers again. "All right, here's what's going to happen … ." When no one looked in his direction, Landon clapped his hands to get their attention. "Hey, idiots, eyes over here! If you want to leave without getting a ticket for underage drinking, you will file past us now."

"That's it? You're not going to arrest us?" Charlie looked relieved.

"I'm not going to arrest you," Landon confirmed. "If you expect to leave here without a ticket, though, each and every one of you will hand over your keys to Marcus before going. If that doesn't happen, I'll start writing tickets."

It was a bluff. Landon didn't carry citation books. Can the FBI even hand out civil infraction tickets?

The assembled teens began to grumble.

"I don't care how angry you are," Landon said. "If you want to leave, those are the terms."

"How are we supposed to get home?" Dakota asked.

"I guess you'll have to call your parents for rides," Landon replied.

"We'll get in trouble," Charlie complained.

"You should've thought about that before you threw a party where a dead body was found," Landon shot back. "Now, who wants to leave?"

The teenagers reluctantly formed a line, filing past Marcus and handing him their keys as they trudged away from the creek. Landon kept his eyes on them, fighting to keep a straight face when Dakota shot him a dirty look while passing. The area was almost empty when Dakota swiveled around.

"How are we supposed to get our keys back?"

"They'll be at the police station tomorrow," Landon replied, clearly enjoying himself. "You can pick them up there."

"Oh, great," Dakota grumbled. "I guess we'll be getting a lecture from Chief Terry while we're at it."

"I have no idea whether he'll have time for that," Landon replied. "Don't forget to take your parents with you when you show up, though. Anyone who tries to claim their keys without a legal guardian won't get them."

"What?" Charlie looked as if he was about to pass out. "My father is going to kill me."

"Your father was in this exact situation a few times in his life I'm sure," I countered.

"So you think I won't get in trouble?" Charlie visibly brightened.

"Oh, you're definitely going to get in trouble," Thistle interjected. "Your dad is just going to be a hypocrite when he grounds you."

Once we were sure they were all gone, Marcus doing a double loop to ensure we had privacy, Landon set me free to do my thing. Unfortunately, there wasn't much I could do without a ghost.

"Can't you make him show up?"

I rolled my eyes. "We've been over this before. I don't control the ghosts. I can only communicate with them."

"It would be more fun if you could control them," Thistle said. "Then you could send them to haunt Aunt Willa and Rosemary."

"That would be fun," I said, stepping away from Landon. He and Marcus opted to clean up the mess – diligent citizens that they are – and focused on their task instead of watching me. I didn't miss Thistle using the abandoned keg to fill her own cup out of the corner of my eye. She was going to be in a world of hurt tomorrow. "I'm not sure … ." I stilled when I caught a hint of movement by the water's edge. "Nathaniel?"

Landon jerked his head up, handing the bag in his hand to Marcus before moving closer to me. "Is he here?"

"I think so," I murmured, straining my eyes in the darkness. He was there. I couldn't really see him as much as feel his presence. He was suspicious. I couldn't blame him. He'd been stabbed eight times and dumped in the creek. We weren't familiar faces.

"Ask who killed him," Landon instructed.

I shot him an annoyed look. "Really? I never would've thought of that."

"Don't get mouthy."

"You don't get mouthy," I muttered, taking a step away from Landon. "Nathaniel, my name is Bay Winchester. My family owns The Overlook. Do you know who I am?"

The bonfire still burned, but the shadows were large outside of the ring of light. It was hard to see his face as he drifted farther down the shoreline.

"Is he talking?"

I shook my head and mimed zipping my lips for Landon's benefit before turning back to Nathaniel. "I know this must seem scary for you," I said, keeping my voice soft and pleasant. "You're probably confused and … searching … for something to cling to. I can help you, if you let me."

Nathaniel floated a few more feet and turned his attention to the water, staring intently. I took another step toward him. "Do you know what happened to you?"

Nathaniel didn't answer. Instead he lifted his arm and pointed toward the water. He was trying to show me something. I carefully picked my way through the heavy brush, stopping when I reached his side. Nathaniel didn't move his arm or his gaze. I peered into the water, but it was too dark to see anything.

I dug into my pocket for my cell phone and touched the button to turn it into a flashlight, lowering it closer to the water in an attempt to glean what Nathaniel was trying to show me. I didn't see anything at first, but the light glinted off something at the bottom of the water when I shifted the phone.

"Landon, do you have one of those bag things?"

Landon glanced around and grabbed a plastic grocery bag from the ground. "Not exactly. What do you have?" He stepped next to me and I pointed to the water. "What is that?"

"Did you find something?" Thistle asked, sipping her beer.

Marcus finally realized what she was doing and knocked the cup out of her hand. "No more alcohol."

"Hey! I'm an adult. I can drink if I want to."

"Don't come crying to me when you're hungover tomorrow and have a headache," Marcus countered. "I don't want to hear it." He's generally passive and lets Thistle have her way, but when he does stand up to her, she has a tendency to listen.

"Fine," she grumbled. "I guess I've had enough."

"Bay, point that light a little higher," Landon instructed, reaching into the water and digging around. He returned after a few moments with a large knife in his hand, the handle made of white plastic and the blade notched and dangerous looking. "Well, I guess we found the murder weapon."

I glanced at Nathaniel. "Do you know who killed you?"

He didn't answer, instead fading into the darkness.

"Did he answer you?" Landon asked, straightening.

"No."

"Well, we're still better off than when we started," he said, dropping the knife into the bag and tying it shut. "I told you that you were helpful, no matter what you think."

"I guess you should take me everywhere with you then, huh?" I teased.

Landon smiled. "I've considered it. Come on. Let's get out of here. There's nothing left for us here ... at least not tonight."

"I don't feel so well," Thistle mumbled, clutching her stomach.

"If you puke in my truck we're going to have problems, Thistle," Landon warned. "You're going to clean it up, too."

"Don't worry," Thistle replied. "I'm not going to make it that far." She doubled over at the waist and vomited, causing everyone to look in a different direction.

"And you said we wouldn't have fun," Marcus said, patting her back as he smiled ruefully in our direction. "I can't take her anywhere."

"I can honestly say that nights with you are never boring," Landon said, shaking his head. "I can't decide whether that's a good thing or a bad thing right now."

He wasn't the only one.

SEVENTEEN

"Do you think we should go inside and help Marcus put Thistle to bed?" I asked, shifting on the lounger behind the guesthouse an hour later and glancing toward the window. I could hear Marcus talking to Thistle, although I had no idea what he was saying.

"She's not our responsibility," Landon replied, pulling me closer to him as we relaxed. "We didn't drink too much and make fools of ourselves."

"Not tonight," I clarified. "We've done it before."

"Yes, well ... we were the good ones tonight," Landon said. "We should be rewarded for not being dumbasses."

"That sounds like a fun rule," I said, giggling as Landon tickled my ribs. "Thank you for being so good with my father tonight."

Landon sighed. "I knew you were going to take this to a serious place," he said. "Can't you ever just have fun?"

"I thought that's what we were doing."

"So did I until you put your serious face on," Landon replied. "Sweetie, I didn't do anything special tonight. You're the one who put things together so you could try to have a new beginning. Try thanking yourself occasionally."

"Oh, and to think I was going to offer to rub myself in bacon grease as a reward."

Landon smirked. "We'll do that tomorrow night."

We lapsed into amiable silence, Landon cuddling me closer as we enjoyed each other's silent company. Eventually Thistle's bedroom light switched off, which meant she was either done puking for the night – or taking a welcome respite.

"She's going to feel terrible tomorrow," I said.

"She is," Landon agreed. "She should be a ball of fun at breakfast. She doesn't have a filter on a good day. On a day when she's hungover, she should be downright terrible."

"Maybe we should hide the knives and sharp objects."

"Maybe we should go into town for breakfast and let them duke it out without us," Landon countered.

"We can do that."

Landon nudged me forward so he could slip his hands around my shoulders, digging in and causing me to groan as he kneaded out the day's stress. "Oh, that feels good."

"If you want it to last more than five minutes, you won't make those sounds," Landon said. "They give me ideas."

"You always have ideas."

"I'm a smart man."

We lapsed into silence again, enjoying the night until … . I lifted my head. "Did you hear that?"

"I didn't hear anything but you moaning," Landon replied. "Why? What did you hear?"

I tilted my head to the side, listening hard. There it was again. Someone was talking. To be more precise, someone was laughing. "I think someone is up by the clearing," I said.

Landon stilled. "How close is that clearing to the pot field?"

"Not very close," I replied. "Why? Do you think it's kids looking for pot?"

"Either that or Aunt Tillie is about to sacrifice someone to her goddess," Landon said, pushing me to my feet. "Come on. We need to check that out just in case."

"What if it is kids looking for the pot field?"

"Then I'll arrest them."

"You would have to admit there's a pot field if you did that," I reminded him.

"Not if I bust them for trespassing and fail to mention the pot." Landon wrapped his hand around mine. "You stay behind me."

I considered arguing. After all, he wasn't armed and I was the one with powers. Instead I let him lead. I didn't sense danger. In fact, I realized what we were going to find about a split-second too late. Landon was already cresting the hill when he saw who was hanging out in the clearing.

"Oh, holy hell!"

I screwed my eyes shut. I knew what I'd see if I opened them. It wouldn't be pretty.

"What are you two doing out here?" Mom asked, causing me to force my eyes open. Yup. I was right. They were getting drunk under the … huh, it wasn't a full moon. Why were they getting drunk?

I strolled closer, warily scanning Mom, Marnie and Twila to make sure no one was naked. Marnie was down to a tank top and cotton shorts, but no one was flashing any bits they shouldn't – at least not yet.

"We heard something in the woods and wanted to make sure it wasn't someone trying to pilfer Aunt Tillie's pot," I answered, glancing over my shoulder to find Landon rooted to his spot. He knew what happened in our ceremonial clearing when alcohol was involved. "Come on, coward," I prodded. "They're not naked yet."

"It won't take long," Marnie warned, chugging from a bottle of Aunt Tillie's homemade wine.

"Where have you guys been all night?" Mom asked, lifting her own bottle to her lips. It must be serious if they were all drinking their own bottle. Aunt Tillie's brew was strong enough to knock you on your ass when you shared it.

"We had dinner at the Dragonfly," I replied.

"Oh, so your fathers are more important than us. Is that what you're saying?" Twila was starting to slur. That was never a good sign.

"Actually, we took the opportunity to eat with them so we could hash things out about that truth spell," I said. "The fact that it got us out of a meal with Rosemary and Aunt Willa was an added bonus."

"You know what?" Marnie asked, wagging a finger for emphasis. I watched as it distracted her and she completely lost her train of thought. It was just as well.

"How was dinner?" I asked, already knowing the answer.

"Aunt Willa is the Devil," Mom said. "She's not a devil. No! She's the Devil. The big one. The red horns and fires of Hell one."

"I could've told you that before she arrived," I replied. "What happened to make you guys come out here and get drunk?"

"Nothing happened," Mom replied. "Rosemary barely talked, and when she did she said something stupid. Aunt Willa wouldn't stop talking, and everything that came out of her mouth was mean."

"So you decided to handle it by getting drunk?"

"I wish I could deny that and come up with something better to say, but I'm too drunk," Mom admitted. "Yes. We're drinking away our pain. Are you satisfied? Where did my wine go?"

"It's in your hand," I replied, nonplussed.

Landon finally got up the courage to join me. "They're dressed."

"That won't last forever," I countered, "unless they get really blitzed and pass out before they get a chance to dance. You might luck out there."

My mother and aunts were notorious for their full-moon rituals. Those usually involved Aunt Tillie's special brew and dancing naked in the moonlight. Landon accidentally saw the ritual a time or two, and he was terrified of seeing it again. He still had nightmares.

"What are you guys doing out here again?" Mom asked.

I shook my head. She was beyond rational conversation. "We're checking on you," I replied. "We wanted to make sure you were okay."

"We're just great," Twila enthused. "Feeling no pain!"

That wasn't going to be the case in the morning.

"Do you want to join us?" Mom asked. "We have plenty to go around. Mystery loves company. Mystery ... mystery ... ."

"Misery?" I suggested, trying to help.

"I know exactly what I'm saying," Mom snapped, wrinkling her nose. "What was I saying?"

"They are hammered," Landon said.

"Do you want to have a drink with them?" I asked, sympathy for my mother and aunts rolling over me. "I don't feel comfortable leaving them out here alone."

Landon sighed. "I was hoping to see you naked," he said. "I don't want to see them naked."

"You should be so lucky," Marnie muttered. "I look good naked."

"That's the word on the street," Landon deadpanned, resigned. "Okay. We're going to join you. If anyone but Bay gets naked I'm out of here, though."

He sat down on the blanket next to Twila, taking the bottle from her hand and gulping a huge mouthful. "This stuff is just as potent as I remember," he rasped, handing me the bottle.

"You have a fresh mouth," Mom said, trying to focus on Landon even though her eyes kept wandering. "Has anyone ever told you that?"

"You have … and Aunt Tillie has … and Bay has," Landon said. He patted the open spot next to him. "Come on, Bay. This was your idea. If any of them get naked, you're going to have to protect me."

I took the spot – and the bottle of wine when he handed it over – and chugged a little bit before giving it back. "You know we're going to regret this, right?"

Landon shrugged and took another swig. "We'll live."

"You might not say that in the morning."

"That's what aspirin is for."

TWO HOURS later Twila was passed out, Marnie was halfway there, and my mother was talking to a tree. I couldn't hear what she said, but it seemed like a lovely conversation.

Speaking of conversations, Marnie had been holding one with Twila for the past half hour. Twila's contribution to the discussion was snores, but Marnie didn't seem to mind.

The good news was that everyone still had their clothes on. The bad news was Landon and I were now officially hammered, too. It was going to be a rough morning.

"What time is it?" Landon muttered, flopping back on the blanket and staring at the stars.

"It's almost midnight."

Landon groaned. "We need to go back to the guesthouse and drink a lot of water and take half a bottle of aspirin each."

"I don't have to get out of bed tomorrow if I don't want to," I countered. "I'm my own boss."

"Well, I have to take that knife to Chief Terry first thing in the morning."

"I'll call and tell him you're sick, and we'll spend the day in bed instead," I suggested.

"That's only fun if you don't feel like throwing up."

"Good point," I muttered, cracking my neck. "I'll tell Mom we're leaving." I struggled to my feet.

"Oh, don't interrupt her and the tree," Landon said. "She probably won't even remember we were here if we leave now."

That was an interesting suggestion. Still, I'd feel guilty if I didn't at least say goodnight. "Just give me a second. Mom! We're leaving."

"Don't yell so loud," Marnie said, covering her ears. "You're giving me a headache."

"That's the quart of wine you drank," Landon shot back.

"You're loud, too," Marnie said, flicking his nose. "You need to adopt an indoor voice when we're ... well, we're outside, but you know what I mean."

"How can you even hear me with Twila snoring so loudly?"

"Maybe Aunt Tillie's zombies will hear her and come," I suggested. "Mom! Did you hear me? We're leaving."

"I heard you," Mom said. "I don't really care. In fact ... ." She reached for the hem of her shirt and whipped it off. Uh-oh!

"Oh, yay!" Marnie said, climbing to unsteady feet and reaching for the back clasp of her bra. "It's time to dance. Where is the music?"

"That is definitely our cue to leave," Landon said, hauling himself up and staggering next to me. "Move your cute little butt. We can't see this. Seeing it again will kill me."

"Do you think we should leave them?"

"They're grown. They can handle themselves. All I want to do is handle you."

I snorted. "All you're going to handle is a bottle of water and your pillow."

"Well, that will be fun, too," Landon muttered. "Let's get out of here. This is about to turn freaky, and I've had my fill of freaky for one day."

"Okay." I slipped my hand into his, both of us taking a moment to collect ourselves before starting the trek home. "I'll see you in the morning, Mom."

"Whatever," Mom said, not bothering to look in our direction as she struggled with her bra.

"What the hell is going on here?" I froze at Aunt Willa's voice, swiveling to find her and Rosemary staring at the scene playing out in the clearing. "Have you turned this place into a brothel?"

"They're communing with nature," I replied, listing slightly and falling into Landon's chest. He wrapped an arm around my waist to keep me upright. "They're not doing anything wrong."

"They're taking their clothes off," Aunt Willa argued. "How can that be right?"

"I ... ." I didn't have an answer.

"Isn't that illegal?" Aunt Willa pressed. "Shouldn't you be arresting them?"

"Naked dancing under the moon isn't a crime that the FBI is interested in," Landon replied, utilizing his "official business" voice. "Besides, it's not as if they're exposing themselves to kids. Who cares?"

"I care."

"That's because you have a big stick up your butt," Marnie said, crying out triumphantly when she finally managed to unclasp her bra. "I did it!"

"We have to go right now," Landon said. "This is getting serious."

"You can't leave until you handle this," Aunt Willa argued. "I won't allow it."

"Well … I guess it's good that you're not my boss then, isn't it?" Landon asked. "Come on, Bay. I need water and aspirin. If we don't leave now I'll be rendered blind."

"You can't leave me with this mess," Aunt Willa snapped. "It's unseemly."

"Then leave them be," I suggested. "They're not hurting anyone, and they'll pass out in the next few minutes. Once they dance, they'll be happy."

"I am not putting up with this!"

I opened my mouth to answer, but didn't get a chance, because Marnie's bra smacked Aunt Willa in the face and caused me to lose my train of thought. Before I realized what had happened, I burst out laughing and started moving toward the guesthouse.

"Have a nice night, Aunt Willa."

Landon stopped in front of her long enough to salute. "And have a happy new year, too."

EIGHTEEN

"I'm dying."

"I'm pretty sure I'm already dead," Landon murmured the next morning, rolling to his side and groaning. "The only reason you can see and hear me is because you're gifted. That has to be it."

I tried to laugh, but it hurt. "Why do we keep doing this to ourselves?"

"Because we're gluttons for punishment," Landon replied, reaching for the bottle of water he wisely stowed on the nightstand the previous evening. "It's always fun and games when you're doing the drinking. The morning after is a stark reminder that we're getting old." He gulped down half of the bottle and then handed it to me. "Well, at least you're getting old. I'm still in my prime."

I wordlessly took the bottle, debating whether smacking him would hurt him more than me. Finally I gave in and guzzled the water. It was too much effort to go after him. "We need more aspirin."

"I'm on it." Landon grabbed the bottle from the nightstand while retrieving a second bottle of water. He popped three tablets in his mouth and swallowed them before handing me a similar dosage. "Medicate up. We have to be down at the inn for breakfast in an hour, and it's going to hurt a lot worse if you don't head it off now."

"I don't have to do anything," I replied. "I'm forgoing breakfast and staying in bed all day. You can find me here when you're done working. If you're lucky, I'll have showered by the time you get back."

Landon smirked. "I thought you were going to say that you would be naked if I was lucky."

"I'm not sure you're going to get that lucky today."

"I guess it's good that I feel lucky whenever I get to spend time with you," Landon teased, snuggling close for a moment. "Even if you do smell like stale wine."

"Ugh."

We cuddled for a moment, content in the quiet, and then Landon slapped my rear end. "Get up," he ordered, climbing out of bed. "If I have to put up with your family for breakfast, you have to go with me. Those are the rules."

"Eat something here."

"You have nothing," Landon replied. "I hope you know that when we're living together we're going to have food in our own house."

I froze, the implications of his words washing over me despite the heavy fog frying my brain. "What did you say?"

Landon must have realized what he said, because his face paled. "I … you know what? I'm not doing this. Yes, I have plans for us to live together one day. I'm sure that's going to freak you out, but I'm not tiptoeing around because you work yourself into a tizzy whenever I mention the future."

"I don't work myself into a tizzy," I protested, my heart flopping. Was that worry? Dread? No, that was excitement. Crap. I'm such a girl.

"You thought I forgot I told you that I loved you a few weeks ago and refused to bring it up because you were terrified I was going to take it back," Landon countered. "I'm not taking it back. I don't want to take it back. I'm not taking this back, either. Get your butt up and get in the shower. I'm hungry and you have to be there when they feed me."

"Why do I have to be there?" He definitely was going to take it back if I kept sounding this whiny.

"Because your Aunt Willa is going to be on a rampage after last night, and if I'm the one dealing with her I'll shoot her."

"Holy crap!" I bolted upright, grabbing my head when the pain rushed to the forefront. "I forgot she was out there last night."

I risked a glance at Landon and found him smirking. "Yes. I think my favorite part was when Marnie whipped her bra off and threw it in her face."

"This is going to get ugly."

"Oh, little witch, it was ugly last night," Landon countered. "We were just too drunk to care. Now, come on! If you promise to keep your hands to yourself we can shower together. If you can't control yourself, though, you're going to take a cold shower alone. We don't have time for mischief this morning."

"You think an awful lot of yourself sometimes," I muttered. "Has anyone ever told you that?"

"You can think a lot of me, too, if you get in the shower," Landon replied. "Chop, chop! We both know the only thing that is going to cure this hangover is food … and there's only one place we can get it. Move! There's bacon calling me, woman!"

"YOU GUYS LOOK ROUGH."

My mother always told me I had a penchant for stating the obvious. Given the look on her face – and the heavy circles under her eyes – she wasn't thrilled with that trait this morning.

"Do you have to be so loud?" Marnie asked, rubbing her forehead as she flipped pancakes on the griddle. "Your voice is like nails on a chalkboard sometimes."

"Don't listen to her," Landon said. "Your voice is beautiful." His rebound rate after a hangover was much quicker than mine. After a shower – which turned out to be more "hands-on" than initially envisioned – he was back to his usual self. I wanted to punch him.

"How are you two not dying this morning?" asked Twila, the impression of the blanket she passed out on the night before still visible on her cheek.

"We didn't drink as much as you guys did," Landon replied, grabbing a slice of bacon from Twila, knowing she was suffering from delayed reflexes. "We also went to bed before midnight."

"And downed a bunch of water and aspirin before going to bed," I added. "We followed that up with more water and aspirin this morning."

"And how do you feel?" Mom asked.

"I'm still a little shaky," I admitted. "Landon is much better than he was. I saw Thistle when we were leaving. She was heading into the shower. She refused to speak. I think she's feeling as bad as you guys are this morning."

Mom's mouth dropped open in horror. "I don't even remember Thistle being there last night! Oh, dear Goddess, we drank so much we forgot Thistle was there!"

"Was Clove there, too?" Marnie asked.

I considered messing with them, but opted to put them out of their misery. "Thistle got drunk at the Dragonfly – and then a little more at Hollow Creek before Marcus put the kibosh on that. She wasn't with you guys last night. She got drunk on her own."

"That's a relief."

"Clove didn't get drunk at all," I added. "She spent the night at the Dandridge."

"She spends every night there now, doesn't she?" Mom asked.

"Pretty much," I said, glancing toward the dining room door. "Have you seen Aunt Willa and Rosemary yet this morning?"

"No," Marnie replied. "Maybe we got lucky and they slipped out in the middle of the night."

"If anything could get them to do it, you tossing your bra on Willa's face could be it," Landon quipped. "Personally, I didn't want to see it. I'm glad I got to see Willa's reaction, though."

Marnie froze. "W-what?"

It seemed I wasn't the only one with memory problems this morning. "You don't remember that?"

Marnie and Mom exchanged horrified looks.

"Do you remember that?" Marnie asked.

Mom shook her head.

Oh, this was definitely going to be fun. "Do you want me to tell you about it?"

"I'm not sure," Mom replied. "What was I doing when Marnie tossed her bra on Aunt Willa?"

"Forget that. What was I doing?" Twila asked.

"You passed out an hour before they showed up," Landon interjected. "You're free from all the embarrassment. Well ... other than snoring like a freight train and drinking enough that you could pass out in the middle of the woods."

"What about us?" Marnie asked. "Wait ... I'm not sure I want to know."

"Well, Mom was having a lovely conversation with a tree when they showed up," I answered, enjoying the discomfort on my mother's face.

"You two were having a great time," Landon said, stealing another slice of bacon. My mother and aunts were too horrified to notice. "I think you were making plans for a bright future together."

"Oh, no," Mom said, burying her face in her hands.

"Oh, it gets worse," Landon taunted.

"Marnie was down to her tank top and shorts when we arrived," I explained. "She took it down all the way when Aunt Willa showed up, and for a finale threw her bra at Aunt Willa's head."

"I was dressed, though, right?" Mom looked hopeful.

"You were at the beginning," I replied. "That's the only reason Landon agreed to hang around."

"Oh, I'm going to cry," Mom whimpered. "What did Aunt Willa do?"

"She ordered Landon to arrest you for public indecency, and when that didn't work ... well ... I have no idea," I admitted. "We stumbled home and passed out after Marnie tossed her bra in Aunt Willa's face. I'm not sure what happened after that."

Mom slapped my arm. "How could you let us do that?"

"Hey! We were drunk, too. You're lucky we didn't start shedding our clothes."

"Yes, that would make a wonderful story to tell my co-workers," Landon mused. "Did I ever tell you about the time I got drunk with my girlfriend, her mother and her aunt, and everyone got naked together? Good times."

"You shut up," Mom hissed, extending a warning finger in Landon's direction. "And stop stealing the bacon."

Landon was nonplussed. "Make me."

"Just ... ." Mom was beside herself as she waved her hands around like a loon. "This is the worst possible thing that could've happened!"

"Oh, no," I countered. "I think that's still to come when everyone has breakfast together."

"Get out!"

THE DINING ROOM was full when we entered, Aunt Willa and Rosemary sitting in their regular places. I briefly considered running, but Landon's insistent hand at the small of my back made that impossible. He pushed me forward and I forced a bright smile for the benefit of the guests.

"Good morning."

Everyone not related to me greeted us with genuine smiles and pleasant words. Aunt Willa and Rosemary remained stony and silent.

"It looks like it's going to be a nice day," Landon said, trying to make conversation as he pulled my chair out so I could sit. He reached for the jug of orange juice and filled his glass before pouring tomato juice into mine, and then settled next to me.

He knew me. It wasn't the simple act of knowing what juice I preferred, he also realized I would be uncomfortable holding random conversations with strangers given my hangover. He forced me out of bed so I wouldn't waste a day and regret it later. He instinctively did things to prove how well he knew me every time we were together. His earlier words about living together one day warmed me. Could he actually want that? It was an exciting – and daunting – prospect.

"I'm surprised you are up so early," Aunt Willa said, her tone snotty. "I would've thought drinking as much as you did last night would make for a rough morning."

"Who drank last night?" Aunt Tillie asked, appearing in the doorway. She was dressed in camouflage pants and a "Keep calm and STFU" T-shirt. She narrowed her eyes as she glanced around the table. "Is that why my wine closet looks considerably lighter this morning?"

"You have a wine closet?" Rosemary asked. "Why?"

"I need a place to put wine," Aunt Tillie replied in her best "well, duh" voice, sitting next to Landon and looking him over. "You don't look too bad."

"That's because we stopped at midnight," Landon replied, sipping his juice. "Your nieces are another story."

Aunt Tillie arched an eyebrow. "Why wasn't I invited to this little shindig?"

"Probably because you're one of the reasons they were drinking," Landon replied, leaning back in his chair. "They were actually having a good time until ... well ... we had visitors."

"What visitors?"

"Aunt Willa and Rosemary," I replied, shooting a quick look in their direction and finding both of them glowering at me. "They came in at the tail end of things."

"That didn't stop us from being mortified and embarrassed," Aunt Willa hissed. "I can't believe you talk about such things at the breakfast table."

"It's the lunch and dinner table, too," Aunt Tillie pointed out. "This table has been privy to many dirty conversations. Why are your panties in a bunch?"

"Speaking of panties, um, Marnie might've thrown her bra in Aunt Willa's face last night," I added, keeping my voice low.

Aunt Tillie snorted. "Now I'm definitely upset that I missed it," she grumbled. "First they steal my wine, then they don't invite me, and now I find out they messed with Willa? I always miss the fun stuff."

"It was not fun," Aunt Willa countered. "It was far from fun. It was ... despicable. The way you raised these girls to act ... it's scandalous."

"Oh, stuff it," Aunt Tillie said. "If you spent a little more time loosening up with some wine and taking off your clothes you probably wouldn't be so intolerable. How hungover are they?"

"Extremely," I replied.

"Well, I guess now is the time to tell them I want an off-road vehicle."

Landon stilled. "What?"

"I've got my eye on a Polaris Ranger," Aunt Tillie explained. "I've been holding off on telling them I'm getting it because they'll pitch a fit about safety ... and helmets ... and wasting money. Now that they're hungover, it's the perfect time to slip it in. They'll agree just to get me to shut up."

"What are you even going to do with something like that?" I asked.

"Ride around."

"Whatever," I muttered.

"That's it?" Aunt Willa's voice was shrill. "No one is embarrassed by what happened last night?"

"Oh, what really happened?" Aunt Tillie argued. "They got drunk and took their clothes off."

"I didn't take my clothes off," Landon said. "Just for the record."

"No. You didn't arrest them for taking their clothes off, though," Aunt Willa pointed out. "That's against the law."

"Not on their own property, it's not," Landon countered. "Take a chill pill ... and lower your voice. You would make dogs uncomfortable right now."

Aunt Willa's mouth dropped open. "That's all you have to say?"

"Pretty much," Landon replied.

"Hold up a second," Aunt Tillie instructed, narrowing her eyes. "What were you doing out in the woods by yourselves in the middle of the night?"

I shifted my attention to Aunt Willa. That was a really good question.

"You know, I didn't even think about that until you brought it up just now," Landon said, swiveling so he could see over my head. "What were you doing out there?"

"What were you doing out there?" Aunt Willa shot back.

"We heard noise in the woods and found them drinking, so we decided to join them," Landon replied, not missing a beat. "Bay lives on this land. We had a reason to be out there. You're a guest. What was your reason?"

"I ... oh, look at the time," Rosemary said, hopping to her feet and cutting off the questioning. "Brian will be here in a few minutes to pick me up. I can't keep him waiting."

Landon made a face. "Brian who?"

"Brian Kelly," I answered. "They hit it off at the newspaper office yesterday."

"Yeah, well, that sounds about right," Landon muttered. "They've both got similar personalities."

"Meaning they're both total a-holes," Aunt Tillie interjected.

"Meaning they're not the type of people getting drunk and ... naked ... in the middle of the woods on a weekday," Aunt Willa challenged.

"I still want to know what you were doing out there," Aunt Tillie pressed. "That's private property."

"Oh, shut up, Tillie," Aunt Willa muttered, crossing her arms over her chest. "I don't have to answer to you."

Landon shifted his eyes to mine. "Something weird is going on here."

"What was your first clue?"

"We need to figure out what they were doing out there last night," Landon said, keeping his voice low. "Whatever it was is obviously shady. That's why they won't own up to it."

"And how do you expect me to get the information out of them? They're not going to tell me."

Landon inclined his chin in Aunt Tillie's direction. "I think we have someone better suited for that assignment."

Aunt Tillie nodded, her smile smug. "Consider it done."

NINETEEN

I left Aunt Tillie to figure out what Aunt Willa and Rosemary were up to, stopping in the driveway long enough to wish Landon a good day at work before grabbing two bottles of water from the refrigerator and hopping in my car.

My headache was ebbing, which was a good sign, because my mind was busy. Landon's offhand statement about sharing a home together had me thinking. What did he have planned for our future?

Before he said "I love you," I wasn't sure we had a future. I knew I loved him, but I convinced myself he didn't love me because it was easier than asking myself the big questions. He walked away when he found out we were witches. That was almost easier, because the decision was taken out of my hands. Now my hands felt very, very full.

The idea of living life without Landon wasn't something I even wanted to consider. The realities of living with him, though, were difficult. His main office was in Traverse City. Did that mean he wanted me to move to Traverse City with him? Did he want to move here and commute? Did he want us to move someplace in between and lock out the rest of the world? Huh. That last one had potential, especially after a really loud breakfast with my family.

Still, I didn't want to leave Hemlock Cove. That didn't necessarily mean Landon would uproot his life and move here. The hangover headache was quickly turning into a full-blown panic attack. I had to focus on something else.

I parked my car near the path to Hollow Creek, grabbed the water bottles, and headed toward my destination. It was the middle of the day, and even though it was nice and warm, no one ever visited the area to cool off. The water was murky and the creek bed mucky. There were better places for family fun and the teenagers didn't want to risk being caught out here during daylight hours when more police officers were on duty.

It took me about five minutes to reach my destination. I hoped Nathaniel would appear again. If it was only me, and I gave him a chance to get comfortable in my presence, he might be more likely to talk.

Instead of searching the area to find him, I picked a spot close to the water and settled in the shade. I opened one of the water bottles and hydrated as I waited. Unfortunately, that gave me plenty of time to obsess about what Landon said regarding future living arrangements.

I was just about to text Clove and Thistle to tell them about the conversation when I caught a hint of movement out of the corner of my eye. When I focused on the spot, it was empty. The hair on the back of my neck rose, and I could feel someone watching me. I was pretty sure it was Nathaniel.

I tucked my phone back in my pocket and got comfortable again, hoping I gave off a soothing vibe. It took only a few minutes for Nathaniel to return. He played at the corner of my vision, refusing to move in front of me as he studied me. I let him continue his game for what felt like forever. In real time it was probably only five minutes. Finally, he filled the space by my feet and met my gaze head on.

"Hello, Nathaniel."

He didn't appear surprised by my greeting. He knew I could see him thanks to the knife discovery the previous evening. In the bright sunlight, his ethereal body was completely transparent in some places and fairly solid in others.

"You can see me."

"I can," I replied. "I saw you last night. Do you remember?"

"Your drunk cousin threw up," Nathaniel replied, his dark head bobbing. "You don't see a chick with purple hair puking very often."

"Probably not."

"Why are you here?" Nathaniel asked, glancing around. "Where is your boyfriend?"

I ignored the question. "Do you know who I am?"

"You're Bay Winchester. You're the editor at The Whistler. You're also part of that crazy witch family that runs The Overlook. That's a stupid name, by the way. Didn't your family realize that was the same name as the haunted hotel in *The Shining*?"

"No," I replied. "They thought the property had a bluff and you overlook things on it. That's as far as the reasoning went. We tried to tell them, but my family is great at talking and very poor at listening."

Nathaniel snorted. "It seems to have worked out for them."

"It has," I said, taking a moment to decide which way I wanted to steer the conversation. "Do you know what happened to you?"

"I'm dead."

"I know that," I said, fighting to tamp down my irritation. "Do you know how you died?"

"I was stabbed."

I hate teenagers. Yes, technically Nathaniel was no longer a teenager. He was still annoying because he acted like one, though. "Do you know who stabbed you?"

Nathaniel shrugged. "I ... maybe."

That was an odd answer. "Does it have something to do with the drugs?"

"What drugs?"

"The ones you were selling," I said, shooting him my best "I'm not an idiot so don't treat me like one" look. "I know you were selling pot. Were you selling more than that?"

"Who told you that?" Nathaniel asked, his expression darkening.

"Everyone in town told me that," I replied. It was technically a lie, but he didn't know that. "Quite a few people said you were selling pot and having money problems. Well, to be fair, some people said you were seen flashing big wads of money and others said you were desperate to find more product because you needed more money."

Nathaniel scowled. He wasn't a handsome boy by any stretch of the imagination, so the expression only made him more unappealing. "I want names," he snapped. "Who talked to you?"

"Grow up," I shot back. "You're dead -- and you're not a child. You might want to act like one, but it won't get you anywhere ... especially not now." I usually approach ghosts with a gentle tone and sympathy. Nathaniel was unlikeable, and I didn't have the patience to play tedious games. "I'm here to help you move on. If you don't want that help, tell me right now, and I'll go."

Nathaniel tilted his head to the side, confused. "Move on to ... where?"

"The other side."

"What's on the other side?"

"I've never been there," I answered. "I know people who have. I know it's better than being trapped here."

"If there's something else, why am I stuck here?"

I licked my lips, giving myself time to decide how to answer. "Most ghosts stay behind because they don't know they died. They wake up thinking they're still alive. Others ... remember dying. They're so traumatized by the event, though, they remain behind because they feel the need for retribution."

"So you're saying I'm still here because I want someone to pay for killing me. Is that it?"

I nodded.

Nathaniel pursed his lips. "I do want someone to pay," he said finally.

"Tell me who killed you and we can make someone pay," I suggested.

"I don't know that I remember who killed me," Nathaniel said. Something about the way he phrased the statement bothered me. "I can't remember everything."

"What do you remember?"

"I remember coming out here and trying to be quiet because all the drunk kids were annoying me," Nathaniel answered. "I remember ... hearing something. Then I remember screams. I think they were coming from me."

It wasn't uncommon for ghosts to block memories of their death. Sometimes they were too traumatic to ever recall. Other times they remember in bits and pieces. Sometimes – although it's rare – the memories come back in a flood when they're finally ready to accept what happened to them. Denial plays a part in almost everything, even when you're a ghost. I had no idea how it would go for Nathaniel.

"Well, let's break it down," I said, my pragmatic side taking over. "Who was here that night?"

"I ... everyone was here," Nathaniel said. "Dakota, Charlie, Michael, Dennis, Hayley, Jessica ... everyone."

Most of those monikers meant nothing without last names. I knew which Dakota and Charlie he referred to – and the fact that they didn't mention being out here with Nathaniel right before he died was irksome – but the other names could belong to several teenagers. "I ... "

The sound of cracking tree branches caught my attention and I swiveled to my left. Nathaniel was so surprised he blinked out of existence. I wanted to call out to him, make him stay so we could continue our conversation, but it was too late.

I rolled to my feet, ready to explode on whoever was coming, but the admonishment died on my lips when I saw Chloe. Her hair was a mess, wispy strands sticking out from a haphazard ponytail. She had dark circles under her eyes and her face was devoid of makeup. If I had to guess, it looked as if she hadn't slept in days.

I scrambled in Chloe's direction, catching her off guard when she realized she wasn't alone.

"Oh ... I ... what are you doing out here?"

Chloe looked so lost I wanted to hug her. But I didn't want to crowd her, and given her earlier attitude, I didn't think she would like it if she thought someone felt sorry for her. "I came to look around," I said. "I wanted to see where your brother died when no one was here and I could actually get a gander at what was going on."

"There's a rumor going around town," Chloe said. "They're saying your boyfriend found the murder weapon here last night. Is that true?"

"We found a knife," I answered. "We're not sure it's the murder weapon, but it probably is."

"Do you think … do you think it hurt? I mean, was it a big knife?" Chloe looked miserable.

I scanned the area, hoping Nathaniel would return when he realized the interloper was his sister. As far as I could tell, though, he wasn't around. "I think it was probably over before he realized what was happening."

Chloe's eyes were hopeful. "Really? Do you think that's possible?"

"I think that dying is probably chaotic," I replied. "I think the body has ways of shutting down pain that it knows the human mind can't take. A lot of people report being numb when they die."

Chloe furrowed her brow. "Numb? How do people report things if they're dead?"

Uh-oh. I tipped my hand a little bit there. "It's just something I read in a book once," I lied. "People who almost died said they didn't feel anything at the time."

"Oh. I guess that makes sense."

Whew! "What are you doing out here, Chloe?"

"I just … ." She didn't answer. Perhaps she couldn't.

"You wanted to see where he died," I finished for her. "You thought you might feel something if you came out here."

"How do you know that?"

"I've known quite a few people who died," I answered. "You can go ahead and look around. The police are done here."

"Are you staying?"

"Do you want me to stay?"

Chloe shrugged, helplessness washing over her face. "I don't know."

"Well, how about I hang around for a little bit and walk around the area with you," I suggested. "If it starts to bother you, I'll go. Just tell me. I promise there will be no hard feelings."

"Really?"

I nodded.

Chloe looked so relieved that my heart rolled. I followed her as she shuffled around, studying her face as she looked at the bank and water. After a few minutes, she turned her attention back to me. "I thought I would feel his presence here or something. Does that make me sound like an idiot?"

"No. That makes you sound like a sister who is grieving."

"I hated him for most of my life," Chloe admitted. "Now I feel guilty because I hated him, and it's too late to take it back."

"I'm sure he knows," I said. "I ... ."

Nathaniel popped back into view about a foot behind his sister. She couldn't see or sense him, and his expression was unreadable as he looked her up and down.

"What were you saying?" Chloe prodded.

"I was saying that I'm sure your brother knows how much you loved him."

Nathaniel made a disgusted sound in the back of his throat. "She's the one who told you I was selling pot, isn't she?"

I opened my mouth to argue and then snapped it shut. Chloe was already unhinged. If she thought I was talking to her brother's ghost she would lose any sanity she had left.

"Don't bother lying for her," Nathaniel sneered, stalking around his oblivious sister. "She's always been a freaking baby. God, I hate her!"

Before I realized what he was doing, Nathaniel reached out with his ghostly hands and shoved Chloe into the water. She tumbled forward, the force of the ghostly movements propelling her several feet into the water.

I was stunned. Most ghosts don't have the ability to alter the human plane, even when they've had years to practice. The most I'd ever seen Edith do was move a pencil, and that took her decades to master. Poltergeists can move things. They don't retain human form because they transform into rage-fueled monsters. Nathaniel appeared to be a mixture of the two.

Chloe surfaced, her hair sticking to her face as she climbed to her feet. "What the hell?"

"I ... ." How could I possibly explain this?

"Are you trying to kill me?"

"I didn't ... ."

"You're the only one here," Chloe said, slogging toward the shore. "You're trying to hurt me! There's no other explanation."

Well, crap. This situation spiraled out of control quickly.

TWENTY

"She tried to kill me!" One hour and multiple screaming fits did nothing to calm Chloe before the cavalry – in the form of Chief Terry – arrived.

"Tell me again what happened," Chief Terry instructed, pinching the bridge of his nose.

After fruitlessly trying to convince Chloe that I wasn't trying to murder her – and offering her a ride back to town, which she promptly turned into a purported death threat – Patty Jamison arrived thanks to a call from her outraged daughter. She in turn called Chief Terry to haul me in for attempted murder.

It wasn't going well.

"I want her arrested," Patty screeched, pointing at me. "She tried to kill my daughter."

"I didn't," I argued. "I didn't touch her."

"How did I get into the creek then?" Chloe asked, gesturing wildly at the water. "I was standing on the shore looking at the place where my brother's body was dumped. The next thing I knew I was flying through the air and landing in the water. That didn't just magically happen."

Technically, that wasn't true. I didn't think now was the time to bring it up, though.

Chief Terry glanced at me. "What were you doing here?"

"I was ... ." Talking to a ghost. Chief Terry knew about my abilities. Patty and Chloe did not. It was probably wise to keep it that way. "I was looking around because I wanted to instruct a photographer on what photos to take for our article on Nathaniel's death. I was going to call him with locations when I got back to the office." That was believable, right?

"She was out here waiting for me because she wanted to kill me," Chloe yelled. "Arrest her!"

"What's going on?" Landon popped out of the woods, his eyes scanning the area until they landed on me. He looked relieved. Instead of rushing over to hug me, though, he put his immovable "cop face" into action. "I heard there was a ruckus down here."

"Your girlfriend tried to kill me," Chloe spat.

"And you are?"

"I'm Chloe Jamison!"

"She's the deceased's sister," Chief Terry supplied. "She was down here ... what were you doing down here, Chloe?"

Chloe crossed her arms over her chest. "What are you accusing me of?"

"I'd like an answer to that, too," Patty said.

"I'm not accusing her of anything," Chief Terry replied, his famous patience on display. "I'm trying to get both sides of the story."

"There's only one side of the story," Chloe said. "She pushed me in the water and tried to kill me."

Landon narrowed his eyes. "Why would she do that?"

"Who knows? Maybe she killed my brother and wanted to take me out, too," Chloe suggested. "Maybe she was doing something out here and she was worried I figured out what it is and had to kill me to shut me up."

"What would she be doing out here?" Landon pressed. "Did you see her doing something?"

"Of course not," Chloe snapped. "She's much too ... diabolical ... to let a teenager know what she's doing."

"Then why would she try to kill you?"

"I ... ugh! You're going to take her side no matter what because you're sleeping with her," Chloe snapped. "Admit it."

"First of all, my relationship with Ms. Winchester is not up for debate here," Landon said. "Second, unless you can give me a proper motive, I have trouble believing a grown woman pushed a teenager into the creek in an attempt to drown her. If she really wanted you dead, why didn't she follow you in there and finish the job?"

"I ... ." Chloe broke off, confused. "I have no idea. Ask her."

"Fine. I will." Landon exchanged a brief look with Chief Terry and then moved in my direction. He grabbed my elbow, leading me far enough away that prying ears couldn't hear our conversation, and then fixed me with a look. "I should've left you hungover in bed this morning."

"This is not my fault," I protested. "I didn't touch her."

"How did she end up in the water? She says you were the only one here."

"I ... it was Nathaniel."

Landon stilled. "Are you telling me a ghost threw her in the water?"

"I don't know," I replied, fidgeting. "If I tell you that, are you going to have to put it in a report? I'm not sure I want that in a report."

"Don't push me, Bay," Landon warned. "Start talking."

"I honestly have no idea how it happened," I said. "I was talking to Nathaniel. He was ... being a pain. I heard a noise and Nathaniel disappeared. It was Chloe. I talked to her. She didn't want to be alone. I followed her around a little bit. Then Nathaniel popped up and he just ... tossed her in the water."

Landon rubbed the back of his neck, conflicted. "How is that possible? I've never seen a ghost touch anyone. Well, Floyd touched people ... and threw dishes across the room ... but no one else. Why can Nathaniel do it?"

"I'm not sure. Floyd was a poltergeist. He wasn't a regular ghost."

"You're not sure?" Landon was getting angrier by the second.

"I don't know what you want me to tell you," I snapped. "I've never seen a ghost able to do what Nathaniel did. It was as if he was overcome by rage. It's almost as if he's a mixture of ghost and poltergeist."

"Does that mean he could tip and become one of the nasty ones?"

I shrugged, helpless. "I don't know."

Landon pressed the heel of his hand against his forehead. "This is a mess, Bay. You have no arguable defense, because if you tell anyone who isn't sleeping with you this nonsense they'll lock you in a padded room."

"I know."

Landon's expression softened. "It's going to be okay," he said. "She wasn't hurt. You have no motive. We can always argue she threw herself in the water and then blamed you. She's grieving. People do odd things when they're grieving."

"Are you honestly instructing me to lie when that girl is struggling to hold on as her entire world crashes down around her?"

"I'm telling you not to do a thing without talking to me first," Landon countered. "I cannot live my life without you. I need you to keep your head together. I … are you smiling? Yes, I said something schmaltzy. Don't let it go to your head."

I pressed my lips together to hide my smile. It didn't work.

"Oh, you're lucky you're cute," Landon muttered, although a small smile tipped the corners of his mouth up. "This isn't going to be a thing. Don't worry about it."

"That's easy for you to say," I said. "What happens when she tells her story to everyone in town and they think I'm hanging around at Hollow Creek trying to murder teenage girls?"

"Then I guess the teenage boys are going to think you're old and dangerous."

I pinched his side, causing him to squirm. "Stop calling me old."

"Stop getting in ludicrous situations."

Chief Terry lifted his chin, sending a silent message for us to return. I longed to put my hand in Landon's, briefly wishing for a few moments of solace. That was a really horrible idea given his official capacity, though, so I fought the urge.

"Mrs. Jamison has agreed that pressing charges probably isn't smart given the ... realities ... of the afternoon," Chief Terry said.

"And what realities are those?" Landon asked, confused.

That was a good question. "I ... ."

"Shut up, Bay," Landon ordered, refusing to meet my gaze. "Did we miss something?"

"Just one thing," Chief Terry said. "Do you want to tell them, Chloe, or should I?"

Chloe screwed her face up into a petulant frown. "I am not making this up."

"Chloe might have found her brother's pot stash before leaving the house this morning," Patty supplied, her voice stilted. "I was not aware that she was ... high ... until Chief Terry pointed out how large her pupils were."

Huh. I'd missed that telltale sign, too. I should've seen that. When you live on the same property with a woman who claims she's curing glaucoma on a daily basis, you learn to recognize certain things. Of course, when you're used to it you also start to overlook it.

"It seems Chloe might be a bad witness today," Chief Terry said. "I think she probably fell into the water and needed someone to blame. Her mother agrees."

"I'm really sorry, Ms. Winchester," Patty said. "Chloe has been dealing with her brother's death, and she's been acting out a little bit. That doesn't excuse the way I blamed you. I hope you can accept my apology."

My stomach twisted with guilt. "I ... ." Landon shot me a warning look. "It was an honest mistake. I don't hold a grudge."

"Of course not," Chloe seethed. "You threw me in the water, and now you're getting away with it."

"That's enough, Chloe," Patty said, jerking her daughter's arm. "We'll be going now. Thank you, Chief Terry, for looking past this."

"I understand she's going through a rough patch," Chief Terry said. "Try to ... I don't know ... toss all of the drugs in the house."

"I thought I had. Thank you … and I'm sorry."

"Don't worry about it," Chief Terry said.

Once it was just the three of us, Chief Terry swiveled quickly. "Did you shove that girl in the creek?"

I took a step back, surprised. "No!"

Chief Terry relaxed. "Good. I didn't think so, but I had to be sure."

I rolled my eyes. "Was that your way of testing me?"

"If you scare people they're more likely to tell you the truth," Chief Terry explained.

"I wouldn't lie to you!"

"I know, Bay," Chief Terry said. "What did happen out here?"

I told him the story, expanding on a few points now that Chloe and her mother were gone. When I was done, Chief Terry was more confused than when I started.

"I don't understand."

"I'm not sure how to explain it to you because I don't understand either," I said. "I've never seen anything like it."

"Well, we did get something out of this," Landon interjected. "We know that Dakota and Charlie were out here that night. Dakota might not crumble under pressure, but that Charlie kid will give up his mother if he thinks it will benefit him."

"What did you guys find out about the knife?" I asked. "Chloe mentioned that there was a rumor going around town about you finding it."

"This town's gossip mill is churning overtime," Chief Terry muttered. "The knife was in the water. It's definitely the murder weapon, but there are no prints to lift. We're trying to run the brand, but odds of us finding the owner seem slim at this point."

"I'm bothered by Nathaniel's admission that a lot of people were out here that night," I said. "If people were out here, why has no one come forward to say they saw Nathaniel that night?"

"What are you suggesting?" Landon asked.

"Maybe they're all hiding something. Maybe they're not trying to cover up a murder. Maybe they're trying to cover up something else. Even if one of these kids is a murderer, keeping the rest quiet would be a monumental task. There has to be a reason no one has come forward."

Chief Terry's shoulders stiffened as he shifted. "You think more than one person knew about Nathaniel's death, don't you?"

"I think that something else is being hidden out here," I clarified. "I don't think most of these kids have it in them to hide a murder. What if they're hiding something else?"

"Like what?"

I shrugged. "Has anyone taken a good look around here?"

"We had people all over this place when the body was found."

"Did they go to the other side of the creek?" I asked.

"I ... ." Chief Terry rubbed his chin thoughtfully. "Now that you mention it, I don't remember seeing anyone searching that side of the creek. It's wide and deep enough that you can't simply wade across. Do you think something is over there?"

I shrugged. "It can't hurt to look, can it?"

Landon and Chief Terry shared an extended look.

"What do you think?" Chief Terry asked.

"I think I've learned not to question her intuition," Landon replied. "She's right. This place should've been searched more thoroughly. Maybe we should look around ourselves first."

"Okay. Let's do it. If anyone throws me in the water, though – ghostly or otherwise – I'm arresting someone."

Landon snickered. "Duly noted."

TWENTY-ONE

"Well, I guess you were right," Chief Terry said three hours later, watching the county crew tear apart one of the biggest pot fields I'd ever seen. "I can't believe this was right under our noses. I feel like a complete and total idiot."

"Hey, you're getting the credit for finding it," I reminded him. "You look like a genius."

"Only because we can't tell people your witchy intuition led us to it," Chief Terry muttered. "Where is Landon?"

"He's over talking to the county guy," I replied, my gaze landing on his broad back as he listened intently to whatever the man was saying. "I didn't even know they had a response team for pot fields. You learn something new every day."

"They have an entire drug team for the county now," Chief Terry explained. "Meth is a huge deal in a few of the other towns. I don't think they've seen a pot field this large in … maybe ever."

"It was the perfect place to hide it," I pointed out. "No one comes to Hollow Creek to swim. No one builds houses out here because the land is too dense and the ground too spongy. No one even bothers to go to that side of the creek. For all we know, they've been planting and cultivating this field for years."

"That's an interesting thought," Chief Terry mused. "How did you know?"

"I didn't know," I countered. "I just had a feeling there was something out here drawing these kids to the area. I had it last night, too. I kind of forgot about it with all the drunken foolishness and nudity."

Chief Terry scowled. "The kids were getting naked out here? Landon didn't mention that."

"The kids weren't getting naked out here," I clarified. "Well, maybe they were. We didn't see that. I didn't see the true drunken debauchery until I got home."

"Do I even want to know?"

I shrugged. "Let's find out," I said. The story was too good not to share. "Aunt Willa has my mother and aunts in an uproar. They're tense and they broke last night. They all went to our ceremonial field and got hammered."

"Where does the nudity come in?"

"Oh, they like to dance naked under the full moon. I thought you knew that."

"It wasn't a full moon last night," Chief Terry said, his cheeks coloring. "I ... I know about the dancing. I just don't like commenting on it."

"You should check it out one night," Landon suggested as he joined us. "You'll never be the same again."

"You saw them get naked?"

Landon nodded.

"I'm not sure how I feel about that," Chief Terry admitted.

"It's not the first time I've seen it," Landon replied, nonplussed. "I make a point to run when I know it's going to happen. Unfortunately, when we tried to run last night we ran into Willa and Rosemary. They were out for a midnight stroll."

Chief Terry frowned. "What were they doing wandering around in the middle of the night?"

"See, that's why you're a good cop," Landon said. "I was too drunk to do anything but laugh when Marnie tossed her bra and it bounced off Willa's head."

Chief Terry's mouth dropped open. Marnie is extremely well endowed. "I ... ."

"It's frightening," Landon supplied.

"You did more than laugh," I reminded him. "You gave Aunt Willa a saucy salute and wished her a happy new year."

Landon snorted. "I forgot about that."

"It sounds like you guys had an eventful evening," Chief Terry said. "How did everyone feel this morning?"

"Like burnt eggs on toast," I replied.

"Nice analogy," Landon said. "It's pretty spot-on, too."

Chief Terry shook his head. "Still, you had a hangover and you figured this out. I'm impressed."

"It was the kids last night that tipped me off," I admitted. "I didn't realize it until ... well, until you pointed out Chloe was high. That was a nice catch, by the way. I didn't notice, and I'm used to hanging around the lone member of Hemlock Cove's glaucoma club."

"What did they do last night that tipped you off?" Landon asked.

"Remember when Charlie started screaming about cops and how everyone should run for their lives?"

Landon nodded while Chief Terry chuckled.

"I swear that kid will be a comedian one day," Chief Terry muttered.

"A few of the kids started running into the water," I said. "At first I thought it was panic. The more I thought about it, though, the more I realized that they would've run into the woods if they didn't know there was a safe way across the creek."

"That's pretty smart thinking," Landon said, winking. "You're right. I thought the kids were just crocked when they tried to run across the creek. I'll bet if we spend some time moving along the creek we'll find a trail that allows people to walk across without going under."

"Also, I don't care how sentimental you claim to be," I added. "There are plenty of wooded areas around Hemlock Cove where those kids could've partied last night that weren't connected to a dead body. There had to be another reason for them to come out here."

AMANDA M. LEE

"The pot field," Chief Terry surmised. "Well, I still feel stupid. We should've known something like this was out here."

"Unless you were specifically looking for it, how would you find it?" Landon challenged. "What we need to do is find out who planted it and how long it's been here."

"Bay brought up a good point," Chief Terry said. "For all we know this isn't new. It could be an ongoing operation. The winters are brutal, so the field would be seasonal. That doesn't mean they haven't been planting it for years, starting a new crop every spring."

"That is a good point, sweetie," Landon said, tweaking my nose.

"You two make me sick," Chief Terry complained.

"Get over it," Landon shot back. "Well, I think our first order of business has to be finding out exactly who knew about the pot field. I suggest we start with Charlie. He'll roll over on everyone else."

"What if he doesn't know?" I asked.

"How could he possibly not know? He hangs around with those kids all the time."

"Yes, but he's a wannabe," I pointed out. "He wants to be part of the group, but I have a feeling they let him hang around only because he acts as their errand boy and does whatever they want him to do. I don't think they're confiding big secrets in him."

"Bay might have another point," Chief Terry said.

"You're on fire today," Landon said, winking.

"Knock it off! Now you're just doing it to irritate me!" Chief Terry scowled in Landon's direction.

"Stop making yourself such an easy mark," Landon countered. "Criminy! It's not as if we're doing something illegal."

"It's still gross."

"Whatever," Landon said, turning to me. "We do need to have a serious discussion."

Uh-oh. Did he already change his mind about sharing a house with me some day? That would be just my luck. "What?" Wow. My voice sounded squeaky enough that Landon sent me an odd look.

"We need to talk about Aunt Tillie," Landon said, scanning the area to make sure no one was close enough to hear us. "The county people are making noise about sweeping various areas for pot fields. They think if there's one, there might be more."

I swallowed hard. "Oh."

"What did you think I was going to say?" Landon asked.

"I ... how do you know that's not what I was thinking?"

"Because I know you," Landon replied. "You got all high-pitched and weird there for a second."

There was no way I could tell him what I was really thinking. "I thought maybe you were going to be schmaltzy again," I lied.

"We'll save that for later," Landon said, grinning when Chief Terry started fidgeting. "I'll schmaltz your cute little behind right off."

"All right, that did it," Chief Terry warned. "I'm going to push you in that creek ... and it's going to be on purpose when I try to kill you."

"Promises, promises," Landon teased, although his face sobered when he turned back to me. "How much do we need to worry about the county boys finding Aunt Tillie's hobby?"

"Oh, man," Chief Terry groused. "This is worse than the flirting."

"It's a real concern," Landon pointed out. "Do you want the Winchesters going down over this?"

"Of course not," Chief Terry shot back. "They can't find that field. We both know she did ... something ... to make sure we can't find it. If we can't find it and we know it's there, they're certainly not going to find it when they start blindly poking around."

"She also fixed it so anyone in law enforcement gets diarrhea when they even think about finding it," I added.

Chief Terry made a face. "Did you have to tell me that? Now I'm not going to be able to stop myself from thinking about it."

"Make sure you have a subscription to a good magazine you can leave near the toilet," Landon suggested.

Chief Terry knit his eyebrows together. "You're a sick, sick man."

"So I've been told," Landon deadpanned. "Bay, you need to have a talk with Aunt Tillie tonight. I know you don't want to – and there's probably going to be some horrible curse coming your way – but she needs to stay out of that area in case anyone is watching the property. Do you understand?"

I nodded. "She already said she wouldn't work in the field. I'm not sure I believe her, though. She'll have to agree after this," I said. "Even she can't find fault with staying away. It's the smart thing to do."

"She's never cared about what's smart and what's completely idiotic before," Chief Terry said. "Do I have to remind you about the time she took three small children to break into a house to save Christmas?"

I pursed my lips. Of course he wouldn't forget that. "I'll talk to her," I said. "I'm going to try to keep my mother out of it, though. She has enough on her plate with Aunt Willa."

"That's another concern," Landon said. "Willa knows about the pot field. She doesn't know where it is – and maybe that's what they were looking for last night – but she knows it exists. She could be petty and call in a tip when she gets wind of this."

I hadn't thought of that. "I'll definitely talk to Aunt Tillie."

"No one is to go in that field until we're sure the county people are gone," Landon said. "It's important, Bay."

"I know. I'll ... figure something out."

Landon ran his hand down the back of my head. "Thank you."

"Well, look over there," Chief Terry said, inclining his chin to the spot over Landon's shoulder. We all stared in the direction he indicated, three teenage faces popping into view from the other side of the field.

"What do you think?" Landon asked. "That's Charlie and Dakota, right? Who is the third kid?"

"That's Stephen Brooks," Chief Terry answered. "He's Andrew Brooks' kid. He's the mailman. It doesn't surprise me that they're running together."

"Charlie is with them," Landon pointed out. "He has to know what's going on."

"They're going to lie and say that they saw all the people and came to check it out," I offered. "You know that, right?"

"I do," Chief Terry said. "I think letting them stew about this overnight is our best move. We'll figure out a plan of action for questioning them tomorrow. For now, I think what's going to happen next will be enough to terrify them."

I was confused. "What's going to happen next?"

Landon pointed toward the field, where one of the county drug enforcers was taking a flamethrower to the plants. "It's standard operating procedure," he explained. "They take samples for the lab and burn the rest."

"The whole town is going to get high," I protested.

Landon snorted. "They won't. It's wet. They're going to watch thousands of dollars in profit go up in smoke in the next few minutes. The county won't leave until the field is razed."

"You know that's going to make their clientele – and maybe whoever else they're working with – very unhappy, right?" Chief Terry prodded. "That could make for some desperate kids. We need to watch them."

"We're already watching them," Landon said, raising his hand to wave at the boys. "They know we suspect them. Now they're going to come up with a lie."

"What will you do?" I asked.

"Rip it apart," Landon replied, grabbing my hand as his eyes twinkled. "Come on. I want to get out of here before I get the munchies. I'm already starving, and you have a chore to do before we eat."

"Oh, yeah, right," I muttered. "I get to lay down the law with Aunt Tillie."

"If she's going to curse you, please ask for the bacon one," Landon begged. "Tell her I'll even pay if that's enough to sway her."

"You make me sick," I grumbled.

"That's what I've been telling you," Chief Terry said. "Why don't you ever listen to me?"

TWENTY-TWO

"This is the worst idea we've had since ... well ... we were old enough to have ideas," Clove announced, peeking around the kitchen door and eyeing Aunt Tillie as she watched *Jeopardy* on the couch in the family living quarters a few hours later. "She's going to curse us with something truly awful."

"We don't have a choice," I argued. "You know what will happen if someone discovers that field. Aunt Tillie wouldn't be the one on the hot seat. Our mothers would be in trouble."

"Don't kid yourself," Thistle said, flattening her slim body against the wall to get a better look at Aunt Tillie. "We'd go down, too, and then Aunt Tillie would be left to rule the roost with her iron fist of death."

"You're in a mood," Clove muttered.

"I have a terrible headache," Thistle said.

"That's what happens when you drink yourself to the point where you puke at a teenage kegger," I pointed out.

"I'm sad I missed it," Clove said wistfully. "I miss all the fun stuff."

Thistle scowled. "You wouldn't have missed it if you didn't spend every night at Sam's place," she said. "What's going on? Are you going to move in with him?"

Clove shifted, surprised by the question. "Why would you ask that?"

"Because you don't really live with us anymore," I answered. "We've noticed your constant absences."

"And we've really enjoyed them," Thistle snarked.

"It's okay, Clove," I said, taking sympathy on my cousin and her deer-caught-in-headlights expression. "If you want to move in with Sam, we understand."

"I don't," Thistle grumbled.

"You'll always have a place with us," I added, ignoring Thistle. "Just because you move in with Sam doesn't mean we're not a family. We'll still ... do stuff."

"You really wouldn't mind?" Clove looked relieved. "I've been considering it. Sam wants me to. It's just ... I was worried about leaving you guys. You know you're going to fight nonstop if I'm not there to cast the deciding vote, right?"

"We're adults," I said, patting her arm. "We'll ... figure it out."

"We will," Thistle agreed. "We're going to figure out that I'm always right."

"Don't make me force-feed you dirt," I threatened.

"Later," Thistle hissed. "We have to deal with ... that ... first."

"Any suggestions?" Clove asked, inhaling deeply and pulling together her limited courage. "How should we do this?"

"I have only one idea," I admitted, shoving Clove through the door.

"That was mean," Thistle said. "Good job."

"Hey, if she's going to leave us, she deserves this," I said, following Clove into the room. "Good evening, Aunt Tillie."

"Whatever it is, I didn't do it," Aunt Tillie said, her eyes trained on the television. "If you want something, the answer is no."

"We haven't even told you why we're here," Clove protested.

"You're here to annoy me."

"You don't know that," Thistle challenged. "We could be here to tell you how wonderful and great you are."

"Do I look like I was born yesterday?" Aunt Tillie refused to move

AMANDA M. LEE

her eyes from the television. She was sending us a message, and that message was clear: I'm not afraid of you.

"We need to have a talk," I said, employing a calm voice as I moved closer. "Something happened today."

"I heard," Aunt Tillie replied, nonplussed. "You found a huge pot field out at Hollow Creek and the fuzz burned it to the ground. That's a total waste, if you ask me."

I narrowed my eyes. "How did you hear?"

"All of the guests were talking about it," Aunt Tillie answered. "I guess it was the talk of the town. I hear there was a run on corndogs and elephant ears at the festival this afternoon."

I scowled. "Landon said it was impossible for everyone to get high."

"Yes, and I'm sure Landon knows everything," Aunt Tillie shot back. "What do you three want?"

"I think you already know what we want," Thistle surmised. "You need to stay out of your field for the foreseeable future. The county guys are looking to conduct searches. No one can see where you go."

"Um ... no."

I wasn't expecting her to capitulate without a fight. Her blasé attitude was irksome, though. "It's not up for debate," I argued. "I promised Landon you would stay away from that field. You're going to do it."

"Um ... no."

"Aunt Tillie, you have to understand where we're coming from," Clove said, trying a different tactic. "If your field is found, our mothers will be in big trouble. Can't you please do this for them?"

"Um ... no."

She was starting to sound like a broken record. "Why do you have to be such a pain in the ass?"

"I think it's in the genes," Aunt Tillie replied, hopping to her feet. "What is Mount Rushmore!"

"What?" I knit my eyebrows together, listening as Alex Trebek gave the correct response as "What is the Andes." I had no idea what the original clue was. "You were wrong. Will you pay attention to us now?"

Aunt Tillie flipped the television off and moved past us, heading in the direction of the kitchen. "Is dinner ready?"

Thistle and I exchanged an incredulous look. She was unbelievable. We followed her into the kitchen, and I hurried around the opposite side of the counter to cut her off. "We're not through yet," I said, blocking the door.

"I don't have to listen to you three. I can do what I want." Aunt Tillie tried to push me away from the door, but I held my ground.

"This is for our family," I said, gritting my teeth. "You have to do what's right for our family."

"I don't have to do anything but eat," Aunt Tillie countered. "Get out of the way."

"Not until you agree," I said.

"Never!" Aunt Tillie threw all of her weight against me, taking me by surprise. My footing slipped and the door flew open as I hit the ground between the two rooms. Thankfully Aunt Tillie lost her balance in the scuffle, too.

Mom's eyes were wide when they landed on me. "What … ?"

"Don't worry about this," I said, forcing a smile for the guests as I rolled to my knees. "We're having a small … discussion … about something in the kitchen. We'll be right out."

I grabbed Aunt Tillie's wrists and wrestled her back toward the kitchen.

"Help me," I ordered Clove and Thistle, both of them hurrying to my side and grabbing writhing appendages as Aunt Tillie huffed.

"I'm going to curse you all to within an inch of your lives," Aunt Tillie warned. "Mark my words!"

"Do you need help?" Landon asked dryly.

I shook my head. "We're good."

It took all three of us, but we finally managed to corral Aunt Tillie in the kitchen. Once the door was safely shut, I rested all of my weight on top of her, pinning her to the ceramic tile. "Agree to our demands."

"Um … no!"

Thistle hopped on top of me, adding her weight to the melee. "Do it, old lady," she snapped. "You owe us after the fairy tale book. This is for our mothers. Don't make us hurt you."

"I'm going to kill you all!" Despite our weight, Aunt Tillie still flailed about. "Clove, if you help me I'll reward you."

Clove looked caught.

"Clove, if you help her I'll destroy you," Thistle threatened.

Clove sighed, resigned. "I'm sorry, Aunt Tillie. We have to do what's best for the family." She hopped on Thistle's back, helping us make a four-person sandwich. The added weight was a struggle for me to deal with. It had to be almost unbearable for Aunt Tillie.

"Agree to our demands," I instructed.

"Do it," Thistle pressed.

"Fine," said Aunt Tillie, her face red with exertion.

"Promise us," I said, knowing she wouldn't go back on it if she said the words.

"I promise," Aunt Tillie seethed.

We reluctantly got off her, everyone pulling themselves together before we joined the rest of the guests.

"Thank you," I said.

"Oh, no. Thank you," Aunt Tillie shot back. "I may have to stay out of that field because I'm not a liar, but that just gives me plenty of time to think of your punishment."

Clove's face slackened. "But ... ."

"I'm a woman of my word," Aunt Tillie said. "I promise to stay out of my field until Landon says it's okay to return. I also promise to make you three pay!" With those words Aunt Tillie flounced out of the kitchen and into the dining room.

"This is going to be horrible," Clove whined.

"And it's all your fault," Thistle said, pinching my arm. "I'm going to make you eat so much dirt ... . You're dead to me. You know that, right?"

I blew out a frustrated sigh. "I think we're all going to be dead when she's done with us."

"SO, I hear there was quite a bit of excitement down at Hollow Creek today," Mom said, her eyes busy as they scanned the flustered faces at the table. "How did you find the field?"

"We just happened upon it while we were out there," Landon replied, squeezing my knee under the table. "It was a fluke."

"Well, it's going to make quite an article for the newspaper," Brian said, his eyes sparkling.

I frowned. I didn't even notice he was at the table. "Who invited you?"

"I invited him," Rosemary said, shooting me a death glare. "Where are your manners?"

"I think they're on the kitchen floor," Thistle supplied, stabbing a piece of chicken. "Where is the wine?"

"You don't need any wine," Marcus countered. "You're not even over last night's bad decisions yet."

"None of us are," Twila said, rubbing her forehead.

"Are you two dating now?" I asked, wrinkling my nose as Brian and Rosemary whispered to each other.

"Would that bother you?" Brian challenged. "If it does, I ... ."

Landon cleared his throat. "I don't think it bothers her for the reason you think it bothers her," he said. "She doesn't like Rosemary."

Mom tried to kick him under the table and made contact with my shin instead. "Ow!"

"What?" Landon returned Mom's glare. "Everyone here knows that no one likes Rosemary. It's not a secret."

"You've got that right," Aunt Tillie said, guzzling her glass of wine and immediately refilling it. "There's nothing to like."

"I think there's something to like," Brian countered. "In fact, I think she should be our first human interest interview."

"Oh, that's so sweet," Rosemary cooed, batting her eyelashes.

"Over my dead body," I said.

Brian frowned. "I'm still your boss."

"Barely."

Thistle snickered, and even Aunt Tillie looked tickled with the conversational shift.

"You're going to interview Rosemary for our next edition," Brian ordered.

"Um ... no," I replied, causing both Thistle and Clove to giggle.

"You have to," Brian said, his voice getting shrill. "I'm the boss."

"No." I reached toward the center of the table and plopped a huge dollop of mashed potatoes on my plate. "Can someone pass the gravy?"

Marnie obliged, watching me with shocked eyes as I doused my chicken and mashed potatoes.

"I'll fire you," Brian threatened.

"Don't go there with her," Landon shot back. "I don't like it."

"No one cares what you like," Brian hissed.

"We both know you can't do that anyway," I said. "William left a stipulation in his will that you can't sell the newspaper or fire me. If you try to sell the newspaper, I get it. If you try to fire me, I get the newspaper. You're stuck with me ... and I'm not interviewing Rosemary."

"You should just give the paper to Bay," Mom said. "She does all the work."

"I work!" Brian's face reddened.

"You do not," Aunt Tillie said. "You sit in your office and try to come up with ideas to make more money in a town that has set advertising dollars. We all know you're a tool. Actually, you and Rosemary have a lot in common. Why don't you run away with her and leave Bay in charge?"

"I second that," Landon said.

"I've about had it with you," Brian warned. "I don't like your attitude."

"Do you want to take it outside?" Landon challenged.

Brian swallowed hard. "I ... ."

"I didn't think so," Landon said, turning back to his plate. "Don't threaten my girlfriend. If you do it again, we're going to have a big problem."

"But ... I'm the boss!"

"You keep telling yourself that, Sparky," Aunt Tillie said. "Everyone knows the real power behind that newspaper. Even though she's on my list, Bay is ten times the newspaper person you are.

"If you're going to stay at this table, shut your mouth," she continued. "You're giving me a headache, and I've been banned from my medicine."

"What is that supposed to mean?" Aunt Willa asked, flabbergasted. "How can you people treat a guest this way?"

"You caught us on a bad day," Mom said, resigned. "We're all hungover. We'll try to do better tomorrow."

"I won't," Thistle said.

"I won't either," I added.

"Well, maybe none of us will," Mom said, reaching for the wine. "I don't think it matters anymore."

Landon leaned closer to me. "This could be my favorite family dinner ever."

"That's good," I said. "Aunt Tillie is going to kill us tomorrow."

"Well, we'd better make tonight count then," Landon said, straightening. "I'm going to need some bacon to take back to the guesthouse when we leave tonight."

"You're such a pervert," Aunt Tillie said.

Landon didn't seem bothered by her assessment. "I can live with that."

TWENTY-THREE

I woke up with my face pressed against Landon's chest and an unsettled feeling in the pit of my stomach. Something was ... off.

"What's wrong?" Landon asked, rubbing my back.

"How can you tell something is wrong?"

"You usually wake up in a gooey pile of mush," Landon replied, pressing his lips to my forehead. "You're tense. I can probably fix that for you if you beg me."

I rolled my eyes. "I ... ." Huh. I knew what I wanted to say and yet my tongue wouldn't form the words.

"Go ahead and say something snarky," Landon prodded. "If you're feisty this morning, that probably bodes well for me."

"You're a very handsome and charming man," I said, frowning. That wasn't what I intended to say. I tried again. "You make the sun brighter and the sky clearer." I definitely didn't mean to say that. "You make the stars shine like diamonds in the sky."

Landon leaned back to study my face. "Are you playing a game?"

I shook my head and grabbed my tongue to shake it for good measure. "I think the sun rises and sets on you." Oh, holy crap!

Landon chuckled. "You can't say what you want to say, can you?"

I mutely shook my head.

"Is this the nice spell? Did she cast it on you guys?"

That was an intriguing thought. "I ... think so." It was a struggle, but the words managed to come out.

Landon pushed himself to a sitting position, dragging me with him and shoving my morning bedhead out of the way so he could look me over. "Let's try something else," he said. "What's my best quality? Try to say something dirty."

I scowled. "You only want me to say something dirty because you hope we can do the act of love," I complained, loathing the schmaltzy words.

Landon shrugged. "Try it anyway."

"I ... um ... sometimes when I look into your eyes I feel I could spend all day in there hanging out," I said. "Oh, no!"

Landon tried to hide his smirk. He wasn't fond of my distress. As curses go, though, this was one of the least destructive in recent memory. "It's not so bad, Bay."

I narrowed my eyes.

"Seriously, sweetie, I ... kind of like it," Landon said, grinning. "I would've preferred the bacon one, but I think this one could have some perks. Tell me how handsome I am again."

"Your face looks as if it was chiseled from fine marble," I said, hating myself as I said the words. "You're like one of those Greek statues that's supposed to show the ideal man." I slapped my hand over my mouth, mortified.

"Oh, this is fun," Landon said. "This is better than the time you had to tell the truth ... especially since that one turned nasty. I didn't know you had such strong feelings about things. Tell me how good I look naked."

I viciously pinched his side, relieved that I could still do mean things – even if I couldn't say them. Landon rubbed the spot over his ribs ruefully. "I guess that answers that," he muttered. "This would be more fun if you could do only nice things to me."

"Aunt Tillie was right about you being ... a perfect gentleman," I said, flustered.

AMANDA M. LEE

Landon barked out a hoarse laugh. "You can't even call me a pervert, can you?"

I shook my head.

"I ... ." The bedroom door flew open, taking us by surprise. Thistle, her purple hair standing on end, stood in the doorway, her chest heaving. "You, too, huh?"

"I'm going to reward that wonderful elderly matriarch with a bouquet of roses," Thistle announced, her forehead wrinkling as she realized what she actually said. "I'm going to gently rub my hand against her cheek and tell her I love her."

Landon's shoulders shook with silent laughter as Marcus appeared in the doorway behind Thistle.

"Thistle is going to have a coronary if this goes on too long," Marcus warned. "She's already told me she loves me more than chocolate chip cookies, that I'm the handsomest man in the world, and if she could sit around and watch me naked all day she'd be the happiest woman alive."

Landon frowned. "Bay won't say anything dirty. I feel left out."

"I'm not going to do anything ... romantic and kind ... until this is over," I said, rolling my neck until it cracked. "This is the best thing that ever happened to me." I felt like crying.

"I'm going to ... ." Thistle broke off and mimed punching an invisible person. She also roundhouse kicked it and pretended to strangle it. If a mime could make money in Hemlock Cove, Thistle would be rich right about now.

"Well that looks fun," Landon said. "I ... ." He was cut off by the sound of the front door slamming and Clove huffily pushing into the room. "Hello, short stuff," he said, smiling. "How are you this fine and wonderful morning?"

"I've never been better," Clove replied, although her face was murderous. "I want to go outside and sing, I'm so happy."

"No!" Everyone vehemently shook their heads. No matter what she believed, Clove was tone deaf and had horrible taste in music.

"I believe that we have you to thank for this, Bay," Clove said. "We wanted to leave our perfect and wonderful Aunt Tillie to do her own thing, because we know she's always right, but you decided that was an improper use of our time." Clove was agitated. "How are we going to make our day even better?"

"I think we should split up and spend the day in bed," Landon suggested, wriggling his eyebrows. "I'm going to get Bay to say something dirty if it kills me."

"Oh, we can't stay in bed, sweetie pie," I said, cringing at my own words. "We have to get up and have breakfast with the best great-aunt in the world."

"And then we have to ... ." Thistle smacked her hand against the wall.

"Okay," Landon said, giving in. "That might be fun, too."

BY THE TIME we got to the inn an hour later, we'd managed to work out a word game akin to murderous Mad-Libs. Landon and Marcus couldn't stop laughing, and I was seriously close to choking them. Landon may be handsome and charming, but he's a pain in the ass when he wants to be.

"The first thing I'm going to do when I see her is wrap my arms around her neck for the biggest hug ever and just squeeze ... and squeeze ... and squeeze," Thistle said, making a face. "I'm going to squeeze her so hard her head pops off like a really pretty dandelion."

"That sounds absolutely delightful," I said. "I'll help you because I love helping my family – especially my beautiful and giving great-aunt. I'll help you until she's blue in the face from ... my love." Or choking. Choking would work, too.

"Of course you love her," Clove interjected. "She's done nothing but give of herself to make sure we have the perfect lives ... and by perfect I mean ... perfect." Clove was having the hardest time getting in the swing of things.

"And by perfect you mean that she always made sure we landed on soft pillows as she knocked us down with her light touch," Thistle corrected, punching the air again for good measure. "I want to lightly touch her right now."

"Okay, that one bordered on creepy," Landon said, opening the door and ushering us inside. "Let's try not to gross me out, shall we?"

"Why would we want to do that?" I challenged. "You've been gracious in our hour of need. You've smiled through our pain and made us want to ... hug you to death, too."

Landon pursed his lips. "You're getting better at this."

"We're fast learners," Thistle said, pinching his cheek as tightly as she could. "It would be to your marvelous benefit to remember that happiness is a state of mind, and our minds will return to the everyday bliss we love most at some point."

"I think she's warning you that she'll kill you if you don't give them a break," Marcus suggested.

Landon jerked his cheek from Thistle's fingers and ruefully rubbed his tender skin. "I'm starting to get that."

We marched into the kitchen and fixed our mothers, who were busily focused on breakfast, with our most serious looks.

"Our lives couldn't possibly be any better thanks to Aunt Tillie," Thistle announced. "For that we would like to spend the entire day with her ... showering her with love and affection."

Mom frowned. "I know Landon said it was impossible, but are you three high from that pot field they burned yesterday?"

Landon snickered, swallowing his smile when I shot him a dark look. "There's been a ... development."

"Do I even want to know?" Mom asked wearily.

"It seems they all woke up with the inability to say what they really feel," Landon explained. "Instead, they can only say nice things."

Mom's eyes widened. "Oh. This is Aunt Tillie's retribution, huh? As far as curses go, this one has potential."

I glared at her. "It doesn't have the right vibe for what I'm trying to accomplish today," I said, hating how fake and happy I sounded. "I need to talk to a few people, and I can't do it when I'd much rather be spreading joy to the world."

"Huh." Mom ran her tongue over her teeth. "Tell me what a great mother I am."

"If there was a queen of all mothers, you would be her," I replied, internally rolling my eyes.

"This is fun," Mom said. "Tell me all the horrible things you did as a child and how sorry you are for them."

I jutted out my lower lip into a pout and bit my tongue. I had no intention of playing that game.

Landon rubbed my back to soothe me. "Listen, I thought this would be fun, too," he said. "We have a problem keeping them this way, though. I at least need the curse lifted from Bay. Thistle and Clove can probably muddle through the day, but Bay can't."

"And why is that?" Aunt Tillie asked, appearing at the bottom of the stairs. "I think she's the one who led yesterday's mutiny. She needs to be punished."

Thistle launched herself at Aunt Tillie, her hands formed into claws as she reached for her neck. Marcus caught her before she could land on our ecstatic great-aunt.

"That's not going to help," Marcus chided. "If you kill her you might be stuck like this forever."

Thistle hung her head. Marcus's words made sense even as her inner nature bucked going along with the program.

"Can't you think of a different punishment for Bay?" Landon asked. "Bacon would be good for me … but she hates it. Do that one."

I slammed my elbow into his stomach.

"Oomph! I'm trying to help you, sweetie," Landon gasped, rubbing his ribs. "I'm not going to be your champion if you keep hurting me."

"I don't think Bay has learned her lesson about turning on me yet," Aunt Tillie said. "I think the curse needs to stay."

"It can't," Landon said, his pragmatic side taking over. "We need her to try to speak with Nathaniel's ghost. I know you don't want to admit it, but Bay was doing the right thing when she asked you to stay out of your field last night. No matter what you say, you wouldn't want any of your nieces going to jail because of that field. I know it."

Aunt Tillie opened her mouth to argue, but Landon shushed her with a look.

"Now, I find the curse hijinks in this family entertaining … some of the time," he continued. "I need Bay in control of her faculties today. The bacon curse would let her keep her wits while still driving her crazy."

"If I make her smell like food, it's going to be one you hate," Aunt Tillie countered. "How would you feel about curling up next to Brussels sprouts tonight?"

"It wouldn't be my first choice," Landon admitted. "That doesn't change the fact that I need her, though. Someone needs to talk with Nathaniel. If he really is turning into a poltergeist like Floyd...."

Aunt Tillie narrowed her eyes. "What do you mean he's turning into a poltergeist like Floyd?"

Landon related my story from the previous day while I stood next to him, arms crossed over my chest, and imagined eighty different ways to kill Aunt Tillie. When he was done, Aunt Tillie was intrigued.

"I've never heard of anything like that before," Aunt Tillie mused. "He could be dangerous. He could be more dangerous than Floyd, because he's being pulled in two different directions."

"The kids who planted that field could be dangerous, too," Landon pointed out. "We burned thousands of dollars of profit yesterday, and someone will want payment for that product. Bay was at the field with us. Three of those boys saw her there, and it doesn't take a rocket scientist to know she's involved in all of this. If they try to go after someone for payment ... I need Bay to be able to protect herself. She can't like this."

Aunt Tillie sighed, still unconvinced. "They all piled on top of me and made an Aunt Tillie sandwich yesterday. Someone has to pay for that."

Landon pursed his lips to keep from laughing at the unintended visual. "You can keep the curse on Clove and Thistle for the day," he offered, earning a hard cuff from Thistle before stepping far enough away that she couldn't reach him. "They'll have a rough day having to be nice to everyone at the store. They won't be in danger, though."

"I still need to cast a curse on Bay."

"I don't care if you make her smell like Brussels sprouts," Landon said. "She did take on Rosemary and Brian last night, though, and you hate both of them. She's had a rough couple of days. Can't you just … let this one slide until the case is solved, and Willa and Rosemary are gone?"

Aunt Tillie sighed, the sound long and dragged out. "And what do I get if I do?"

"What do you want?"

"I want a Polaris Ranger," Aunt Tillie replied, not missing a beat. "It should be red, and tricked out with all the bells and whistles."

Landon glanced at me, conflicted. "I don't think I have the money to pay for that right now."

"I don't expect you to pay for it," Aunt Tillie countered. "I'm not heartless and greedy. Well, I'm not greedy enough for you to go broke buying something for me. I want to be able to buy it myself and not hear one word from any of you about it being dangerous."

"Fine," Landon said, giving in. "Go nuts. It's your money."

"I also want to leave the curse on Thistle and Clove until sunset."

"I can live with that," Landon said.

"I can't live with … the idea that I'm thrilled with the suggestion," Thistle said, groaning and kicking the cabinets.

Aunt Tillie beamed. "We have a deal."

Great. I would be free and clear in moments. I risked a look in Thistle and Clove's direction and found them scorching me with duplicate scowls. Whoops! I guess I had one little problem left to deal with.

TWENTY-FOUR

After an uncomfortable breakfast that included Thistle and Clove saying some truly sweet things to Aunt Willa and Rosemary (which made them unnecessarily suspicious and paranoid), I fled The Overlook before my cousins could get me alone. Landon knew what he was doing when he arranged for Aunt Tillie to spare me, and I couldn't help but wonder whether that was part of her retribution. She wanted Clove and Thistle to be angry with me. It played into her game.

Landon was worried. He didn't say it, but I could read it in the set of his shoulders and the furtive looks he cast in my direction during breakfast. He wanted me to stay home and keep my nose out of this case, yet he knew it was impossible given where we were with the investigation. I was the only one who could talk to Nathaniel. That made me important.

After waiting two hours for Nathaniel to show at Hollow Creek, I gave up and headed back into town. Landon and Chief Terry were brainstorming at the police station, and I figured three minds were better than two. Plus, I kind of wanted to mess with Landon after he messed with me over this morning's curse. He had it coming.

I parked in front of The Whistler, figuring I could stop in and check my email and the page count for this week's edition before heading to the station, when movement caught my eye across the way. Three figures – two I'd seen enough of in recent days to recognize outright – headed behind the high school. It was Charlie and Dakota. I had a feeling the third figure belonged to Stephen Brooks, but I hadn't gotten a good enough look to be sure.

I decided to follow them, stopping long enough to text Landon what was going on and then pocketing my phone. He would be angry, but I felt I performed due diligence by texting him my location. I wasn't exactly thrilled with the way he teased me about the curse. Well, to be fair, I was actually more worried about Clove and Thistle jumping me when I wasn't looking. It was easier to blame him, though.

I kept close to the high school as I approached, attempting to hide my shadow and listen before confronting them. They were animated as they talked.

"This is a nightmare," Dakota said.

"What are we going to do?" Charlie asked.

"We're not going to do anything," Stephen replied. "It's out of our hands."

"I don't think they're going to agree that it's out of our hands," Dakota countered. "They're going to blame us for losing everything."

I waited for them to continue, but when they didn't I realized it was time. I rounded the corner, taking the three boys by surprise. "Who is this 'they' who is going to blame you?"

Dakota frowned. "Are you following us?"

I considered lying, but it felt a waste of time. "I saw you when I was parking at The Whistler," I replied. "I texted Landon to tell him where I was going, and then … yes … I followed you." I put the Landon tidbit out there right away in case they had any ideas.

"Were you listening?" Charlie asked, fidgeting nervously.

Dakota roughly cuffed him. "That's why she wants to know who 'they' are, stupid!"

"Oh, right," Charlie said, lowering his eyes.

Despite the fact that I knew they had been up to illegal activities –

and one or more of them might be involved in Nathaniel's death – I couldn't help but feel sympathetic regarding Charlie's plight. His biggest problem was that he had no backbone and was desperate to fit in. I remember being desperate to fit in when I was his age. Of course, as a Winchester, I didn't lack a backbone. It was genetically impossible.

"So, are you guys in trouble now that the pot field has literally gone up in smoke?" I asked.

Stephen narrowed his eyes to dangerous slits. "We have no idea what you're talking about."

"I'm sure you think that's going to fly, but it's not," I said. "We know you guys are involved. What we want to know is whether you're involved alone or you have someone else working for you."

"You don't know jack shit, lady," Stephen snapped. Up close and personal I recognized him from the night of the party. He was one of the only kids who didn't try to run. He stood back and watched everyone else panic while Dakota and Charlie mucked things up for the entire group. He puffed out his chest in an attempt to scare me. I refused to take a step back. "You're crazy if you think we had anything to do with that field."

"I might be crazy," I conceded. "I often think my family is going to drive me there eventually. I'm not wrong about this, though. I think you guys planted that field. I also think you're in over your heads with whoever 'they' are. Are 'they' the ones who killed Nathaniel?"

Charlie shouted, "We don't know anything about that."

"I know that's not true, Charlie," I argued. "I know you guys were at Hollow Creek the night Nathaniel was murdered. I don't know whether you were directly involved, but I'm pretty sure Nathaniel's death is tied to the pot field, too."

"And what makes you say that?" Stephen challenged.

"Nathaniel was a known drug dealer who was seen flashing money all around town," I replied. "He was also reportedly in financial trouble. Is that because you guys tried to cut him out of the business? Did he go out there that night to steal product? Is that why he's dead?"

"We had nothing to do with Nathaniel's death," Dakota said. "We're not killers. How can you even think that?"

"Because you three are calling attention to yourselves right now," I said. "You're the ones the police are looking at."

"Oh, my mom is going to be so mad at me," Charlie whimpered. "This is going to be worse than your dad going nuclear about having to go out and get your truck after the other night, Stephen."

"Shut up," Dakota said, smacking the back of Charlie's head hard enough to whip it forward. "You're being a baby."

"Don't hit him," I warned.

"Don't tell me what to do," Dakota shot back.

"I think our nosy friend here needs a lesson in what's acceptable, don't you?" Stephen asked, taking a step forward.

Uh-oh. I didn't like this one bit. "Did you miss the part of the conversation where I told you that I texted Landon where I am? Just for the record, I told him who I'm following, too."

Stephen slowed his pace, but only marginally. "I think you're bluffing."

"Go ahead and touch me and find out," I challenged, my voice stronger than my courage. I didn't like the vibe Stephen gave. Charlie was a definite follower, and Dakota fancied himself a big man in a small pond. Stephen was something else. There was true menace clouding his soul.

"Oh, I'm going to touch you," Stephen hissed.

"If you touch her, I'll break your hand."

The sound of Landon's voice caused my heart to flip, and not in the ridiculous romantic way it usually did. I forced my gaze to remain on Stephen, refusing to back down as Landon approached.

"We weren't doing anything," Charlie offered, his voice quaking. "Please don't shoot my thing off."

"Shut up, Charlie," Landon snapped, his eyes flat as they fixed on Stephen. "I'm not kidding. If you touch her, you'll regret it."

"She's the one who came here hassling us, man," Stephen said, taking a step back and allowing me to release a pent-up breath. "We were minding our own business...."

"I don't care if you were helping old people cross the street," Landon said, cutting him off. "Don't even look at her."

"Why would we want to look at her, man?" Dakota asked, rolling his eyes. "She's ... old."

Oh, well, great. That was just what my ego needed today.

"Get moving," Landon ordered, stepping behind me and resting his hand on my shoulder.

"This is a free country," Stephen argued. "We can hang out here if we want to."

"Get moving or I'll arrest you," Landon countered.

"For what?"

"Whatever I can make stick," Landon replied. "I'll start with threatening Ms. Winchester and then hold you until I have the evidence to charge you for the pot field. That's going to be a felony. You'll do big time for that one."

"We had nothing to do with that field," Charlie said, his voice weak. "I swear I'm innocent."

"No one believes you, Charlie," Landon said. "You might want to talk this out with your parents. The first one to come in and confess gets the best deal. I'm thinking that's your only course of action."

"We don't need deals, because we're innocent," Stephen said. "My father told me that you don't have a case. You don't have anything on this. You and your ... girlfriend ... are poking around to see if you can find anything. Everyone knows that you can't."

"I guess we'll have to wait and see on that one, won't we?" Landon's voice was harsh.

"I guess so," Stephen challenged. He stared Landon down for a moment and then broke eye contact. "Come on, guys. We don't have to put up with this."

Landon waited until they were gone before grabbing my shoulders and forcibly swiveling me so I faced him. "Are you trying to kill me?"

I frowned. "I texted you what I was doing," I argued. "What more do you want?"

"I want you to keep your head in the game and not risk our entire future because you're in a foul mood," Landon snapped. "What were you thinking?"

"I was thinking that they were doing something hinky behind the high school, and I wanted to see what it was," I replied, miffed. There was no need for his attitude. "That's why I texted you who I was following and where I was going. I thought those were the rules."

"There are no rules if you die on me, Bay," Landon raged. "I … you … we … I can't deal with you being in danger. It kills me."

I softened my stance at his admission. "I only wanted to listen. They said something about 'they' being angry about everything being lost. I think they're working for someone."

"Oh, you don't think the high-schoolers are drug kingpins? I'm shocked!" Landon waved his hands in the air for emphasis. "Think, Bay! You cannot die on me. I can't take it."

I pinched the bridge of my nose. Between Landon's meltdown and Clove and Thistle's imminent payback, I was having a terrible day. "I don't want to die on you," I replied, lowering my voice. "I don't want you dying on me either. That doesn't mean I go after you yelling because you're in a dangerous situation."

Landon tugged a restless hand through his hair. "I know I'm being a hypocrite," he said, his voice shaky. "It's not fair. I'm not going to pretend it's fair. You sit at home all week wondering about me and I pitch a fit when you do anything.

"I can't seem to help myself," he continued. "The thought of something horrible happening to you … it paralyzes me sometimes. When I got that text and knew what you were doing I thought my heart might actually explode."

"I can take care of myself," I reminded him. "I did it for a long time before you came along."

"That's not good enough for me, Bay," Landon said. "I need to know you're safe. I'm sorry. I think I've been pretty good about including you … and bringing you along on adventures … but I draw the line at you dying on me. You can't die on me. I forbid it."

I pursed my lips to keep from laughing. "Well, I forbid you dying, too."

"I think I can live with that," Landon said, reaching out to snag my hand. "I don't want you to stop being you. You have intuition ... and power ... and heart. You also have a mouth that doesn't know when to quit sometimes. Just ... be careful."

"I will," I said. "I'm sorry you're upset."

"I'm sorry I'm upset, too," Landon said, pulling me in for a hug. "I think Aunt Tillie cursing you to smell like bacon might make me feel better."

"You have to let that go," I hissed. "It's starting to bug me."

"It's going to bug you a lot worse if she curses you to smell like Brussels sprouts and I don't stop complaining for days," Landon said, linking his fingers with mine and dragging me around the building. "Come on. If you're good I'll buy you lunch."

"Just no Brussels sprouts, right?"

"Definitely not," Landon said.

I pulled up short when we rounded the corner, frowning when I saw Nathaniel floating next to a nearby tree.

"What is it?" Landon asked.

I didn't answer him. "What are you doing here, Nathaniel?"

"You're on the wrong path," Nathaniel said, his eyes flashing as his wispy aura darkened. "You're not looking in the right place. Those guys are my friends. They wouldn't hurt me. They're too ... cowardly ... to do that."

"If we're on the wrong path, who did kill you?"

"It wasn't them," Nathaniel said, his expression grim. "It's right in front of you if you bother to see it. It's ... right in front of you."

I opened my mouth to question him further, but he dissolved before I got a chance. Landon flicked a worried look in my direction, but patiently waited.

"He says it wasn't them," I said finally.

"Do you believe him?"

"He has no reason to lie."

"Did he say who did it?" Landon pressed.

"He said it was right in front of my face but I wasn't seeing it," I said. "I think we're missing something else."

"I think that's the story of our lives," Landon said. "We'll figure it out. We always do."

I hoped he was right. Nathaniel was destined for an afterlife of pain if we couldn't put him to rest. A killer was running free, and I worried Nathaniel was only the first victim if we didn't figure this out soon. Things were getting out of hand.

TWENTY-FIVE

"I can't go in there."

"You have to go in there."

"They want to kill me."

"They're actually low on the list of people who want to kill you today," Landon said, pushing me into Hypnotic and watching Thistle and Clove spin in unison in my direction. "Well, I might've been wrong on that front. They look pretty ticked."

"Welcome to our store," Clove intoned robotically. "We're thrilled to see you."

"Yes," Thistle said. "We're very glad to see you." She took a step in my direction, causing me to slam into Landon when I involuntarily stepped back.

He put a reassuring arm around my waist. "If I leave her here with you guys, are you going to play nice?"

"Yes," Thistle said. "I have a very nice game I want to play with her."

Landon sighed. "Why don't I believe you?"

"Because we lack the ability to tell the truth right now," Clove said. "We're really happy about it, too."

"Hey, look at that," Landon said. "You're starting to get the hang of sarcasm."

"You are such a ... wonderful man," Thistle said, scowling. "I want to do wonderful things to you."

"You know what? I'm staying to eat with you guys after all," Landon said, moving toward the couch in the middle of the store. "I offered to buy Bay lunch, but she insisted on seeing you guys first. I think she's feeling a little guilty because Aunt Tillie lifted the curse on her and not you guys."

"Thanks to your boundless wisdom, that is our happy lot in life today," Thistle agreed, making a face as she slapped her forehead.

"This can't go on," I muttered. "She's going to have an aneurism if she keeps this up ... or accidentally poke her own eye out. You have to call Aunt Tillie and get her down here."

Landon balked. "Why would I do that?"

"Because I need them to go back to Hollow Creek with me, and they can't go like this."

"You're not going back to Hollow Creek without me, and I can't go this afternoon because Chief Terry and I have a meeting with the county guys," Landon replied. "They want to start conducting searches right away and they're going to show us a search grid."

"What happens if ... ?"

"I don't know, Bay," Landon answered honestly, knowing exactly what I was going to ask. "I'm doing the best I can, sweetie. If Aunt Tillie says the field can't be found, then I have to believe her. If they find it ... ."

I knew what he wasn't saying. If they found Aunt Tillie's field, there was absolutely nothing he could do for us. He would kick, scream and fight – but we would be in real trouble. "We need Aunt Tillie down here right now."

"Bay, I don't think that's a good idea," Landon said, clenching his jaw. "We just had this talk."

"We just had this talk when it was about you and me," I clarified. "This is about my family, too. I need to go down to Hollow Creek. Nathaniel said the answer was right in front of my eyes. My heart is telling me that I need to go back there. I know you don't like it ... ."

"Fine," Landon said, giving in. "If you go down there I want Clove and Thistle with you. If they're going to be of any use, the curse has to be lifted. I'll call Aunt Tillie."

"Oh, thank you, kind sir," Clove said, throwing her arms around Landon's neck. "I've always loved you."

"Okay, now I'm starting to get uncomfortable," Landon said. "You'd better prepare yourselves … because this is going to take a lot of groveling."

"**ABSOLUTELY** NOT!"

Aunt Tillie arrived at Hypnotic thirty minutes after Landon called, and wasted no time shutting him down. I think she only came to town so she could see our faces when she did it. She's a mean little thing when she wants to be.

"You have to do it," Landon pressed. "Bay needs to go out to Hollow Creek, and she can't go alone."

"There's nothing stopping Clove and Thistle from going with her," Aunt Tillie countered. "They'll just be really nice when they go."

"I need to know they can say a spell to save themselves if it comes to that," Landon argued. "I need to know Bay is safe."

"Why wouldn't Bay be safe?" Aunt Tillie was convinced we were lying to get out of our punishment.

"Because Bay followed Stephen, Dakota and Charlie behind the school, and I found that Stephen kid threatening her," Landon replied.

"Bay is an idiot sometimes," Aunt Tillie grumbled, not surprised in the least by my actions. "Do you think he killed Nathaniel?"

"Nathaniel showed up," I answered. "He said they didn't kill him, and that I was looking in the wrong place."

"If they didn't kill Nathaniel, why would they go after you?"

"I think they're upset about the pot field," I explained. "I overheard them. There was a lot of chatter about 'they' being upset. They're either working with someone or for someone."

"That sounds delightful," Clove said.

Aunt Tillie rolled her eyes. "Okay. I admit it. That's annoying." She snapped her fingers. "The curse is lifted. Go forth and say something nasty."

"I'm going to make you eat dirt for this, Bay," Thistle seethed. "It's going to be filled with worms ... and beetles ... and grubs."

"And we're back," Landon said, sending Aunt Tillie a rueful smile. "Thank you."

"I'm not doing it because of you," Aunt Tillie scoffed. "I'm doing it because I don't want Bay getting hurt." She plopped down on the couch, kicking Landon's legs out of the way so she could get comfortable. "Let's break this whole thing down and look at it from the proper perspective, shall we?"

I hate it when she talks down to us.

"We know the field was planted on the far side of the creek," Aunt Tillie said. "How were they getting to it? That area isn't accessible unless you want to hike three miles in from the road. I doubt they were doing that on a daily basis."

"We think there was a shallow pathway through the creek that the kids knew about," I answered. "When we busted the kids drinking out there, a few of them ran into the creek. That seemed like a stupid idea until ... well ... until we found the pot field."

"That would mean more than a few kids knew about the field," Aunt Tillie pointed out. "That's not a very smart way to run a business. The more rats in the maze, the more people to eat the cheese."

"That was truly profound," Thistle deadpanned.

"They're teenagers," Landon said. "Teenagers aren't known for being smart business partners."

"We need to go out there," Aunt Tillie said, rising to her feet. "You've got me curious now."

"You're going with us?" I was flabbergasted. Aunt Tillie's idea of an outing was walking to her greenhouse so she could smoke her glaucoma medicine in peace. "Why?"

"I don't like anyone threatening my family," Aunt Tillie replied. "That's my job."

"And you do a bang up job of it," Clove said.

"You're not still under the spell," Aunt Tillie said. "You don't need to be nice."

"Oh, I wasn't being nice."

Aunt Tillie smirked. "Let's go out there while it's still early," she said. "If anyone is searching out there, we'll use a spell to track them. If Bay is right and there is something left at Hollow Creek, these kids won't be able to control their impulses. They'll go for it sooner rather than later."

"And what will you do if they come after you?" Landon asked.

Aunt Tillie's smile was nothing short of evil incarnate. "Well, then they'll find out I can't control my impulses either."

Landon grinned. "May the Goddess have mercy on their souls, right?"

"Oh, honey, given my mood no one is going to have mercy on their souls."

"THIS PLACE IS JUST as much of a pit as I remember," Aunt Tillie said, making a face as we spread out to search the banks of the creek an hour later. "It smells, too."

Clove wrinkled her nose. "I don't smell anything."

"That's because I have the olfactory senses of an elephant. I can smell things mere mortals can't detect."

Thistle shot me a dubious look. "Did she just explain something?"

"Don't you idiots watch the Discovery Channel?" Aunt Tillie asked. "Everyone knows that elephants have the best sense of smell. I'm like an elephant."

Thistle opened her mouth to say something, but Aunt Tillie silenced her with a look.

"I'll restore the curse."

Thistle sighed. "Fine. You're an elephant. Can you use your keen sense of smell to find whatever Bay thinks is out here?"

"What do you think I'm trying to do, fresh mouth?"

"It would help if we had an idea what was out here, Bay," Clove suggested. "Are we looking for something big or small?"

I had no idea. I only knew we were looking for ... something. "I can't explain it," I said. "I know we're supposed to find something out here. I'm sorry I can't be more precise."

"Well, I guess we should split up and start looking," Thistle said. "At this rate we'll be having dinner out here."

"We've been out here for five minutes," I argued.

"It feels longer."

"It does," Aunt Tillie agreed. "We need to cast a spell to find what we're looking for."

Clove knit her eyebrows together. "A locator spell? Isn't that dangerous if someone sees us out here and we have a ball of light zipping around?"

"If someone sees us out here they're probably looking for something illegal – or remnants of the pot field to smoke – so they wouldn't be able to tell anyone without looking like a creepy drug addict, would they?" Aunt Tillie challenged.

"I guess I never thought about it that way."

"And that's why I'm the brains of the operation," Aunt Tillie said, causing Thistle to snort. "You're still on my list, missy. See what happens if you push me. I'm out here to keep Bay safe. I can restore that curse with a snap of my fingers."

Thistle waited until Aunt Tillie looked in another direction to stick out her tongue.

"I saw that," Aunt Tillie said.

"Let's cast the spell," Clove suggested. "I don't like being out here. Ever since we found that cave with the dead body inside, this place gives me the creeps."

I stilled. *It's right in front of your eyes.* "The cave."

"That would make sense," Aunt Tillie said. "What happened out here was all over town. People probably figured if no one found that cave for decades, there's probably no reason for anyone else to find it now."

"Do you remember where it is?" Thistle asked.

I tapped my lip as I scanned the tree line. "It's over there."

We trudged in that direction, forming a line with me taking up the

AMANDA M. LEE

front and Thistle keeping a watchful eye at the rear. After a series of missteps – each one causing Aunt Tillie to grumble something about "idiots" and "couldn't find their butts with two hands and no place to move" – I found the entrance.

"We need a light," Clove said. "I'm not going in that dark hole again without a light. You can't make me."

"Why are you such a baby?" Aunt Tillie sniped, pressing her eyes shut briefly and then snapping her fingers to conjure a small ball of light. "Do you think I would let you go in that hole without a light?"

"Bay did."

"Yes, well, Bay approached three boys who may be murderers on her own this afternoon," Aunt Tillie shot back. "She's an idiot."

"I love you, too," I muttered, following Aunt Tillie's ball of light into the cave. Given its size, I didn't expect much illumination. Once we were inside, though, it expanded and gave off an almost homey vibe – well, for a cave.

"Someone needs to clean this place," Clove muttered, stepping around a large rock.

"Oh, yeah," Thistle deadpanned. "We should place an ad. Do you want to clean a dark and dank hole? Well, we've got just the place. It's next to Hollow Creek, the former home of a dead body, and the occasional spot for murderers. Fill out an application here."

"It must be a relief for you to be mean again," I said, something clicking in the back of my mind and making me turn around.

"You have no idea," Thistle said. "I told the mailman I loved him."

"I was there," Clove said. "He thought she was coming on to him. He asked what color her underwear was and she had to tell him. Sometimes I think Mr. Brooks is creepy. If he didn't wear those stupid shorts to deliver the mail, he would freak me out. I ... do you see something?"

Everyone moved in behind me as I knelt, the clicking getting louder in my brain. I lifted a piece of discarded wood and tossed it to the side, revealing a small tin box – one of those tins that once contained expensive tea sold at the grocery store. It looked relatively new.

LIFE'S A WITCH

"What's inside?" Clove asked.

"She hasn't looked inside yet, you ninny," Thistle snapped.

"Good grief. I'm already missing that curse," Aunt Tillie muttered, causing my cousins to clam up. "Be careful opening it. There might be a snake inside."

The suggestion was ludicrous, and also made me internally shudder. "Why would you say that?"

"I saw a movie where someone found a tin can like that in a cave and it was filled with snakes."

"What movie?"

"Open it," Aunt Tillie hissed.

I pried the lid off and peered inside as the ball of light moved lower. I slipped my fingers into the narrow opening and pulled out a huge wad of money.

"Holy crap," Thistle said. "How much is that?"

I counted it, going over it twice to make sure, and whistled. "Five thousand bucks!"

"I think you should give that to me for safe keeping," Aunt Tillie instructed. "I'm the most responsible one here."

"I'm not giving you this money," I said. "We have to turn it over to Landon and Chief Terry."

"Do you think it's Nathaniel's money?" Thistle asked.

I glanced around, hoping he would make an appearance if that was the case. He didn't. "I have no idea. I think it's too much of a coincidence for it not to be tied to the pot, though."

"Is this what you were looking for?" Aunt Tillie asked.

I nodded.

"Does that mean I can curse them again? Thistle is really bugging me."

"I will lock you in this cave and forget where you are," Thistle threatened.

"Let's get out of here," I said, ignoring both of them. "I don't like it in here. This means something. I just don't know what. We're missing something big ... and I hate that feeling."

TWENTY-SIX

I found Aunt Tillie loitering around her greenhouse when I got back to The Overlook a few hours later. She was messing around with an empty pot, and she appeared lost in thought. I cleared my throat to announce myself.

"Did Landon decide to give me that money after all?"

I shook my head and smiled. "Landon and Chief Terry were surprised and made me go back and show them exactly where I found it. They're not sure how they're going to write it up in the report."

"What do they think it means?"

"They're as stumped as we are," I said, moving further into the greenhouse. "Can I ask you something?"

"No, I don't plan to curse you guys with the nice spell again," Aunt Tillie replied. "It wasn't nearly as much fun as I thought it would be. I think I might be slipping in my old age."

"That's not what I was going to ask ... and thank you. Landon asked me to tell him how great he was for what felt like forever because of that spell. I'm not interested in that right now, though."

Aunt Tillie stilled. "You want to know why I lifted the curse early, don't you?"

I shook my head. "That's also not what I was going to ask," I said. "Now that you've brought it up, though, why did you?"

Aunt Tillie shrugged. "I'm not really angry with you guys," she said finally. "Don't get me wrong, wrestling me to the ground like that was undignified, and I'm still going to get you back, but you're not my problem right now."

"Is Aunt Willa your problem?"

"She's the Devil."

I tugged on my limited patience and leaned against her potting bench, crossing my arms over my chest as I studied her. "What's the real deal with you and Aunt Willa? You don't even act as if you're from the same family."

Aunt Tillie sighed and tossed her trowel into the pot. "I don't ever remember getting along with her," she said. "I always got along with Ginger. We were ... close. We were close like your mothers are close. I still miss her."

"I wish I could've met her."

"She would've hated you," Aunt Tillie said, although her eyes twinkled as she shuffled over to the shelf next to the wall. "Actually, she would've loved all three of you. She would've gotten a kick out of Thistle's mouth. She would've enjoyed Clove's whiny quality. She would've loved your ambition and the way you hold things together in a crisis. I think she missed out on a lot because she didn't get to know you three."

I was dumbfounded. That was one of the nicest things Aunt Tillie had ever said to me. "Why didn't you just agree to stay out of your pot field when I first asked you? You said you would that first day, so why was it such a big deal when I asked you the second time? We could've avoided all of that ... melodrama ... if you had."

"Maybe I didn't want to stay out of my field. Did you ever consider that?"

"That's the first thing I considered," I conceded. "You may be stubborn and set in your ways, but you're also unfailingly kind when it's important. You're the most loyal person I know.

"I realized today when you went to Hollow Creek with us that you

AMANDA M. LEE

didn't do it out of boredom or because you were yearning for adventure," I continued. "You were doing it because you were legitimately worried about us. If we were going to get in trouble, you wanted to be there to get us out of it."

"I think you're delusional," Aunt Tillie said. "I thought nothing of the sort."

I didn't believe her. "You would never purposely put us at risk," I said. "You were never going to go back to that pot field even before I asked, were you?"

Aunt Tillie sighed. "Do you know your biggest problem?"

"I think it's this nagging voice in the back of my head that keeps telling me the bottom is going to drop out because I'm really happy these days," I answered honestly.

"Oh, good grief," Aunt Tillie muttered, rolling her eyes. "Is this about Landon? The boy is smitten. He's not going anywhere. I know you're worried because he walked away the first time, but I knew he would come back. He needed time to think."

"He said the other day that he envisions us having our own home one day," I said. "He thought it would freak me out – and it did, well, kind of. When I thought about it more, though, I realized I wanted that. The problem is … ."

"Our family," Aunt Tillie supplied. "We're joined at the hip and lip – not in a gross way, so don't get some weird lesbian fantasy."

I fought the urge to shake her. We were having a moment, even if she insisted on being belligerent during it. "Clove is going to move in with Sam. She's going to do it soon."

"I figured that," Aunt Tillie said. "She's always been the one who needs stability. Sam gives her that. I wasn't sure I liked him at first."

"And now?"

"He saved your life and he dotes on Clove," Aunt Tillie answered. "I have no reason not to like him."

"And you love Marcus," I pressed.

"He's a good boy." Aunt Tillie's smile was genuine. "He's funnier than he realizes, too. He makes me laugh."

"No matter what you say, I know you like Landon, too."

"I never said I didn't like him," Aunt Tillie shot back. "He's just a bossy pain in the ass. That's why he's good for you. You need someone to occasionally kick you to get you moving. You've always been the most sensitive one in some ways."

"You're the one who says Clove is a baby all the time," I reminded her.

"Clove is a baby. You're sensitive in other ways. You can't help it. The sensitivity comes with your gifts. Landon helps that. He accepts you for who you are and encourages you to spread your wings. That's what you need."

"Tell me about your relationship with Aunt Willa," I prodded, bringing the conversation full circle. "I think you know why she's here."

"You're giving me too much credit," Aunt Tillie countered. "I've never understood a single thing that woman does. You're mistaking my relationship with Willa for the one you share with Clove and Thistle. You may not be sisters by birth, but you are in your hearts.

"I had that relationship with Ginger, and I miss it every single day," she continued. "I can't say the same for Willa."

"Do you think she wants that type of relationship with you?"

Aunt Tillie snorted. "No. She doesn't like me any more than I like her. She's here for a different reason ... and before you ask, no, I don't know what it is. I've been racking my brain trying to figure out what her endgame is here. It's ... beyond me."

"She has to want something," I said. "No one would put up with the shenanigans she's seen unless they had a specific reason. I'm worried. I'm worried about Mom and you most of all."

"Don't worry about me," Aunt Tillie lightly scolded. "I made a promise many years ago that I would outlive Willa and dance on her grave. She'll never beat me."

"I hope not," I said. "We need to figure out what she wants. She's been here for almost a week now. She's seen Marnie's boobs, us wrestle you down in the kitchen, and all of us be mean to her. We need to know why she's here. I don't like her being so close when we don't know what she's up to."

AMANDA M. LEE

"I agree with that," Aunt Tillie said. "I ... ." She broke off when the daisy in the corner started wailing. I looked closer and realized it was an actual flower and it was ... making a screeching noise.

"What the ... ?"

"Someone tripped the wards in the field," Aunt Tillie said, moving toward the window and narrowing her eyes. "Someone is trying to steal my stash! That's just despicable. Don't these people realize I need that pot for my glaucoma?"

"Do you think it's the police?"

"It's not dark yet, but it will be soon," Aunt Tillie replied, pointing toward the sky. "There's a storm coming. I don't care how inept I think the police are. They wouldn't come out here looking for my field right before a storm."

"Then who?" I already knew the answer before I finished asking the question. "It's the kids. They need product to replace what's lost."

"We'd better get out there," Aunt Tillie muttered. "They can't find it, but I don't want them traipsing around my property. Now, where is my gun?"

BY THE TIME we got to the field the storm was moving in. Aunt Tillie insisted on collecting her combat helmet and shotgun before departing. I thought about arguing, but the gun might be a welcome distraction if we ran into someone.

We opted to remain away from the field in case someone was watching from the trees. We didn't want to tip anyone off about the entrance.

"Do you see anything?"

I shook my head. "I can feel someone, though. I ... the storm is going to be a big one."

"Yeah, we're definitely due for one," Aunt Tillie replied. "The humidity has been cranking up for days. "I ... there!" She extended her arm to the line of trees to our left. I narrowed my eyes, frowning when I recognized the trio of figures.

"What are you doing out here?"

They didn't answer or move.

"Stephen, Dakota and Charlie, I see you," I said, raising my voice so it would carry over the rising wind. "This is private property. What do you think you're doing out here?"

No response.

"Okay, I'm going to start shooting," Aunt Tillie said, pumping her shotgun. "I have the right to protect my property from snot-nosed little punks who threaten my life. Do you feel lucky, punks?"

"You can't shoot them," I whispered. "They're not doing anything."

"They don't know that," Aunt Tillie said, aiming her gun at a spot high on the tree they hid behind.

"I ... wait. What are you doing?"

"Watch and learn." Aunt Tillie pulled the trigger before I had a chance to cover my ears, the deafening roar stunning me for a moment. I watched with grim detachment as a high branch fell, causing the boys to race out of their hiding place and stop about fifteen feet away from us.

"What are you doing here?" My ears rang, so I focused on their lips.

"We were only going for a walk," Stephen sneered. "That's not against the law, is it?"

"It is when you're on private property."

"There aren't any signs," Dakota said.

"I'll show you a sign," Aunt Tillie snapped, raising the shotgun again.

I couldn't even get an admonishment out before the boys scattered, their excited exclamations telling me they were running for it and not looking back. "That was stupid," I chided. "We both know why they were here. We should've gotten them to confess before you scared them off."

"They're teenage boys, which means they're naturally stupid," Aunt Tillie replied, nonplussed. "That doesn't mean they're going to admit to trying to steal pot before a thunderstorm."

"You know they could turn you in for firing that gun, right?"

"Only if they want to admit what they were doing here," Aunt Tillie replied. "Besides, I'll deny it."

"How are you going to explain this to Chief Terry and Landon?"

"I'll say I was shooting skeet and had no idea they were out here," Aunt Tillie answered. "You need to learn to think on your feet. The easiest lies are often the best."

"If that's true, why do you tell so many outrageous lies whenever you get caught doing something wrong?"

"I'm old and I have to get my jollies somewhere," Aunt Tillie said. "I ...."

The sound of footsteps to our right caused us to swivel, Aunt Tillie with her gun at the ready. Instead of teenage boys, though, our new foe was much worse.

"What in the hell are you doing out here?"

Aunt Willa and Rosemary seemed surprised by our presence – and terrified of the gun. They gripped each other's arms as they exchanged a worried look before focusing on us.

"I ... we were out for a walk and we got turned around," Aunt Willa said. It was clearly a lie. "We're trying to find our way back to the house."

Aunt Tillie narrowed her eyes. "You're full of it."

"You're carrying a gun," Rosemary said.

"You always were a bright one," Aunt Tillie deadpanned.

"Why do you have a gun?"

"We were hunting," I lied.

"Hunting?" Rosemary wrinkled her nose. "For what?"

"Rabbits," Aunt Tillie and I replied in unison, causing each other to laugh.

"I don't think that's what you were doing at all," Aunt Willa said.

"Well, I don't really care what you think we were doing," Aunt Tillie shot back. "We know you weren't lost out here. This is the second time you've been caught wandering around our property without permission. Do you know what happens the third time?"

Aunt Willa remained silent, although I could see her throat working as she swallowed.

"You become the rabbits if we find you a third time," Aunt Tillie informed them. "Come on, Bay. It's time for dinner, and we need to get inside before the storm hits. I hope we're having rabbit. It will get me in the mood for future hunting."

Love her or hate her, you have to admit the woman has style. I didn't bother to hide my smile as I followed Aunt Tillie toward the inn. Things weren't looking up, but they were definitely getting more exciting.

TWENTY-SEVEN

"Why are you wet?" Landon looked me up and down as I flipped on the library pedestal fan and stood in front of it to dry my hair. We were almost back to the inn when the rain started. I could be a lot wetter, so I wasn't going to start complaining ... well, at least not yet.

"I was outside with Aunt Tillie when the storm started."

Landon sipped his drink, his eyes thoughtful. "How did that go?"

"Yeah. Is she still mad she didn't get the money you found?" Marcus asked, reclining in one of the chairs across from the couch. He'd been discussing something with Landon when I entered, and I didn't bother to make apologies about interrupting them. They often whispered to each other when they thought no one was looking these days.

"She's actually ... ." I didn't know how to answer. Even though my conversation with Aunt Tillie ended with us running through the woods and her firing a shotgun to amuse herself, what happened before was fairly eye opening.

"What's wrong?" Landon asked, leaning forward. "Is she going to curse you again?"

I chuckled. "No. She says she's not really angry with us, and the curse wasn't nearly as much fun as she thought it would be," I replied. "She's still going to punish us, but it will probably only be with ill-fitting pants and zits."

"What's bothering you then?" Landon pressed.

"She's worried about Aunt Willa and why she's here," I answered. "She's angry with Willa and she misses my grandmother. I think it's a lot for her to take on right now. We were easy marks."

"Wow. I wouldn't have thought I would ever hear you taking up for Aunt Tillie like this," Landon said. "It sounds like you had a nice talk."

"We did until ... ." I pursed my lips. This next part was going to royally tick him off. "Someone tripped the wards while we were in the greenhouse. She has somehow rigged a real daisy to make screeching sounds when it happens. I need to ask her about that, because it was wicked cool, by the way.

"When we ran out there, we found Stephen, Charlie and Dakota lurking by the pot field," I continued. "They couldn't find anything and ... well ... I should probably mention that Aunt Tillie put on her combat helmet and grabbed a shotgun before we left the greenhouse."

Landon leaned forward, his face murderous. "What?"

"It's about to get worse, so you might want to brace yourself," I warned. "I tried to talk to them and they refused to come out. I could see them hiding behind a tree. I didn't want to move too close to them because I knew you would have a heart attack and kill me if they didn't do it first ... ."

"I am so terrified to hear the ending of this story I don't even know what to do with myself," Landon muttered.

"I have a feeling I know how this ends," Marcus supplied.

"Before I could stop her – and I really tried, I promise – she fired the gun and ... ."

Landon hopped to his feet. "Please tell me she didn't shoot one of those kids and leave him out there to bleed to death!"

I scowled. "Yeah, that sounds exactly like something I would do," I deadpanned.

Landon's expression softened. "I'm sorry." He held up his hands to placate me. "The idea of that woman running around with a gun and easy targets is horrifying. Please continue."

"She hit a tree branch and it fell down, so they scattered," I explained. "They told us they were lost, but I didn't believe them. I wanted to question them further, but Aunt Tillie ... had other ideas."

"I can imagine," Landon said, brushing my hair out of my face. "Well, at least she didn't kill anyone." He pushed me closer to the fan and ran his fingers through my hair to untangle it. "Those kids are obviously desperate to get their hands on product. They're not even trying to hide that fact now. That means we're dealing with something bigger."

"Like organized drug dealers?" Marcus asked.

Landon nodded. "I don't like that everyone keeps trying to come out here to get product," he said. "It's as though there's a big pink elephant in the room. Everyone knows it's there, but they can't see it."

"That would make it an invisible pink elephant," I said. "If we had one of those we would be rich and never need to work a day again. We could live on love and hide from everyone we don't like."

"You're cute," Landon said, tweaking my nose. "I still think these kids have to be working with a larger distributor to be this bold. Someone must expect money from them in lieu of the pot we burned."

"And we took the money from the cave," I interjected. "They're probably doubly desperate now. Do you think they know we took it?"

"I think Chief Terry's secretary has a huge mouth," Landon replied. "I think that she tells everyone in town what's going on whenever she can because she likes being the center of attention. She knows you guys were the ones who found the money. That means everyone will know before the day is out."

"I know this is going to sound strange, but I'm more worried about Aunt Willa right now," I admitted. "They were out wandering around the woods, too. They seemed surprised when they happened upon us."

"Oh, good grief," Landon grumbled. "She didn't shoot at them, did she?"

"No, but she did give them a second warning and threatened that they wouldn't like it if we caught them a third time," I said, smiling at the memory. "We told them we were rabbit hunting and if we found them wandering around the property we would make them the rabbits next time. Aunt Tillie had a lot of swagger in her step when she sauntered off with her gun. She even managed to pull off the combat helmet."

Landon chuckled. "That actually sounds funny," he said, moving away from me and settling back on the couch. "We still have a problem because of that field. If those kids are in real trouble, they'll keep coming out here, because Aunt Tillie isn't as terrifying as whatever they're facing."

"How are you going to combat that?" Marcus asked.

"There's only one way I can think of," Landon said, rubbing the back of his neck. "We're going to have to haul all three of those kids in and offer them protection for information."

"What if they killed Nathaniel?" I asked, turning so the fan could blow at the back of my hair. "You can't offer them a deal until we know who killed him, and he's not exactly being forthcoming."

"I know. It's … a mess." Landon sighed.

"I need to go find Thistle," Marcus said, getting up from his chair and moving around me. "She's probably saying every nasty thing she can think of now that the curse has been lifted. No poor schmuck will be safe now that she's in control of her tongue again."

Once it was just the two of us, Landon fixed me with a curious look. "What else did you and Aunt Tillie talk about?"

"What makes you think we talked about other stuff?"

Landon shrugged. "I don't know. You seem … calmer."

"Do you generally find me overly dramatic?"

Landon cocked a challenging eyebrow. "Do you really want me to answer that?"

I made a disgusted sound in the back of my throat. "We mostly talked about how much she missed my grandmother, and how Clove is going to move in with Sam soon."

"That's not all you talked about," Landon countered. "You told her what I said about us living in the same house one day, didn't you?"

"Did she already tell you that?" My cheeks started burning.

"Ha! I knew it!" Landon said, shuffling to my side. "She didn't tell me. I know you've been constantly thinking about it. I know you."

"I guess you do," I conceded. "I feel strange that you know me so well."

"Get used to it," Landon said, smiling. "You know you kind of look like an angel with your hair flying up like that. Only someone who knows you would realize you're really an evil witch."

"You're so funny."

Landon gripped my chin and gave me a kiss. "I love you, Bay. Everything is going to work out like it's supposed to. Stop freaking out and enjoy it."

"You sound like Aunt Tillie."

"This is the only time I will ever take that as a compliment."

THE DINNER TABLE was busy with chatter when we arrived, and it seemed Aunt Tillie and her gun warred for top billing with news of the pot field burning.

"This is all so exciting," one of the female guests enthused. "We have drugs and guns ... and combat helmets. It's like a television show."

"That would only work if it was *The Walking Dead* and I was paired up with Daryl," Aunt Tillie replied dryly. "If you try to stick me on something like *Dancing With the Stars*, we're going to have a problem."

"And that's before everyone realizes you have negative rhythm," Thistle supplied.

"I liked it much better when you were being nice this morning," Rosemary said, smiling as Brian handed her a dinner roll. Why is he here again? I hate him.

"Yes, well that wasn't my natural state," Thistle countered. "I'm much happier this way."

"So as long as you're happy and everyone else is miserable, you're okay with that?" Aunt Willa challenged.

"Yes."

"We all like her better mouthy," Aunt Tillie said. "I thought I would like her nice, too. It turns out I was wrong. See, it does happen occasionally."

"Like when you threatened me with a gun?"

"No, I was definitely right when I did that," Aunt Tillie replied, causing Aunt Willa to scowl.

"When did you shoot at them?" Mom asked. "You weren't out in the storm, were you? You'll get sick if you're not careful."

Aunt Willa was incredulous. "That's what you're worried about? You're not upset that she held a gun on me?"

"You're obviously still alive," Landon interjected. "She couldn't have gotten very close."

"That's a great attitude for law enforcement to have," Aunt Willa hissed.

"Hey, if she actually shot you – or was aiming at you – I might be more concerned," Landon said. "I happen to know that she didn't aim that gun at you and was shooting at other things, so you're only making trouble to make trouble."

"What was she shooting at?" Clove asked.

"Teenagers," I replied. "They were out by the … trees … looking around."

"That's not good," Thistle said, reading between the lines. "Do they know we found their money?"

"What money?" Marnie asked.

"Landon claims everyone in town is going to know we found that money by the end of the day," I said. "I don't know whether it was about the money as much as it was about the … oregano."

"That's code for marijuana," Rosemary explained to Brian. "Apparently Aunt Tillie grows her own illicit drugs."

"I've heard that," Brian said. "People can look as long as they want. They'll never find it if it's true. I think it's an urban legend. When I was living here I spent months looking for it. I never found a thing."

"I knew it!" Aunt Tillie hopped to her feet. "I knew you were a busybody."

"Hey, I thought it would make a good story," Brian countered. "Who doesn't love an article about a little old lady growing weed?"

Aunt Willa raised her hand.

"You weren't looking for it because you wanted to print an article about Aunt Tillie," Landon argued. "You were looking for it so you would have something to hold over Bay's head. You think if you can get her to quit the newspaper you'll be able to get around the stipulations of your grandfather's will. You're not fooling anyone."

"Is that true?" Mom was aghast. "Of course it's true. You're a snake. That makes total sense."

"I am not a snake!"

"You're worse than a snake," Thistle said. "A snake has human nature working against it – and mostly just wants to slither around and amuse itself. You want to slither around and undermine everyone. You're a ... snake turd."

"Good one," Aunt Tillie said.

"I want to know what you and Rosemary were doing on the property in the first place, Willa," Landon said. "This is the second time you've been wandering around. You don't strike me as a nature girl."

"Landon has a point," Marnie said. "Although ... I want to go back a second. Why does no one ever tell me the good stories? I would've loved to see Aunt Tillie threaten Aunt Willa with a gun."

"Hey, I missed the best story of the week," Clove argued. "I didn't get to see Mom whip her bra at Aunt Willa's head. I feel so left out."

"That's what happens when you move in with someone and don't tell your mother," Marnie shot back.

"I haven't moved in with Sam," Clove protested.

"Yet," Sam supplied. "We're doing it soon, though."

"Sam!" Clove's eyes bounced from face to face. "I ... we're ... um ... ."

"Oh, calm yourself," Aunt Tillie chided. "Everyone knows you're going to move in with Sam. We've been talking about it for weeks."

"But ... why didn't anyone tell me?" Clove whined. "That would've made my life so much easier."

"That's why we didn't tell you," Aunt Tillie said, focusing on Aunt Willa. "Why have you been searching the property? Did you hide a box of money out here when we were kids or something?"

"I grew up on this property," Aunt Willa replied. "I have a right to look around."

"You don't live here any longer," Aunt Tillie reminded her. "You don't have any rights where this property is concerned. I own it now. It's all mine. When I die in fifty years – and I don't plan on going a minute before then – the property will pass to Winnie, Marnie and Twila in equal shares. They will then pass it on to their girls."

"That's where you're wrong," Aunt Willa said. "I still have a claim on this property."

"Here we go," Landon muttered. "I had a feeling it was something like this."

He wasn't alone. I just couldn't figure out how she thought she would get control of Aunt Tillie long enough to wrest ownership of the property away from her.

"You don't have a claim on this property," Aunt Tillie said. "Ginger and I bought your share of the property because you weren't interested in staying here. We had it appraised and paid you fair market value. I have the documents showing you signed over your share."

"Yes, but I was hoodwinked when that happened," Aunt Willa said. "I didn't know the real value of the property. I happen to know it's worth a million dollars now. I want my share."

"There was no value in the property when we made the deal," Aunt Tillie argued. "We built the value in the property by expanding the house and building the inn. That's where the value comes in. You had nothing to do with that."

"We?" Mom raised an eyebrow.

"I supervised you building the inn," Aunt Tillie shot back. "That counts."

"Fine," Mom said, holding up her hands. "It doesn't matter, though. Aunt Willa has no claim on this property."

"My attorney thinks otherwise," Aunt Willa said, crossing her arms over her chest.

"Then your attorney is a moron," Landon suggested. "Wait … isn't Rosemary your attorney? If so, she's definitely an idiot. Aunt Tillie has the land deeds. She's the owner. You don't have any legal standing here."

"How are you even involved in this conversation?" Aunt Willa challenged.

"I like to spread my wisdom near and far, no matter the topic," Landon replied, blasé.

"Well, keep quiet," Aunt Willa ordered. "You have no say in this."

"Don't talk to him that way," I said. "He's a part of our family. You're not."

"Thank you, sweetie," Landon said, handing me a roll.

"All of this is crazy," Aunt Tillie said. "I knew you were up to something. Even I didn't think you were this stupid, though. Go ahead and file your lawsuit. I'm going to make you pay my legal costs when it fails, though. I'm also going to laugh at you in public, including taking a trip south to follow you around just so I can point and laugh in grocery stores and restaurants."

I pursed my lips to keep from giggling at the visual.

"I guess we'll just have to settle this in court then, won't we?" Aunt Willa said, making a face. "I intend to win."

"Well, good luck," Aunt Tillie replied. "I don't ever lose. It should be interesting."

TWENTY-EIGHT

"How are you feeling this morning, my witchy wonder?" Landon asked, his tone teasing as we walked to The Overlook. He was having a good time making nicknames out of "witch" lately. I found it annoying and charming at the same time. I wonder what that says about me.

"That's a weird question. Why would I feel anything but hungry?"

"You have a little spring in your step," Landon replied. "I would like to take credit for it ... heck, I'm going to take credit for it because I'm fairly certain I'm the reason you're smiling. But I think something else is going on, too."

"If you must know, I'm relieved we found out what Aunt Willa is up to. It's like half the weight has been lifted from my shoulders. Now all we have to do is find a murderer and track down whoever would be stupid enough to partner with teenage kids to sell drugs. That sounds pretty easy to me."

Landon snorted. "I love it when you're in a good mood. You almost seem like a little kid because you're so wide-eyed and agreeable."

"I am always agreeable."

"Says the woman who once went an entire night saying 'I know you are, but what am I' to Thistle when she decided to start an insult contest."

I rolled my eyes. "You seem to be in a good mood, too," I said, switching the conversation around on him. "Am I the reason you're happy?"

"You're definitely part of it," Landon replied. "I also think there's going to be some bacon in my future. I can't decide which one of you gets top billing in my morning."

I elbowed his ribs playfully. "It's a good thing you're handsome, because otherwise there would be absolutely nothing in this relationship for me."

"Except my charm, body and bedroom prowess, right?"

"If that's what you need to tell yourself," I replied, pushing open the back door of the family living quarters and frowning when I found the sofa empty. "It's seven. Aunt Tillie should be watching the morning news programs so she has something to complain about over breakfast."

"Maybe Willa snuck in here and smothered her in her sleep," Landon suggested.

"That's not funny."

"Wow. You're Team Tillie from the get-go today. I'm impressed."

"She's my great-aunt and I love her," I sniffed.

"She's also on your good side because she told you what a catch I am and how you do nothing but make life harder for yourself when you freak out over my intentions," Landon said.

"Your ego gets bigger and bigger with every breath."

Landon grinned, his status as "world's most charming man" on full display. "It's a good thing I have you to bring me back down to earth, isn't it?" He gave me a quick kiss and then pulled me toward the kitchen. "Maybe she's already at the table. She's probably eating my bacon even as we speak."

That didn't sound likely, but I followed Landon anyway. When we found the kitchen empty, I knew something was wrong.

"Where is my bacon?" Landon asked, looking around with a forlorn expression. "I ... we ... something terrible has happened here."

I shot him a sympathetic look and then flicked his ear. "My family is missing."

"Hey, if they left us bacon we could've celebrated that fact," Landon replied, although he kept moving through the kitchen and pushed into the dining room. That's where we found the first signs of life – although the guests looked terrified. "What's going on?"

"Where is my family?" I asked.

No one answered. Instead, the energetic woman from the night before merely extended her hand in the direction of the foyer. I scampered in that direction, visions of Aunt Tillie standing over Aunt Willa's dead body flitting through my head. It was going to be hard to hide a body with county police personnel descending on the area.

"This is illegal! I will call Mark Geragos and sue you for discrimination!"

Aunt Willa was screeching when we rounded the corner. The first thing I noticed – other than her exposed tonsils – was two packed bags resting on the floor in front of the check-in desk.

"What's going on?"

Everyone ignored me.

"Who is Mark Geragos?" Twila asked, confused.

"He's a famous lawyer," Marnie replied. "I suggest you get him for your plan to sue us for our property, Aunt Willa. We all know Rosemary isn't smart enough to handle the case. If you hire him for both maybe he'll only bill you once."

"You cannot do this to me," Aunt Willa seethed. "I'm a paying guest."

"And we reserve the right to refuse service to anyone," Mom said, tapping the sign behind the desk for emphasis. "Get out!"

"This is kind of neat," Landon said, leaning against the desk and crossing his arms over his chest. "Someone pull her hair. I want to see if that bun is real or a wig."

Aunt Tillie's eyes gleamed as she reached forward, but Mom slapped her hand back before she could grab a hank.

"She could sue us if you did that, Aunt Tillie. Think!"

Aunt Tillie glanced at me, smiling broadly. She was enjoying this little scene. I didn't blame her.

"You cannot kick me off of my own property," Aunt Willa said. "It's against the law."

Mom turned to Landon. "Well?"

"Oh, well, good," he said. "I was feeling left out. Um ... while property disputes really aren't my area of expertise ... since the deed is in Aunt Tillie's name they can kick you out."

"Of course you would say that," Aunt Willa spat. "You're sleeping with the enemy ... literally."

"Hey!" I had no idea where to go with my outrage. "You're a horrible person."

Landon slipped his arm around my shoulders. "I think lack of food is getting to you, sweetie," he said. "That really wasn't your best effort."

"I knew it as soon as I said it."

"I'm not leaving," Aunt Willa said. "You can't make me. This is my property."

Mom shot Landon a "kick her out if you ever want me to cook for you again" look.

"I have no jurisdiction in this," Landon said. "If you want an official presence, well, it's going to have to be Chief Terry."

"That's who I want then," Aunt Willa said. "I want someone who isn't tied to this family to tell you guys how wrong you are. Call him."

"Call him," Landon agreed. "While Winnie is doing that, Aunt Tillie needs to get the deed so we have visual proof."

Aunt Tillie kicked her heels together and saluted. "It would be my pleasure. Can I get my gun, too?"

"Don't even think about it," Landon warned.

"So, what do we do?" Twila asked. "We have to get breakfast on the table, but we can't leave them without a chaperone in case they try to steal something."

"I have never been this insulted in my whole life!" Aunt Willa bellowed.

"I have a feeling you'll be saying that again in twenty minutes," Landon replied. "Twila and Marnie, you can go and fix breakfast. Bay and I will watch Willa. Just a request, but if you make bacon and bring it to me here, I'll make sure Chief Terry pats her down to make sure she didn't steal the silverware on her way out."

"I'm going to fry you up a whole pig," Marnie promised, narrowing her eyes to dangerous slits as she glanced at Aunt Willa. "You're just lucky you're not the pig."

Landon's smile was cocky when the four of us remained. "I can tell already this is going to be my favorite breakfast ever."

"And I didn't even have to get naked," I said. "I think that reflects poorly on me."

"You're all deviants," Aunt Willa grumbled. "You're sick and terrible miscreants."

"I can live with that."

"HOW CAN you people be having a crisis before breakfast?"

Chief Terry looked as if the last place he wanted to be was in the center of a scene from Witchpocalypse Now.

"I blame Aunt Willa," I offered.

"I blame her, too," Landon added, rubbing his nose against my cheek. He was in a good mood this morning, and it was making him frisky.

"Do not make me turn the hose on you two," Chief Terry warned. "All this canoodling is giving me heartburn."

"I think the fact that you're using the word 'canoodling' is what's giving you heartburn, because it signifies you've been traveling through time, and that's bound to have an effect on the body," Landon countered.

"Bay has been a terrible influence on you," Chief Terry said. "I was worried you were going to be bad for her, but it turns out she's turned you into a ... ."

"Deviant," Aunt Willa supplied.

"I was going to say whipped and horny puppy," Chief Terry replied. "What seems to be the trouble here?"

"She's the Devil," Aunt Tillie answered.

"Can you be more precise?"

"She's the Devil from Hell."

Landon pursed his lips to keep from laughing as I opted to help. "Aunt Willa announced to everyone that she's going to take us to court because she believes she was screwed over on land rights forty years ago."

"That's despicable, but predictable," Chief Terry said. "Why am I here?"

"Our moms kicked them out this morning, but they refuse to leave because Aunt Willa claims she owns part of the property," I answered.

Chief Terry groaned. "Seriously. I've got a dead man and a razed pot field. This is the silliest ... ."

"Good morning, Terry," Mom said, appearing in the doorway with a heaping plate of eggs, hash browns, toast and bacon. "I thought you would like to eat something because you had to go out of your way to see to our little domestic dispute."

Aunt Willa made a face. She had no idea what was going on, but it was hilarious to watch her try to figure it out.

"Where is my bacon?" Landon asked.

"It's in the dining room." Mom didn't even bother looking at him.

"I'm the one who watched them to make sure they didn't steal any silverware. My bacon should be served to me out here."

"Then make Bay put on an apron and serve you," Mom suggested.

Landon shot me a hopeful look.

"Don't even think about it," I warned. "Do I look like the type of person who wears an apron?"

"I don't care if you wear an apron. You can be naked as far as I care. I just want my bacon."

"Hey!" Chief Terry extended a warning finger in Landon's direction. "You're on my last nerve." He popped a piece of bacon into his mouth and rewarded Landon with a smug smile. "And you're totally missing out."

"Bay, I'm going to have to start cursing people if he eats all my bacon," Landon said.

"Curse Aunt Willa," I suggested. "She has it coming."

"Does anyone care about the law here?" Aunt Willa wailed.

Chief Terry rolled his eyes and snapped his fingers in Aunt Tillie's direction. "Let me see the land deed."

"I'm only giving you this because I want you to kick Willa out on her fat behind," Aunt Tillie said. "We're going to have a talk about you snapping your fingers at me like I'm a dog later, though."

Chief Terry blanched. "I didn't mean … ." He didn't bother finishing, instead taking the land deed and scanning it. "This says Tillie Winchester owns all the land and it has the county's seal on it. You're fresh out Willa. They have the legal right to remove you from the property."

Aunt Willa wasn't about to give up. "I want a second opinion."

"Well, I'm the top cop in town, so I'm all you've got."

"I want someone else in law enforcement to verify that document." Aunt Willa had the family stubborn streak. I had to give her that.

"Will that make you leave?" Chief Terry asked.

Aunt Willa nodded.

Chief Terry handed the deed to Landon, taking Aunt Willa by surprise.

"It looks legit to me," Landon said, handing the deed to Aunt Tillie and grabbing a slice of bacon from Chief Terry's place.

"Now I'm really going to beat you," Chief Terry warned before turning to Aunt Willa expectantly. "There's your verification."

"He doesn't count," Aunt Willa screeched. "He's sleeping with the enemy."

"That's not going to help your case," Chief Terry replied dryly. "When you say 'enemy,' I picture an eight-year-old with pigtails and a stuffed dog. When you say 'sleeping,' I want to punch someone. I can't punch a woman, but I might make an exception in your case."

"And he can't punch me because I'm strong and manly, and he knows he would lose," Landon added, sneaking another slice of bacon from Chief Terry's plate.

"I will beat you if you steal one more piece of my food."

Landon was nonplussed. "They have the right to kick you out, Willa. You should have the grace to leave with a little pride intact."

"That shows what you know," Willa hissed. "I will never leave this property to you ... people. I know what you are and what you've been doing out here. I'm going to own the whole thing before it's all said and done. Just you wait."

"Well, you might want to try owning it from another location," Chief Terry suggested. "This one belongs to someone else, and she wants you gone."

"That's right," Aunt Tillie said, doing a little jig next to the desk.

"What are you doing?" Willa asked. She was quickly becoming unhinged.

"I'm dancing on your metaphorical grave!"

TWENTY-NINE

"I can't believe I missed it again!" Clove wrinkled her pert nose in disgust as she organized herbs behind the counter at Hypnotic two hours later.

"That's what happens when you move in with your boyfriend and don't tell anyone," I teased, reclining on the couch and studying Thistle's newest candle. It was a sugar skull ... and it was beautiful. "I want one of these."

"Do you really like it?" Thistle asked. "Sugar skulls are all the rage. I thought adding them to the store would be a good idea because they fit the horror atmosphere and still look pretty."

"It's amazing," I said. "Maybe I'll get Landon one. He's feeling flirty today."

Thistle snorted. "I'm working on a candle for you to give to Landon," she said. "To be fair, I'm working on one to give to Marcus, too. I'm going to include you, though."

"What is it? If it's boobs I don't want it. I don't want to be jealous of a candle."

Clove giggled. "It's not boobs. Do you think I would let her sell candles shaped like boobs in our store?"

"Once you move out you're never going to see what I'm working on," Thistle said. "It's going to be glorious."

Clove frowned. "Aren't you going to miss me even a little bit?"

"Nope."

I took pity on my cousin. "I'll miss you."

"Only because she usually takes your side in an argument," Thistle said. "Now we're going to be going at each other without a tiebreaker. That's going to be glorious, too."

I rolled my eyes and focused on Clove. "When are you going to move?"

"I'm not sure," she said. "I'm not leaving until all this Aunt Willa stuff is settled."

"That's probably smart," I said. "You'll want to be close if one of our mothers really does achieve the impossible and manages to make her head explode with only the powers of her mind."

"Oh, please," Thistle scoffed. "If anyone could manage that it's Aunt Tillie. Did she really dance on an imaginary grave?"

I nodded. "It was … odd."

"That's hilarious," Thistle said. "I can't believe I missed it."

"It was one for the record books."

We lapsed into comfortable silence for a few minutes, Clove and Thistle taking care of various tasks while I studied the candle. Thistle was a gifted artist. I don't know how a mind so full of evil thoughts could make something so beautiful.

"Where is Landon?" Clove asked, as if realizing for the first time he wasn't with me.

"He's at the police station," I replied. "They're hauling Stephen, Dakota and Charlie in for questioning today."

"Twenty bucks says Charlie cracks first," Thistle said. "That kid has 'narc' written all over him."

"I didn't think he could possibly be involved at first," I admitted. "The fact that he seems to not only be involved but also actively participating with the other boys indicates otherwise, though."

"He might actually be able to get off with a peer pressure defense,"

Clove suggested. "He wants to fit in so badly that he'll do almost anything."

"I think Stephen is the brains behind the operation," I volunteered. "At first I thought it was Dakota, but when I watched them interact the other day Stephen seemed to be the one in control and Dakota appeared to be along for the ride."

"That's probably true," Thistle said. "I've talked to that Dakota kid a few times at festivals, and he doesn't strike me as bright."

"I'm not sure how bright any of them are," I countered. "You would have to be stupid to sell drugs in a town this small. Everyone knows the gossip mill is out of control. Word was bound to get out."

"The only reason it got out is because Nathaniel was murdered," Clove pointed out. "If he hadn't died, their secret would still be safe."

"Yeah, that bugs me, too," I said. "If Nathaniel was part of the group, why did they kill him? Heck, I'm not even sure they are the ones who killed him. Whoever they were working for could've done it. It's just … ."

"If professionals did it, why did they dump him in an area with ties to the field?" Thistle said. "It doesn't make sense. If professionals took Nathaniel out – or even adults who knew a thing about murder investigations – they would've dumped him somewhere else."

"Hemlock Cove isn't big, but the surrounding woods are dense," I said. "Dumping the body in a remote location would make a lot more sense."

"Maybe we're looking at this the wrong way," Clove suggested. "Maybe whoever Stephen, Charlie and Dakota are working with didn't kill Nathaniel. Maybe someone who knew they were selling drugs to area kids killed him and purposely dumped the body close to the pot field so the police would find it."

Now that was an interesting theory. "Who would do that?"

"Has anyone lost a kid to a drug overdose around here?" Thistle asked, knitting her eyebrows together. "I can't think of anyone. Carter Mortensen's kid almost died in a car accident when he was high, but they put him in rehab and he's been straight ever since, from what I can tell."

"I can't think of anyone," Clove said. "That doesn't mean there's not someone out there we didn't hear about. If I were a parent, I might lie about how my kid died if I thought it would sully his memory."

"Clove's theory makes a lot of sense," I said, running the possibilities through my mind. "It just doesn't feel ... right ... though."

"Does Stephen, Charlie or Dakota killing Nathaniel feel right?"

I shook my head. "That doesn't feel right either," I admitted. "I don't care how stupid those kids are, dropping Nathaniel's body at Hollow Creek was a boneheaded move. I don't think they did it.

"For the sake of argument, though, let's say they did murder him and left the body behind," I continued. "It was several days before Nathaniel was discovered. That's plenty of time to realize what they did and try to move him."

"Okay, if someone with a vendetta against drugs doesn't feel right, and the other two options don't make sense, what are we left with?" Thistle asked.

"Nathaniel was stabbed eight times," I reminded them. "That's not a drug hit. That's personal."

"So we're missing something," Clove surmised.

"We're definitely missing something," I agreed. "For the life of me I can't figure out what, though."

TWO HOURS later I was still on the couch and no further along in my mental investigation. I had nowhere to go, and without an update from Landon I was stuck.

"Let's order lunch," Thistle suggested. "I'm starving."

"Let's get Thai," Clove said. "We haven't had that in ages."

"I can live with that," I said, swinging my feet off the couch and turning to my cousins. "I ... ." The sound of the wind chimes dinging over the door caught our attention. I expected a customer. What I got was a nightmare.

"What are you doing here, Aunt Willa?" Thistle asked, no pretense of warmth on her face. "You're banned from the inn. In case you're slow, that means you're not allowed here. We also reserve the right to refuse service and I would rather cater to trained snakes than you."

"They would be cuddlier," Clove added. She generally wasn't big on insults, but Aunt Willa's attitude and intentions were enough to make her mean. That said volumes about the nastiness of Aunt Willa.

"I'm not here to shop," Aunt Willa shot back. "There's nothing in this ... den of Satan ... that I would ever want."

"Then leave," Thistle suggested.

"I'm here to talk to the three of you," Aunt Willa said. "I wasn't actually expecting to find Bay here, but since she apparently only works when she feels like it – and talks back to her boss whenever the mood strikes – I guess I shouldn't be surprised."

"Brian isn't my boss," I countered. "He's the idiot sitting in the front office who dreams up stupid ideas but never works. There's a difference. I didn't treat his grandfather the way I treat him. William was a wonderful man. He knew what his grandson was and his limitations. That's why he drew up his will the way he did."

"You girls sure think a lot of yourselves, don't you?"

Thistle rolled her eyes. "That's rich coming from you. Get out of my store."

"Not until I say what I came here to say," Aunt Willa shot back.

"Then say it."

"I am owed money on that property," Aunt Willa said, her voice calm and even. "You might not want to believe it because your mothers refuse to see my sister for what she is, but I was swindled.

"Now, I don't want this to get ugly and I don't want you to lose your home," she continued. "I will take your home from you if it becomes necessary, though. I deserve my share of that money."

"Do you think we're somehow going to help you fight against our mothers?" Clove asked, confused.

"I think you are more ... realistic ... about what's going to happen here," Aunt Willa clarified. "You know I have a case. You can save your family a lot of agony by telling them to give me my money."

"Are you done?" I challenged.

"No ... ."

"Shut up," I snapped, cutting Aunt Willa off before she could get a full head of steam. "You don't have a case. You know that. I'm not sure what you're doing here ... maybe you've run into financial problems or something ... but you're not entitled to our land."

"I was born into the same family you were, Bay," Aunt Willa hissed. "My parents left a will stating that anyone with our mother's blood was to be given a share of the property. The land rights run through her. There were three children. That means I get a third of the land."

"You did get it," Thistle argued. "You got it, and sold it to Aunt Tillie and our grandmother because you thought this area was beneath you."

"Don't bother denying it," I added. "We know what happened. When you left, Walkerville was a struggling community. The land was worth practically nothing. You got your payout and you were happy because you thought you stuck Aunt Tillie and Grandma with property you didn't want."

"Our mothers turned that property into a goldmine," Clove chimed in. "They put their blood, sweat and tears into that inn. They designed it and they're the draw thanks to their hard work and cooking. They worked their A-S-S-E-S off and they reaped the rewards. You don't have anything to do with that inn, and you don't deserve a dime."

"Who are you spelling for?" Aunt Willa asked, glancing around.

"You, dumbass," Thistle replied, earning a scorching glare from Aunt Willa. "If you try to take that inn from our mothers, you're going to have a lot more than Aunt Tillie to deal with."

"That's right," I said. "Our mothers are beloved in this community. They volunteer their time and they're good people. No one likes you here. No one will take your side. A judge certainly isn't going to take your side."

"No matter how well your mothers are liked in Hemlock Cove, Tillie is hated here," Aunt Willa said. "People will take my side to get rid of her."

"That's where you're wrong," I argued. "Aunt Tillie isn't hated."

Thistle arched a dubious eyebrow.

"She's not hated," I repeated. "She's feared. Do you really think the people of this town want to risk going after her? She'll burn every single one of them to a crisp before she lets you take that land. You know that, right?"

"I see she has you snowed, too," Aunt Willa scoffed. "You're afraid of her because you think she has magical powers. Let me tell you something, my dears, she doesn't have magical powers because they don't exist."

I stilled, exchanging a confused look with Thistle. Powers came with being a Winchester. Our mothers mostly dabbled, yet they still had power. Had Aunt Willa deluded herself into believing she wasn't paranormal because she was so desperate to be normal? That's the only excuse I could muster.

"I think you're living in La-La Land," I said finally. "Whatever you think you're going to accomplish here, you're going to fail. Whatever misery you think you're going to mete out to Aunt Tillie, it's going to come back on you. That's called karma."

"And we all believe in it," Clove added.

"Then you'll all be sorry together," Aunt Willa said. "Rosemary has been talking to our lawyer. She's quite brilliant in legal circles. You know that, right?"

"The only circle Rosemary looks brilliant in is the one in your own head ... or the Ring-Around-The-Rosy one at your local kindergarten," Thistle replied. "You're an idiot if you think you can touch that property. I'm almost happy you're doing this. It's going to be so much fun to watch you lose."

"And what happens when I win?"

"Then we'll get to watch Aunt Tillie dance on your actual grave," Thistle answered. "That will be fun, too."

THIRTY

After Aunt Willa's visit – and huffy exit – I was on edge. I paced Hypnotic until Thistle and Clove couldn't take another second of my nervous energy and threatened me with a dirt sandwich or banishment. I knew Aunt Willa didn't have a claim on the land, but whenever someone messes with my family I want to do something horrible to them. Unfortunately, that was Aunt Tillie's job in this particular situation.

I headed toward The Whistler, thinking I could get some work done – or at least waste an hour shopping on Etsy – when I saw Rosemary walking through the front door of the office. Ugh. What is with her and Brian? It's incredibly annoying. Well, there was no way I was hanging out with the two of them. Of course, it might be fun to eavesdrop. Oh, who was I kidding? Edith could do that. I'm never going to choose the path that might lead to projectile vomiting, and that's all I could think of whenever I looked at Rosemary.

I cast a glance in the direction of the police department, tempted to see how Landon and Chief Terry were doing with the three teenagers of terror. They didn't want me there for obvious reasons. It was unprofessional to have the local news reporter sit in on an interrogation. It was even worse for the FBI agent in charge to bring his girlfriend along.

With nothing better to do, I found myself walking in the direction of the Jamison house. I was lost in thought – possibilities about Nathaniel's death and fitting retribution for Aunt Willa warring for supremacy – when I happened upon Chloe as I rounded the corner that led to her house.

"What are you doing here?" Chloe asked, her eyes narrowing. "Are you here to finish me off?"

I sighed. Coming to the Jamison house was a bad idea. I'd forgotten that Chloe was laboring under the misassumption that I tried to kill her. "How are you doing, Chloe?"

"How do you think I'm doing?" Chloe asked, her tone scathing. "My brother is dead. My mother is a mess. She's decided I need rehab because the pot is clearly driving me insane. My life is perfect. I should be on one of those Real Housewives of … Whatever shows."

When she put it like that … . "Chloe, I know that life seems as if it's stacking up against you right now," I said. "Things will get better. I know it doesn't seem like it now, but you will find a way to move past this."

"I'm sorry, are you actually offering me sympathy after you tried to kill me?"

"I didn't try to kill you," I replied. "I … you misunderstand what happened."

"How? We were standing next to the water, and the next thing I knew I was flying through the air and landing in the middle of that filthy mess. There was no one else there."

There was no rational way I could explain what happened, so I decided to change the subject. "You should know that Stephen, Dakota and Charlie have been taken in for questioning today," I offered. "Landon and Chief Terry are talking to them right now."

Chloe furrowed her brow. "For what?"

"Well, for everything," I said. "You heard about the pot field, right?"

Chloe rolled her eyes. "Everyone heard about the pot field. It's the

AMANDA M. LEE

lead story in the Hemlock Cove ... oh, wait. You write for The Whistler. There's no way to make sense of that."

I was starting to think rehab was a good idea. Chloe was definitely scattered. "Did you know about the field?"

"Everyone knew about the field," Chloe replied. "The only people who didn't know about the field were the cops and ... well ... you."

That was interesting. Teenagers are prone to exaggeration, but I had trouble believing the pot field managed to remain secret given the number of parties at Hollow Creek. "How long was it there?"

"Um ... I don't know," Chloe said, shrugging. "It's been there as long as I can remember. I first heard about it when I was in middle school. I didn't know what Nathaniel was talking about when he mentioned it, but he was definitely talking about it then."

"So, what? Are we talking, like, four years here?"

"That sounds about right."

Holy crap! Teenagers today are much better at keeping secrets than we were at that age. Aunt Tillie would've sniffed out a secret pot field within days. She wouldn't have needed years. "Who planted it?"

"I ... ." Chloe tilted her head, considering the question. She didn't want to rat out her friends. I got that. The truth was going to come out no matter what, though. Charlie was going to spill his guts faster than a zombie on *The Walking Dead*.

"The police are going to find out one way or another," I prodded.

"I have no idea who planted it the first time," Chloe said, resigned. "Every year a group of kids takes over the field from another group of kids. They get ... selected."

I frowned. It was like a pot popularity contest. "Was your brother one of the chosen ones?"

"He was one of the popular boys."

That wasn't an answer. "Nathaniel was one of the popular ones, so he ran the field with a couple of his friends," I surmised. "It gave him extra money. When he went to college, he lost out on that money, and your mother didn't have any extra to give him. Did he try to take over the field again when he came back this summer?"

"I have no idea."

She was lying. I was on the right track. I knew it. "Who are they working with?"

"Who is who working with?" Chloe asked. She looked genuinely confused.

"They have to be working with someone," I pressed. "I overheard Stephen, Dakota and Charlie worrying about what 'they' would do. Who is the 'they' those boys are talking about?"

"I have no idea." Chloe crossed her arms over her chest, defiant.

"Chloe, you're not protecting anyone but the people who killed your brother," I said. "Is that what you want? Do you want your brother's murder to go unsolved?"

"I don't really care," Chloe said. "I'm not ratting on people. That's not who I am. I don't know a lot about my brother because he was always mean to me, but I know what he would think of anyone who talked to you guys. I'm not going to do it. There's nothing you can do to make me."

"You're making a poor decision here," I said. "You're going to regret it."

"I think I'll live," Chloe shot back. "I'm not taking advice from the woman who tried to drown me in the same creek my brother died in. I know that's something I would regret."

I watched Chloe flounce away in the direction of downtown. Her pace was brisk and yet her shoulders dipped. She was a troubled girl, and I had a feeling it was going to get worse before it got better.

I lifted my eyes to find her mother staring at me through the bay window at the front of their house. Her face was … dark. She probably thought I tried to kill Chloe, too. I lifted my hand in a half-hearted wave, but Patty didn't return it. There was no way she was going to talk to me. This was another dead end.

I was out of options. Again.

I FOUND myself back at Hollow Creek an hour later. I'm not good with down time when I'm waiting for answers. I'm impatient. I can't help it. I blame Aunt Tillie. She set a poor example on that front. I hoped Nathaniel would make an appearance so I could question him. He was the only one with the answers I needed.

I scuffed at the dirt as I walked, debating how I could reconcile what Chloe said with my emerging theory regarding the pot field and her brother's death. If it really had been up and running for years – and I had no reason to doubt that – the pot field served as a money-making endeavor for years. Still, how could the kids simply hand it over to the next generation without putting up a stink? Someone had to organize it. Someone had to make rules and force the kids to follow them.

If Nathaniel came back and thought he was going to step into his old job, that might be enough to propel someone to kill him. It wouldn't be enough to propel someone to stab him eight times, though. That still bothered me.

"What are you doing back here?"

I shifted when I heard Nathaniel's voice, fixing him with a hard look. "I'm trying to figure out what happened to you," I answered. "You're not talking, and there are a lot of things about this that don't make sense."

"You've ruined everything," Nathaniel said. "You ended the parties. You burned down the field. There's nothing left here. You ruined it all!"

"You're left here."

"And now I'm alone, thanks to you," Nathaniel spat.

His reaction made me inexplicably sad. Sure, he was a drug dealer and rampant asshat, but he was still a sad and lonely young man. "You don't have to stay here, Nathaniel," I reminded him. "In fact, you're not meant to stay here. You can move on."

"Maybe I don't want to move on."

"Do you know what will happen to you if you carry on like this? You'll turn into a poltergeist. Do you know what that means?"

"I've seen the movie," Nathaniel replied dryly. "The original was much better than the remake."

"That can be said about every movie," I shot back. "A poltergeist is rage. That's all it is. If you give in to what you're feeling, you'll never have any peace. Is that what you want?"

"I can't have what I want, can I?" Nathaniel challenged. "I wanted a future. I wanted to be someone. I died as a Hemlock Cove nobody. What's worse than that?"

"You died someone," I said. "You might not have been who you wanted to be, but you were still someone."

"And who is that?"

"You were a son. You were a brother. You were a human being. That's gone now. You can still have an afterlife if you allow yourself to release the rage."

"I don't want to do that," Nathaniel said. "I want to be angry. It's the only thing I have right now."

I shook my head. Apparently stubbornness was a shared trait in the Jamison family. "Tell me who you were working for," I said, changing tactics. "Chloe said this field has been operational for years. Every year a new group of students took over the operation. You were forced out, but you tried to come back, didn't you?"

"I did a good job," Nathaniel seethed, his aura flashing red. "I should've been left in charge. Those idiots who were running it this year ... well ... you saw what happened. They killed the entire business."

"Who were they working for?"

"I don't snitch," Nathaniel said. "I'm not telling you that."

"Even though they killed you?"

"They didn't kill me," Nathaniel replied. "They tried to force me out of the business and cut me out of the profits, so I have no love for them, but they didn't kill me. Besides, I stole their cash stash as payback. They got what was coming to them for trying to block me."

The money in the cave. "If they didn't kill you, who did?"

Nathaniel's face contorted, his eyes traveling to a spot over my shoulder. I refused to let him distract me, though. I needed answers and I was sick of him refusing to answer my questions.

"Who killed you, Nathaniel? It's important. I need to know."

"Why don't you turn around and find out."

Oh, crap. Not again.

THIRTY-ONE

Behind me? If whoever was behind me didn't do it first, Landon was definitely going to kill me this time. Crap on toast!

I turned quietly, my shoulders stiff, and found .... No way!

"What are you doing here?"

Chloe's eyes darted in eight different directions before landing on me. Her hair was a mess, as if she'd been dragging her hands through it for lack of anything better to do. Her eyes were wide, pupils dilated. She was stoned, although she looked a little more than that. She appeared to be verging on the edge of mania.

"I was out here ... looking around," I replied, choosing my words carefully. "I was upset after talking with you and I wanted to clear my head." I risked a glance at Nathaniel out of the corner of my eye. He glowered at his sister. This wasn't good. How could I have missed this?

"You were upset after talking with me?" Chloe arched her eyebrows suspiciously. "Why doesn't that seem likely?"

Probably because she was stoned and paranoid. Marijuana doesn't generally make people violent, so I had a feeling there was some sort of upper involved here, too. Crap, crap ... double crap. Why did I come out here without telling anyone? I'm such an idiot sometimes.

"Are you looking for someone else to drown?" Chloe's eyes flashed in the same instant Nathaniel's aura mimicked the change. They were tied together in rage.

"I think I'm going to leave you here to ... talk to your brother in private," I said, taking a wide berth as I stepped around Chloe. "You guys probably have a few things to discuss." I hoped I could get to my car and call Landon before locking myself away from the Jamison siblings. If Nathaniel was going to explode on his sister again – which looked likely – he had the capacity to kill her. Whether Chloe killed her brother was irrelevant right now. I wasn't going to let the girl die if I could help it.

"Talk to my brother?" Chloe was more belligerent than confused. "My brother is dead! How can I talk to him?"

"Tell her you can see me and I'm here," Nathaniel suggested. "I want to see her face when she finds out her secret isn't safe ... that stupid, little ... ."

I ignored the rest of his outburst. "Many people go to the locations where their loved ones died so they can feel close to them," I said. "You came out here to talk to your brother, right? There's no other reason for you to be here." Unless you're a true psychopath and you're reliving the crime because you get off on it, I silently added.

Chloe shook her head. "I came here to relive his death."

Oh, well ... crappity, crap, crap, crap. If I didn't have bad luck I would have no luck at all today. "What do you mean?"

"She means she stabbed me to death and left me to rot," Nathaniel hissed. "Ask her about it. I want to hear what she says. I want to know why."

"Shut up," I hissed, causing Chloe to jerk her head in my direction.

"Who are you talking to?"

"I'm talking to you," I replied without missing a beat.

"Were you telling me to shut up?" Chloe challenged.

"Of course not. I ... ." I scanned her hands. She didn't look armed. That didn't mean she wasn't dangerous. Given Nathaniel's rage, I knew he was dangerous. This whole situation was starting to get ugly. "Chloe, I think that maybe you and I should head back to town. You look a little ... hyped up."

"Hyped up?" Chloe snorted. "Haven't you heard? I'm an addict. My mother is going to send me to a lockdown facility. Do you know what that means?"

"It means she's going to have to go cold turkey," Nathaniel sneered. "She deserves it. She's a ... whore!"

His vehemence took me by surprise. Sure, it was looking more and more likely that Chloe killed her brother, but his outright hatred for his own flesh and blood was surprising.

"It means you probably have some tough days ahead of you," I answered, flexing my fingers. "Once you dry out, though, you'll feel like a new person." I hoped that new person wasn't still homicidal. What? Sometimes I'm an optimist.

"I don't want to dry out," Chloe seethed. "I don't want the edge off. If the edge is off, then I'll have to remember ... ."

Oh, here it comes.

Nathaniel leaned forward, intent on his sister. "Admit what you did to me, you bitch! Tell her how you murdered me and then tossed me in the creek like I was garbage." He was screaming. I had to get control of this situation.

"Why did you kill Nathaniel, Chloe?" I decided to put all of my cards on the table – while keeping a safe distance from Chloe's human hands and Nathaniel's ethereal ones. They both could do damage.

Chloe's face turned from miserable to shocked. She opened her mouth, working it, although no sound came out. Finally, she collected herself enough to address me. "How did you know?"

"I ... ." What was I supposed to tell her? "Nathaniel told me ... and you kind of just told me now, too." There was no sense in lying. If she melted down, it would give me a chance to put distance between us. If she didn't believe me, it might be a good thing, because people fear the insane. If she did believe me, though, I might actually be able to get somewhere.

"Nathaniel told you? How?"

"What have you heard about my family, Chloe?" I asked. "The first day I ran into you on the street in front of your house, you mentioned that we were witches. You said you didn't believe it, that you thought it was all an act to fit in with Hemlock Cove's rebranding. What if I told you that all of it is true?"

"I would say you were crazy!"

"That would be your right," I said. "I'm not crazy, though, and I have been talking with your brother."

Chloe considered the statement, taking time to scan the area around me. "Is he here now?"

Well, that was interesting. Would she believe me after all? "He is."

"And he told you I killed him?"

"He did," I said. "Although, to be fair, he refused to tell me for days, and only now told me when you approached. I had no idea who I would find behind me."

"What did he say?" Chloe asked, her voice low.

"He said that … he understands and he forgives you," I lied, taking a chance.

"Don't tell her that," Nathaniel screamed, lashing out with his rage and shoving me. The force wasn't hard enough to topple me, but it did cause me to wobble before regaining my footing. "Tell her the truth!"

"Was that Nathaniel?" Chloe asked, her eyes widening to almost comical proportions. "Did he … do something to you?"

"He has some issues," I gritted out, rubbing my arm in the spot where Nathaniel made contact. The skin was cold. That was interesting. His rage was hot, but his ghostly anchors kept him cool to the touch. I had no idea what that meant. I was in uncharted territory here, and I didn't like the feeling.

"Is he the one who threw me in the water?" Chloe asked, realization dawning. "He is, isn't he?"

"He's angry about you killing him, Chloe," I said, deciding not to risk Nathaniel's wrath again. "He feels as if he's been cheated out of a great life. He mentioned dying as a nobody when he should've been somebody."

"Of course he feels that way," Chloe spat, her expression unreadable as her eyes darted from one spot to another. She was desperate for a glimpse of Nathaniel. I realized she wanted to believe I was telling the truth, yet she was still doubtful. I had to prove myself to her. "He always thought he was destined for big things ... even though he never wanted to work. He thought big things would just somehow magically happen to him."

"You take that back," Nathaniel raged.

"Nathaniel, you need to calm down before you do something that you'll regret," I warned, fixating on the enraged young man.

"How will I regret anything?" Nathaniel scoffed. "I'm dead."

"You still haven't moved on," I reminded him. "I told you there was a better place out there for you to go to. There's also a worse place. If you do something horrible now, you'll go there."

"Send him to the bad place," Chloe ordered, narrowing her eyes. "He has it coming."

These two were quite the pair. Chloe was a killer who showed no remorse, and Nathaniel was a murder victim with absolutely no redeeming qualities. I had no idea how to approach either of them. "I'm not in control of sending him anywhere," I said. "He has to choose to let go."

"Why won't he let go?"

I shrugged helplessly. "Most murder victims who remain behind do so until their killer is caught," I offered. "Some have other reasons ... like seeing their family one last time or ensuring the safety of someone they love. Nathaniel doesn't like you, but he seems more upset that I ruined Hollow Creek's booming pot business."

"That's so typical," Chloe said. "All he's ever cared about is money and himself. He didn't care who he hurt in the process. He's a ... jackass."

That was putting it mildly. "Let's start from the beginning, Chloe," I said, keeping my voice soothing and calm. "Tell me what happened the night Nathaniel died."

"Why? I'm going to jail no matter what." Chloe was back to being morose. That's another thing I hate about teenagers. They think the universe revolves around them. "What can it possibly matter at this point?"

"I need to know if I'm going to help you," I replied honestly.

"Help her? She killed me!"

"Shut up, Nathaniel," I ordered. "You're not helping matters. I've offered you what I can at every turn and you've been nothing but a spoiled brat. I'm focusing on your sister now. Be quiet."

Nathaniel was taken aback. Thankfully he clamped his mouth shut and let me focus on his sister.

I turned back to Chloe. "Did you come out to Hollow Creek to party that night?"

"I wasn't supposed to," Chloe admitted, resigned. "Nathaniel told me to stay away from here after ... what happened. He said I was being a bitch and he didn't like me around. He didn't care about what happened, though. He only cared about himself."

Huh. What happened? I filed that away to pursue later and let her talk at her own pace.

"I was so ... angry with him," Chloe said, her eyes taking on a far-off quality. "He didn't see it. Either he was too stupid to see it, or he was too self-involved to see it. The more he ignored the situation, though, the more I wanted to make him pay.

"I didn't come out here to kill him that night," she continued. "I don't want you to think I did, because it's not true."

"Okay."

"When I got to the party, Stephen and Dakota were being jerks," Chloe explained. "I wasn't surprised, because they're always jerks. They think they're kings, even though Hemlock Cove is too small to have kings."

Nathaniel snickered. "She's not wrong about Stephen and Dakota," he said. "Those guys are idiots."

"What happened next?" I pressed.

"Stephen started making comments about me being a slut and wanting to take me into the woods," Chloe replied. "He ... touched my hair and face. I told him to knock it off, but he wouldn't listen. After what happened that first time ... I couldn't stand it. I kicked him in the nuts and ran."

A chill washed over me. I was starting to get an inkling of what happened to Chloe, and it wasn't something I wanted to entertain. I didn't think I would get a choice in the matter, though. Chloe needed to unload. I was her only option.

"I was crying and I got turned around," Chloe said. "I knew where the pot field was because I followed Nathaniel once when he was in charge. I wanted to see where he was getting his money. When I saw him ... it finally all made sense."

"Did Nathaniel know you were aware of the pot field?"

Chloe nodded. "He yelled and screamed at me for hours," she said. "I tried to apologize. I told him I wouldn't tell anyone. I thought that he would be nicer to me once I knew his secret. I was wrong."

"I was trying to protect you, you idiot," Nathaniel muttered.

"Did you find Nathaniel in the field that night?" I asked.

"He was stealing," Chloe said. "He had a knife and he was hacking parts of the plants down and sticking them in a bag. I surprised him when I showed up, but he couldn't risk screaming at me in case someone at the party heard him."

"How did you get out to the field without anyone noticing?" I asked Nathaniel.

"I hiked in from the road," Nathaniel replied dully. "I parked out there and made the long walk. I knew there was no way Stephen and Dakota would allow me out there. I needed money."

"What about the money you stole from them?" I pressed. "Why did you bury it in the cave?"

"I was going to use it to start my own business," Nathaniel replied. "I knew they kept a can buried out here. I knew where it was, and I moved it. I needed product first. I was going to pay them back when I got on my feet."

I was pretty sure that was a lie. Whether he was lying to himself or me, though, I couldn't be sure. "So Chloe found you in the field and you were stealing," I said, rolling my neck until it cracked. "I'm assuming there was some sort of scuffle. Did she kill you with your own knife?"

"She went crazy," Nathaniel said, his voice gaining strength. "She started slapping and hitting me. I tried to stop her, but before I even realized what was happening she grabbed the knife and ... it was over."

"Why did you stab him, Chloe?" I asked. "More importantly, why did you stab him so many times? That indicates rage."

"It was his fault," Chloe said, her voice cracking. "Everything was his fault. He left me alone with ... him. He ruined my life."

"What is she talking about?" I asked Nathaniel, shooting him a sidelong look. "Who did you leave her with?"

"How should I know?" Nathaniel asked, nonplussed. "She's crazy. She's the murderer."

"And you're a thief who obviously did something to your sister," I shot back. "Who did you leave her with?"

"I think that would be me."

I froze when I heard the new voice, dumbfounded. Apparently it was Crazy Criminal Day at Hollow Creek, and things were about to get a whole lot worse.

THIRTY-TWO

*A*ndrew Brooks stood about ten feet away from us, his mailman uniform – shorts included – wrinkled from the hike to the creek. His face didn't reflect the kind man I thought I knew.

I guess it shouldn't have surprised me. Stephen worried about what "they" would do. I knew at least one adult was involved. Discovering that adult was Hemlock Cove's lone mailman, though, was surreal.

"You're a long way off your route," I said finally, going for levity. "Did you come out to see where they burned the pot field? Everyone has been curious about it. It's on the other side of the creek. You should check it out."

I hoped he would take my airhead routine as an easy out.

"Yeah, that's exactly why I'm here," Andrew deadpanned. "I'm here to take a look at all my plans after they went up in smoke."

I wanted to cry – or tell him he was a moron. I couldn't, though. I had to keep Chloe safe. "You know what? I'm not going to play dumb. It belittles us both." I opted to change tactics. "Why didn't you run after the pot field was discovered? You had to know it was only a matter of time before it would come back on you."

"Run where?" Andrew challenged. "I'm a mailman. Where could I go that the authorities wouldn't find me?"

Despite the fact that I knew Andrew was dangerous, I had trouble reconciling the man I thought I knew with the notion of an imminent threat. He wore linen shorts with socks, for crying out loud. That's cause for mocking, not concern.

"Why are you out here now?"

"I was looking for Chloe," Andrew replied. "I followed her from town. I wanted to ... talk to her."

I risked a glance at Chloe. She cowered at my side, her hands shaking. I knew what happened to her. I knew Andrew was the culprit.

"How did you get involved with Chloe?" I asked, hoping my questions would keep Andrew talking long enough to figure a way out of this. "Did Nathaniel give her to you as some sort of payment?"

Nathaniel balked. "What are you talking about? I ... oh." His eyes shifted to Chloe and her overt reaction to Andrew. For some reason – maybe it was wishful thinking – I didn't think Nathaniel was aware of what Andrew did to Chloe. Now her resentment and anger started to make sense.

"Chloe and I had a fling," Andrew replied. "She wanted it."

"I didn't," Chloe whimpered.

"How did you ... hook up?" My stomach turned at the distasteful implication, but I didn't want to set Andrew off.

"Nathaniel brought her by one day when we were divvying up the proceeds," Andrew replied. "She was so cute in her little skirt, and she kept smiling at me. I knew what she wanted, and she was sad because her brother was mean to her. Nathaniel left her at my house while he ran an errand. She seduced me."

"That's not true," Chloe protested. "He ... ."

"I know what he did, Chloe," I said, my voice low. Playing Andrew's game was one thing. Blaming Chloe for an adult raping her was quite another. I would never stoop that low. "He's not going to touch you again. I promise."

"I didn't know," Nathaniel said, his face drawn. "I ... she acted funny when I picked her up that day. I just thought she was stoned. I … oh, man. I … ."

I didn't have time to deal with Nathaniel's ghostly meltdown when I was almost positive Andrew was about to get violent. "You can still run, Andrew," I suggested. "You have a few hours in which you can get away from town. Your kid is in custody, but you can still get away. You're wasting time here."

"That's pretty funny, Bay," Andrew replied. "We both know that your boyfriend will hunt me down. I knew the minute they hauled those boys in this morning that it was over."

"Really? I would've thought you realized it was over when they discovered Nathaniel's body."

"I thought Stephen or Dakota killed Nathaniel at first," Andrew admitted. "When I questioned them about it, though, they both denied it. I knew it couldn't be Charlie. That kid … he's an idiot. I told Stephen not to bring him in on this. It looks like I was right, doesn't it?"

"I have no idea." I rubbed soothing circles across Chloe's back. She looked like an animal caught in a trap. I worried she would bolt.

"Do you really think Charlie isn't serving me up to Chief Terry and your fed right now?" Andrew asked. "Come on, Bay. You're smarter than that. Isn't that why you're here?"

"I came out here to … look around," I said. "I knew we were missing a piece of the puzzle. I had no idea you were that piece."

"I thought you were here because you were going to do something witchy."

Andrew was testing me. I remained quiet.

"That's the rumor about your family," Andrew continued, taking a predatory step in my direction. "People whisper about the Winchester witches every time they see one of you. People say Tillie can even control the weather." Andrew laughed, the sound full of evil mirth. "Can you believe that?"

I guess that meant he'd never heard the story about Aunt Tillie bringing down a lightning storm on a former classmate who tried to kill me a few weeks ago. "Aunt Tillie can do pretty much anything she sets her mind to," I said. "If she wants to control the weather, she'll do it."

"And yet she used a shotgun to scare my boys away the other night," Andrew said. "Oh, you didn't think I knew about that? I sent them. I know she has a field out there. Our only shot of getting any money out of this season is that field. It's my next stop."

I had no idea whether Aunt Tillie's diarrhea curse would work on a mailman, but if anyone deserved it, Andrew Brooks was that person. It would be doubly funny in those stupid shorts. "You can't find that field," I replied, not bothering to deny its existence. A plan was starting to form. If I could get him to leave Chloe at Hollow Creek and go with me to The Overlook, I could save the girl and level the playing field. "It's warded."

Andrew furrowed his brow. "What does that mean?"

"It's magically hidden," I explained. "No one can find it. In fact, the more you think about it, the more likely you are to get diarrhea." Huh. That sounded more threatening in my head.

Nathaniel snorted. "That is awesome! I've always liked Ms. Tillie. She's funny."

"I'll tell her you said so," I muttered.

Andrew glanced around, confused. "Who are you talking to?"

"No one."

He didn't believe me. "You just said something to … someone. It didn't look like you were talking to Chloe."

"She was talking to Nathaniel," Chloe whispered. "He's here."

"You've got to be kidding me," Andrew chortled. "You told her you were talking to her dead brother? That's just priceless. You Winchesters are pretty keen on everyone thinking you're witches, aren't you?"

I ignored the dig. "You're in a bad place here, Andrew," I said. "The drugs are going to send you away for a long time. The rape … is going to make you very popular in prison. You should run now."

"Rape? I didn't rape anyone," Andrew argued. "She wanted it. She shouldn't have been wearing that short skirt if she didn't want me to take notice."

He was truly sick. "She's a teenage girl and you're an adult," I countered. "Trust me. No one who has ever seen you in those shorts wants to have sex with you, especially a teenage girl."

"She wanted it!"

"I kept telling him 'no,'" Chloe protested. "I was screaming and crying."

"This is all my fault," Nathaniel said. "I ... I don't know what to do."

I had a few ideas. Unfortunately, I couldn't give them voice without Andrew overhearing. If I thought he was unarmed, I could force Chloe to run and fight him on my own. If he had a knife – or worse, a gun – things would go badly. I needed to give Chloe her best chance at escape.

"Was this your idea or did you stumble on the kids already doing it?" I asked, drawing Andrew back to the original conversation and playing for time.

"Actually, I found Josh Baldwin hiking into the woods with a huge bag one day," Andrew replied. "Do you remember Josh?"

I nodded.

"I parked on the road and followed him," Andrew recounted. "The field was a lot smaller then. It was really seven plants, and it was hidden well. I didn't approach him that day. I wanted to think things over.

"My first thought was to sneak back out here and steal all of his product," he continued. "I knew I could sell it in certain circles. The more I thought about that, though, the more I realized I was opening myself to trouble. If one of those people was an undercover informant, I would lose everything. That didn't seem worth it for a couple of bags of pot.

"That's when I realized I had a prime opportunity in front of me," Andrew said, relishing being the center of attention. "I followed Josh again a few days later. He was terrified when I found him. We made a deal: He did all the work and he split the profits with me in exchange for me keeping my mouth shut. I even made up an imaginary partner who was violent to threaten him. It worked like a charm."

That explained who "they" was. "If it was only seven plants, that couldn't have been much profit," I pointed out.

"Not that first year, no," Andrew agreed. "Josh was happy to get out from under my thumb when he left for college the next year. That first summer's money kept me in beer for the entire year. I wanted to expand on it.

"I picked one kid to run the field each year," he continued. "It was the easiest way. They never got greedy because it was for a short period and I never had to worry about getting in trouble with the kids were taking all the risks. My imaginary friend served as an appropriate threat to keep them in line. It was perfect."

"How did you pick them?"

"You'd be surprised what a mailman knows about the people in a community," Andrew replied. "While you were all dismissing me, I was getting a peek into all of your lives. For example, did you know Tillie has been getting catalogs because she's shopping for an off-road vehicle?"

"She told us. She wants a Polaris Ranger. A red one."

Andrew faltered. He clearly thought he was telling me something I didn't already know. "Well, did you know that Sam and Clove are going to move in together? They've already been making plans, including getting catalogs to order furniture."

"She's not moving until we deal with a domestic issue," I replied, nonplussed. I enjoyed deflating him. "We have a few things to get settled before she can go."

Andrew frowned. "Did you know that Marcus hopes Thistle will move in with him once he gets the stable renovated?"

"Not really," I admitted. "It's not a surprise, though. He's been whispering about his plans with Landon when he thinks no one is looking."

Andrew was becoming frustrated. "Did you know your boss is trying to figure out a way to get you to quit? I heard him talking with some chick about it yesterday."

"It came up at dinner."

"Well, your family is an anomaly," Andrew snapped. "You're all co-dependent and tell each other everything. The rest of the town has secrets. I picked kids who were trying to keep secrets."

I snorted. He thought he was smart. I had my doubts. "I'm guessing you went after kids who had a subscription to Playboy. Am I right?"

"How did you know that?" Nathaniel asked.

"My brother had a subscription to Playboy," Chloe offered. "He thought my mom didn't know, but she did. She said 'boys will be boys' and left it at that."

"Oh, man," Nathaniel said, making a face. "I can't believe Mom saw my … ."

"No one cares about your spank magazines," I hissed.

"Who are you talking to?" Andrew yelled. "That's the second time you've done that."

"She's talking to Nathaniel," Chloe answered. "I already told you that." Her courage was growing. That meant she was probably getting ready to do something stupid. Great. That was one thing I didn't need.

"Are you honestly saying that you believe Nathaniel is here?" Andrew asked.

I glanced at the ghost in question. "I think that there are probably a lot of things about this life – and the next – that you don't know," I said. "Your brain is too small to grasp certain things. After all, you're the smart guy who utilized teenage kids with big mouths to run your pot empire. How smart can you be?"

"You had better watch your mouth, Bay," Andrew threatened. "I've always liked you. Things are going to go badly for you either way today. It doesn't have to hurt, though."

I swallowed hard. "Well, if we're being honest with one another, I guess I should tell you that I'm not going to let you hurt Chloe or me," I countered. "You should probably leave now."

Andrew chuckled harshly. "I like your spirit, kid. It's not going to help you, but … ." His hand moved toward the bag on his waist. It was one of those modified fanny packs, which only made him look more ridiculous. I realized I was out of time.

I grabbed Chloe's arm and pushed her in the direction of the trees. "Run!"

Chloe was bewildered. "What?"

"Run," I repeated. "Don't look back."

Chloe didn't have to be told twice. She bolted for the trees. Andrew, a small gun in his hand, moved to follow, but I stepped in front of him. I didn't have a lot of options, so I did the only thing I could think to do, and slammed my fist into his face.

Andrew reared back, surprised, and groaned at the pain.

"Ow!" I shook my hand as the pain washed through it.

"That was pathetic," Nathaniel said.

"Oh, shut up," I grumbled.

"That's going to cost you, Bay," Andrew said, reaching for my hair.

I jerked back, tripping over a fallen tree and skinning my knee against the rough bark as I fought to keep one foot firmly planted on the ground. Nathaniel, his aura glowing a bright shade of orange, stepped between us.

"Tell my sister I'm sorry," Nathaniel said, his face grim. "Tell her … I know that she didn't mean to kill me. I realize what happened now. I … was a bad brother."

"Nathaniel, what are you doing?" I was confused.

Andrew made to lunge through the ghost, but Nathaniel grabbed his wrist and twisted it, causing the formerly amiable mailman to howl. He didn't let go of the gun, though, instead squeezing the trigger and firing a wild shot into the ground.

"What's happening?" Andrew howled.

"If you kill him, you might not go to a good place," I warned, fighting for solid footing and taking a step back. "I know you're avenging your sister, but … I can't guarantee what will happen if you do this."

"Maybe that's my penance," Nathaniel said. "I let this … piece of trash … ruin her life. She got so scared she killed me. Maybe I deserve this."

"There are other options," I said, taking another step away as Nathaniel's aura flared. He was about to do something I'd only ever heard stories about. I realized now what he was turning into. He was about to become a poltergeist. He was going to be a sacrificial one, though. "You're going to burn so hot your soul won't survive."

The skin on Andrew's arm sizzled as he clawed at the invisible hand holding him, and his screams rocked me.

"I don't want to survive," Nathaniel replied. "I'm already gone. Tell Chloe I'm sorry. Try to help her."

I nodded and turned, resigned. I didn't want to see what was coming. I pointed myself in the direction of the trees, putting one foot in front of the other as Andrew whimpered, cried out and ultimately fell silent.

I was almost to the trees when Landon and Chief Terry bolted into the clearing, guns drawn. When Landon's eyes landed on me they were filled with surprise. "Bay?" He raced to my side and pulled me to him, pressing his face against mine. "I thought … ."

"What happened?" Chief Terry asked, confused. "What … ?"

"It was Andrew Brooks," I said, glancing over my shoulder. His body was on the ground, mostly untouched except for a few red splotches on the side of his neck and arm. "He was in charge of the pot field."

"We know," Landon said, pushing my hair from my face. "Charlie told us. I … what happened to him?"

"Nathaniel." I didn't know what else to say.

"Where is Nathaniel now?"

"He's gone."

"Did he move on after avenging his death?" Landon asked, refusing to let me pull away from him even though I started feeling sick to my stomach.

That was a sticky question. I could protect Chloe and blame Nathaniel's death on Andrew. It was Nathaniel's final wish, after all. I couldn't lie to Landon, though. I wouldn't. It wasn't fair and it wasn't right. "No. He … ."

"Mr. Brooks didn't kill Nathaniel," Chloe announced, popping out of the trees. Tears streamed down her face, but she was otherwise stoic. "I did."

Chief Terry glanced at me for confirmation, seemingly surprised at Chloe's arrival. All I could do was nod.

"Okay, Chloe," Chief Terry said, holding out his hand and

remaining calm. "We're going to figure this out. I need you to come with me, though. Okay?"

Chloe nodded, stopping in front of me long enough to offer a wan smile. "Thank you for protecting me. I'm sorry I thought you were trying to kill me the other day. I ... understand ... now."

"Chloe, before he left, Nathaniel wanted me to tell you something," I said, fighting off tears. "He said he was sorry. He said he didn't want you to be punished. He said ... he understood."

"Is he in a better place now?" Chloe looked hopeful.

I wasn't sure whether the truth would help or harm her, but I didn't have the energy to lie. "He's no place now," I replied. "He sacrificed his soul to protect us. I ... he's gone. There is nothing left of him."

"Oh," Chloe said, her voice small. "I ... oh."

"You were the last thing he cared enough about to sacrifice himself for," I supplied. "He knew what was happening. He wanted to protect you."

"I guess ... it's better late than never," Chloe said, a fresh round of tears sliding down her cheeks.

Chief Terry gently tugged on her arm. "Come on, Chloe. We'll get your mother and start talking this over. It's going to be ... okay." It was an empty promise, but something told me Chloe was already on the way to healing. What came after that was anyone's guess.

THIRTY-THREE

"Are you okay?" Landon let himself into The Overlook's library several hours later and lifted my legs so he could settle next to me on the couch.

I dropped the book I was pretending to read on the nearby table and fixed him with a hopeful look as I struggled to a sitting position. "What's going to happen to Chloe?"

Landon sighed. "I asked you a question."

"I'm fine," I said. "He didn't touch me. No one did."

After hours at the police station, two of which involved me telling the real story to Landon and him coaching me how to respond for the taped interview that followed, Chief Terry sent me home. They still had hours of paperwork ahead of them.

Instead of returning to the guesthouse, I hunkered down in the library. Mom checked on me a few times, worry creasing her forehead with each visit, but otherwise left me to my thoughts. I had a lot of them.

"I'm not going to yell at you for going out to Hollow Creek alone," Landon said.

That was a relief because I couldn't figure out what he possibly had to be angry about.

"No one could've seen that ... entire thing ... coming," Landon said. "I'm just glad you're okay. Although, to be honest, you seem a little shaky. Do you want to talk about what happened to Nathaniel?"

I shrugged, noncommittal. "I'm not sure," I said. "He was turning into a poltergeist. I told him. He ... knew ... what he was doing. He chose to burn so brightly that he could touch our plane of existence, but he lost any chance of passing over into another when he did it."

"I don't pretend to understand anything you just told me," Landon said, choosing his words carefully as he rubbed his thumb against my cheek. "It sounds to me as if Nathaniel tried to do the right thing in the end. You couldn't have stopped him."

"I know."

"The coroner says that Andrew's throat closed due to extreme heat," Landon said. "It cut off his air supply. He has no way to explain it."

"What does that mean?"

"Nothing," Landon replied. "It's going to be recorded as an unexplained death. Because Andrew is a drug dealer and rapist, no one is going to look further into it."

"What about his wife?"

"She has her hands full with Stephen's defense," Landon explained. "Charlie cracked first. I'm sure that doesn't surprise you. He's getting the best deal. That's probably the safest outcome for the three of them. He's least likely to do something this stupid again."

"How did you know to go to Hollow Creek?" I asked. "I didn't tell anyone where I was going. Clove and Thistle thought I was going to The Whistler."

"Well ... ." Landon looked uncomfortable. "I'd like to be the big hero in this scenario, but I can't. I wasn't looking for you. I thought you were still at Hypnotic. We saw the mail truck. When Charlie told us what was going on, we immediately started a search for Andrew. He's the reason we were out there."

I laughed, although it didn't feel genuine. "That's okay," I offered. "I went out to Hollow Creek to get Nathaniel to admit who killed him. I didn't expect it to be Chloe."

"I know you're worried about her," Landon said, tugging my arm to he could draw me closer for a hug. "I ... she has a lot of stuff ahead of her. I can't tell you that things are going to work out for her because I don't know whether that's the case."

"She didn't mean to kill Nathaniel."

"I know that," Landon said. "Given the rape and the emotional duress she was under, she's probably going to be able to plead down to manslaughter. Nathaniel's death wasn't premeditated, although she had time to rethink her actions, because it took her an hour to drag his body down to the creek. She said she thought he would sink.

"Chief Terry and I have been talking, and we're both going to offer recommendations that she serve her sentence in a mental hospital instead of prison," he continued. "She can't get off without any punishment. That's not how the system works."

"How long?"

"I don't know that either," Landon answered. "It will probably be five years."

That seemed like a lot of time for a teenage girl to lose, but it wouldn't be the end of the world. "Well, at least they'll be able to treat her drug issues."

"She's going to be held in a hospital until her trial," Landon supplied. "We've already arranged it. She's starting treatment tonight. Her mother is going with her to get her settled."

Something niggled the back of my mind. Patty Jamison's face as she stared out the window of her home earlier in the afternoon bothered me. "Did she know Chloe killed Nathaniel?"

"She says she had suspicions. Why do you ask?"

"I saw her this afternoon," I replied. "There was just something off about her."

"Part of Chloe's treatment will include counseling sessions with her mother," Landon said. "I think both of them need to work together if they're going to salvage what's left of that family."

"That's probably for the best," I said, resting my cheek against Landon's shoulder. "What about you? Do you have to head back to Traverse City tomorrow morning?"

"I told my boss I had stuff to finish up here tomorrow," Landon said. "That's kind of true. I think he knew I was exaggerating about what's left. He told me to email him my reports and enjoy a nice weekend with you."

I brightened. "Does that mean we can still go to the fair?"

"Yes."

"Will you win me a stuffed animal?"

Landon grinned. "Yes."

"Are you going to give me anything I want because you think I'm depressed?"

He tickled my ribs. "Yes. It's not going to start until after dinner, though. I'm starving, and I think you need the fuel."

"I'm not sure how much I can eat," I admitted, letting him pull me to my feet. "I can't get the sound of Andrew dying out of my head."

"Well, I'll liquor you up and make sure you pass out before bed, then," Landon said. "You need sleep."

"I don't want another hangover."

"Then I'll just give you enough to make sure you're sleepy."

"Okay." I wasn't in the mood to argue. I slipped my hand in his as we left the library, tilting my head to the side when the unmistakable sound of Aunt Willa screeching assailed my ears. "Really?"

"That did it," Landon said, stalking toward the front foyer. "I'm going to arrest her. It's going to be the high point of my day."

We pulled up short when we got to the lobby, our eyes busy as we took in the scene. Thistle sat on the front desk, swinging her legs as she enjoyed the show. Clove was more reserved in the spot next to her. I headed in their direction, skirting behind Mom, Marnie and Twila as they held a struggling Aunt Tillie away from Aunt Willa.

"What's going on?" Landon asked. "I'm ready to arrest them if it becomes necessary. I think we've dealt with enough for one day."

"I heard," Thistle said. "You should've taken us out to Hollow Creek with you. Clove is glad she missed the show, but I would've enjoyed a little mayhem with my afternoon misery."

"Next time," I promised.

"What is Willa doing here?" Landon asked, pushing me between

Thistle and himself to get a better look. "Is Aunt Tillie trying to kill or curse her?"

Thistle shrugged. "I think it's probably a little of both," she answered. "No one in the town has a room to rent, and she demands we accommodate her or give her money to get a room out of town."

"That's not going to end well," Landon said, squeezing my hand before releasing it and moving into the melee. "What's going on?"

"I want my money," Aunt Willa said. "I've had enough of this."

"You aren't owed any money," Landon replied. "You've been banished from this property. Either get out or I'll arrest you."

"That seems beneath an FBI agent," Rosemary pointed out.

"Well, since I've already had to arrest a traumatized teenager who killed her brother ... and see a dead body ... and worry about my girlfriend ... arresting Willa seems like it would be a fun end to a crappy day. I won't know until it happens, but I'm willing to give it a shot."

"You can't arrest me," Aunt Willa said. "This is my property."

"Not according to the law."

"My mother's will clearly states that the property was supposed to be divided equally between her heirs," Aunt Willa argued. "I have a case ... and I'm going to win."

"No, you're not," Aunt Tillie said, jerking her arm from Mom and taking a step forward. She was deadly serious. "I tried to protect you from this for as long as I could, but I'm beyond it now. You're not a part of this family, Willa."

"Just because you say it – and you probably even believe it, for that matter – that doesn't make it true," Aunt Willa sniffed. "I'm owed what's coming to me."

"I couldn't agree more," Aunt Tillie said, snapping her fingers in Thistle's direction. "Hey, fresh mouth, give me that envelope that's on the desk behind you."

Thistle scanned the desk, and handed a thick envelope to Aunt Tillie. It looked old.

"What is that?" I asked.

"It's Willa's comeuppance," Aunt Tillie replied, opening the envelope. "This is a letter my mother attached to her will. We didn't know any of this until after she died, and when we found it, Ginger insisted we keep it to ourselves. She didn't want it becoming public knowledge."

"Oh, this sounds fun," Landon said. "I love a good family secret. What's in it?"

"Willa is not our full sister," Aunt Tillie replied, waving the sheet of paper for emphasis. "She's our half-sister."

Aunt Willa's face drained of color. "You're lying!"

"I'm not," Aunt Tillie replied, her eyes sparkling. Whatever was coming was going to devastate Aunt Willa, and Aunt Tillie relished her role as spoiler. "We do not have the same mother and father."

"That doesn't matter," Willa argued. "Even if I don't have the same father...."

"We have the same father," Aunt Tillie clarified. "We do not have the same mother."

"How is that possible?" I asked. "Isn't Aunt Willa the youngest?"

"She is," Aunt Tillie confirmed. "Our father had a wandering eye. He slept with half the women in town. One of those women was Willa's mother. Because our father had no money, and was something of a tightwad, the woman had no way to care for Willa.

"Even though she didn't want to do it, our mother took Willa in and raised her," she continued. "She tried to treat her like the rest of us, although as much as I loved her I'm not sure she managed to do that. My mother knew what kind of person Willa was, though. That's why she worded her will the way she did."

"She wanted you and Ginger to have the option of leaving Willa out of the property division if it became necessary, didn't she?" I asked, things clicking into place. "If Aunt Willa got out of hand, which she obviously is prone to do, you and Grandma had the option of cutting her out of the inheritance entirely."

"Yes," Aunt Tillie confirmed. "I wanted to do it right away. Ginger insisted on paying Willa her fair share. She always was a Mary Sue about things like that."

I pursed my lips to keep from laughing.

"Ginger didn't want Willa to know she wasn't really one of us,"

Aunt Tillie said. "I was going to make her aware of the issue when she tried to take Twila years ago. I knew it was a money grab. She wanted Twila's inheritance. There was no way I would let that happen."

That explained something else, too. "That's why she's not magical," I mused. "Earlier today, she mentioned that you were delusional thinking you had powers. She doesn't have magic because she doesn't share in our matriarchal line."

"You're smarter than you look, Bay," Aunt Tillie said, although she winked to let me know she was kidding. "Either way, this letter proves that Willa has no claim on this property. She can get out and ... stuff it."

Aunt Willa's expression was murderous. "I don't believe that letter," she said. "I'm still taking this to court."

"That's fine," Aunt Tillie replied, nonplussed. "We can go through the whole rigmarole if you want. We'll get DNA tests. When you lose, though, I'm going to stick you with all of our legal bills. How does that sound?"

"Grandma, I'm not sure we should do this," Rosemary offered, her voice low. "If Aunt Tillie is right ... ."

"She's not right!"

"If she is, though, we could be on the hook for thousands of dollars in legal fees," Rosemary said. "Do you really want to risk that?"

"You said we had a fool-proof case," Aunt Willa charged, whirling on Rosemary. "You said ... ."

"I know what I said," Rosemary replied, gritting her teeth. "Now I'm saying something different. If this is true, you don't have any claim on the property."

"But ... I want my money." Aunt Willa was too stubborn for her own good. She had that in common with Aunt Tillie.

"You already got your money," Landon said. "You should probably go. If you don't, I will arrest you for trespassing. I'm not messing around. We've had a long day and you're the last thing we want to deal with."

"This isn't over," Aunt Willa warned as Rosemary pulled her toward the door. "I'm going to ... do something."

Aunt Tillie followed Aunt Willa, giddiness practically wafting off of her as she started to dance. "I don't want you to think this changes everything, Willa," she said, pushing the door open so Rosemary would have an easier time dragging her grandmother out of the building. "You're still my half-sister. As my half-sister, I want you to know that you're a bitch. See, that's still the same."

"I ... no!" Aunt Willa was on the verge of losing it. "This isn't what was supposed to happen!"

"The good news for you is now I only have to do half a dance on your grave," Aunt Tillie said. "It will be half the work, but twice the fun." She slammed the door in Aunt Willa's face, cutting off some colorful swearing, and turned to us. "I'm starving. Let's eat."

"Another fun day in the Winchester house," Landon said, chuckling as he prodded me toward the kitchen. "Aunt Tillie is in a good mood."

"She is."

"I think I'm going to ask her for a favor." Landon moved in Aunt Tillie's direction. It took me a moment to realize what he was about to do.

"I'll never sleep with you again if you make me smell like bacon," I called to his back. We both knew it was an empty threat.

"Oh, come on, little witch," Landon teased, wriggling his eyebrows. "It will be fun for the both of us. I promise."

Oh, how bad could it be?